P9-CJY-114

A STAY BY THE RIVER

ALSO BY SUSAN ENGBERG

Pastorale

A STAY BY THE RIVER

STORIES BY

SUSAN ENGBERG

VIKING

VIKING
Viking Penguin Inc., 40 West 23rd Street, New York, New York 10010, U.S.A.
Penguin Books Ltd, Harmondsworth, Middlesex, England
Penguin Books Australia Ltd, Ringwood, Victoria, Australia
Penguin Books Canada Limited, 2801 John Street, Markham, Ontario, Canada L3R 1B4
Penguin Books (N.Z.) Ltd, 182–190 Wairau Road, Auckland 10, New Zealand

First published in 1985 by Viking Penguin Inc.
Published simultaneously in Canada

LIBRARY OF CONGRESS CATALOGING IN PUBLICATION DATA
Engberg, Susan, 1940–
A stay by the river.
I. Title.
PS3555.N387S7 1985 813′.54 85-5336
ISBN 0-670-80620-X

Acknowledgment is made to the following periodicals in which some of the stories in this book appeared originally: *Ascent*: "A Stay by the River"; *Indiana Review*: "Boiling River"; *The Massachusetts Review*: "Riffraff"; *Ploughshares*: "Northern Light" and "Household"; *The Southern Review*: "Common Happiness"; and *Wisconsin Academy of Sciences*: "A Daughter's Heart."

"A Stay by the River" was reprinted in *Prize Stories: The O. Henry Awards*, 1977. "Boiling River" won first prize in the *Indiana Review* Fiction Contest, 1984. "Household" appears in *The Ploughshares Reader*, 1985.

Printed in the United States of America by
R. R. Donnelley & Sons Company, Harrisonburg, Virginia
Set in Garamond #3

FOR MY FAMILIES

CONTENTS

MORGAN AND JOANNA

It was a warm Thursday night of full moon, toward the middle of the bloom of May. Dressed in a terry-cloth bathrobe, her feet bare, Joanna Christiansen sat before an open ledger, beside an open window in her upstairs apartment, marking in a few last numbers. Here she was, back home in Rosedale: chastened by both illness and baffled love, nearly recovered from both, and now determined to see if something new could grow up from old roots. After ten years of working and attending art classes off and on, she had borrowed ten thousand dollars for her venture of opening a gift shop in the old stone house on Spring Street that had been willed her by her maternal grandmother. Her father, a widower and longtime foreman of the Greenwoods Fish Hatchery outside of town, had shaken his head in doubt, but gone ahead and put down his name as co-signatory on the loan, perhaps in deference to those family women, so unlike his own stolid, laconic self, perhaps in calculation for his old age. Anyway, the papers had indeed been signed, behind the Greek Revival facade of the only bank in town, and now Joanna was well into the project. She closed the ledger and turned off the stained-glass lamp.

Her love had been for a young painter named Rob, prodigiously talented, ascetic in appearance, opinionative, enthralling, and she had lived with him in the city for over a year before discovering that his monthly allowance did not come from his father, as he had said, but from a woman twice his age whom he had still been secretly managing to please. Already weakened and deeply frustrated by recurrent urinary infections, Joanna had been unable at last to revise her love to accommodate his deception. Her first, wounded recoil had become, with intermittent returns to their former embrace, a progressive withdrawal toward the core of herself. She no longer wanted to live each day with him; she could not bear to continue the struggle for herself too close to his vicinity. But not a day went by that she did not wonder about him, or about herself, for having opened herself to him. She had glimpsed something vast and hopeful in her love for him; to have been deceived had flung her into self-doubt, as if she had been the one untrue. When he still pressed himself on her by telephone—"permanent mates" was what he called himself and her; she was, he said, his "Botticelli woman"—she could only ask for time alone.

Now she stretched far back in her oak desk chair and then leaned into the window opening to look down on her little terrace of potted flowers below. The source of all yearning was what was so mysterious. Sometimes it seemed that you only knew your secret self in retrospect, only after you had already opened the gates on your tenderness.

Across the river at this moment, Morgan Peters ran along the old quarry road toward home between darkened ditches and dew-glimmering fields. He had been to the quarry for his first swim of the season, and what he had thought about in the cold, dark water, floating with the moonlight far above the steam machinery submerged by surprise more than half a century ago, was how he would like to see Joanna Christiansen diving from a limestone ledge, Joanna without her work clothes, her checkbook, her cans of wall paint, diving toward him across the distance that came of her being his employer. Nothing would need to be said. Instantly she would know that if he had been a little gruff sometimes in his daily manner, a little reticent, it was because he had been waiting, a carpenter hiding behind his tools, for a sure sign that he was outliving his past, that the time had come for him to be pleasing.

Joanna might be giving such a sign, in the music she played as they worked, the food she occasionally offered, the way she had come to ask his opinion or call out his name when she returned from an errand: Morgan! Look at this! The woodworking he had done for her, especially some of the display cases, was the best his hands had ever managed. Now he would like to be the one to inspire her to imagine what else might be waiting in him for her touch.

From the quarry road he turned onto the county blacktop and in a quarter of a mile plunged down the dirt lane that led to his river cottage. His skin burned in the cool air; his fingertips pulsed; his eyes saw what belonged to him. Now that Joanna's house was almost finished—all that remained was the outside trim painting and some carpentry on the side stairs leading to her second-story apartment—he longed for her, in turn, to visit his life: the canoe pulled up from the river and overturned beneath the willow tree; the new stand of raspberry canes and the freshly tilled garden; the single, ingenious, comprehensive room with its central stove and slanted wall of glass, made from cast-off storm windows, overlooking the river to the southeast.

He wanted to watch her eyes as she stood in the doorway.

Would she see, as he sometimes did now, the broken pieces from his childhood charmed into a new dignity, separate from his family's feuding and tragedy and shame? Would she understand the pressure that was building inside him from the silent but stirring portions of himself—how he was coming to visualize a modest extension of his land up and down the river and into the woods, a cabin grown in successive additions like something alive, an enlarged garden and jams made from berries and children who looked as fresh as hope? His line would bring up fish for a little kingdom. The plain things he made with his real hands would be thought wonderful. What he thought would now by someone else be thought wonderful. The moment for his own life would have come.

The moon, rising higher, cast the shadow of the bridge on the Plover River and began to clear the tallest branches of the linden tree in front of the gift shop on Spring Street. There it emerged, high and full, lighting upon Joanna in her bathrobe as she watered the clay pots of geraniums and petunias clustered by her front steps. She raised her watering can in a salute to the moon, dependable friend, messenger of returns.

Month after month, the winter of her return had passed. Heavenly, spice-scented viburnum bloomed this week beside the steps. She had been guided home. Forces larger than her understanding had been at work all along, she felt, urging her to retrace her steps. She was recovering herself. Her body was strong enough no longer to be such a burden, and the ache in her heart had subsided to an essence. She was devoting herself to, she was trusting in, a few plain actions that seemed to her without defect. The first weeks in this house she had slept as if she had not slept for years. There were moments when she thought simply, her mind rooted in a new awareness, that all she needed now was sweet time, in this place.

Before she was fully awake the next morning, Joanna heard electric saw screams and hammer pounding and felt tremors passing through the house. Morgan was at work very early. Sunlight rushed down the hallway from the kitchen.

She called to him through the doorway at the top of the outer stairs, "You're at work very early." He was replacing one of the bottom treads with redwood. A gilding light rushed along the side of the house, and there was a penetrating scent of cut wood, like a revelation of tree heart. It was a day to open all the doors and windows.

"Shall I make some coffee?" she called down. He nodded. "All right. Come up in ten minutes."

Taking off his black knit hat, Morgan entered her kitchen for the first time since he had put up the new ceiling. Now he looked up at his handiwork—and hers, the painting—where a blob of reflected light trembled above her head. "It looks OK," he said.

In the high school he had known Joanna's name, that was all, the name of someone remotely circling in the upper classes, but perhaps he had marked her specially—the thought had come to him—because he remembered the look of her passing in the hallways, very thin even then, her books held across her chest. He did not remember that they had ever spoken; he did not remember if hers had been among the faces of Rosedale he had recalled during his years in the army.

"Yes," she said, "it's a very good ceiling." She poured coffee into the mug he held across the table. Tiny particles of sawdust were collected in his beard and in the blond hairs on the back of his hand.

"How's progress?" she asked. His hands were broad across the knuckles, with long, squarish fingers. The left hand was now fisted around his hat, jammed against his knee, his elbow akimbo. "Why are you frowning?" she asked. He was a good worker; she had been lucky to hear about him at the old hardware store, which had once been owned by her grandparents.

Very faintly she remembered him from school; he might have worn the same sort of hat. Sometimes now he wore his army jacket to work.

He bent toward his coffee. "I'm not frowning."

"Yes, you are. There." She touched her own forehead and then pointed to his.

"That's not a frown. That's concentration." He tried to smile but felt that his mouth was only grimacing. An old anguish came down upon him, a sense of being locked up without warrant but without hope. He lowered his eyes to the steam.

"How many days for the stairway, do you think?" asked Joanna, but then, just as he was about to answer, taking courage from the very good ceiling she said he had made, the telephone rang. Anguished, locked inside himself, burdened by the past, he could hear her voice from the hallway. It sounded shaken. She named a name as she hung up. Rob, was it? Who was this Rob, anyway? Morgan pulled on his hat and stood abruptly to leave.

"I'm sorry," said Joanna from the doorway. "What were you going to say about the stairs?"

The sun grew hotter on the stairway during the morning, and Morgan took off his hat and then his wool shirt. A fierceness flowed through him and into his hammer. For the third time he missed a nail entirely and badly dented the redwood. He sat down on the step and lowered his forehead to his arms. There was a sensation of swarming inside his head, and when he opened his eyes, the over-bright sky seemed to be receding rapidly, caving in upon itself, leaving him exposed. He gathered his tools, used the washroom in the basement, then hunkered down in the striped shade beneath the stairway to eat his lunch. He could hear Joanna's music and the banging of the back door as now and then she threw out another empty carton. She was filling her shelves today. She was happy, he supposed. He wished he could get closer to that happiness, that assurance. Traffic along Spring Street was picking up, with people getting an early start for the weekend at the lakes. He closed his eyes and rested his head against the stone wall.

He would like to tie a blindfold around Joanna's eyes and lead her to his truck—right now, this minute—and drive her to his cabin and untie the scarf and say, "Look."

"You!" his mother would scream to his father in the night, in a lower part of the ramshackle house. "And your own brother!" Around his bed the attic room would seem to recede until nothing stood between him and the northern cold.

He could take off the blindfold and say to Joanna, "Look," and then watch her face to see if it was true that his life was being put together, bit by bit, by his own hands, under the bright green willow.

He had a short nap, sitting up under the stairs, and when he woke, his head felt clearer. It could be easy.

She was halfway up a stepladder when he rang the string of brass bells by the front door and then entered.

"Morgan, look at this," she said above the music.

He came closer to the woven piece she was unrolling, in which the thick horizontal strands of wool reminded him of layers inside the earth. His eyes still felt as if he had just woken up.

"Well?"

"I like it," he said. "It makes me think of the quarry. Have you ever been to the old limestone quarry?"

"Of course," she said, "but years and years ago."

"I went swimming there last night."

"You did? But wasn't it too cold?" Her head was turned away from him now as she hooked the weaving to the wall.

Her body twisting, her arms reaching, she felt him watching her, and when she turned back, his eyes were large and questioning, his hands empty.

"I'll take you there right now," he said abruptly.

"Right now?" She gestured to the strewn floor, where her

boxes of treasures—the candles, the soaps and lotions, the aprons and smocks, the weavings and hand-knitted sweaters, the baby clothes and table linens, the pottery and baskets made of pine needles, the framed compositions made of dried flowers, the jams, the embroidered pillows—all at once looked strangely desolate, as if they had been washed ashore from a wreck. "How can I? I can't."

But she smiled at him because of his eyes and the emptiness of his hands. Her own hands, too, were empty. She shrugged, smiling. A complete, stunning spring day poured through the door behind him.

In a rush came old doubts to scatter her sense of soothing momentum. Folding her arms on the top of the ladder, for steadiness and to stall for time, she said to Morgan, "I wish I could." But he had already hunched his shoulders and jammed his hands into his pockets and was turning to leave.

"OK," he said. "The quarry's not going anywhere."

As the afternoon intensified in fineness, Joanna was sorry that she had not at once accepted Morgan's idea, but when she went outside to look for him, his truck was gone. She didn't want to unpack another box. Actions that only yesterday, and through the vicissitudes of winter, had been straightforward to her, today in the tempered spring did not seem as convincing. She turned off the radio, brushed her hair quickly, and started out for the hatchery, even though her father wasn't expecting her until their usual six-o'clock Friday dinner.

Joanna drove north down Spring Street and then east on Main, past the bank and the stores, on out beyond the bin and feed companies, the implement lot, the tanks of propane and ammonia, to a stretch that signaled home—a serpentine watershed valley crossed at intervals by grassy earth dams, ringed by rounded, wooded hills, now delicately greening. At the end of the valley a rustic sign, set among oak trees, marked the entrance to the hatchery. The slope below the house, which overlooked dozens of long ponds, was today smeared yellow with dandelions. In winter, snow would fill this quiet clearing, but upon the ponds, fed by springs and artesian wells, always constant in temperature between 40 and 50 degrees, the flakes would at once disappear, as if eaten by the fish. Winter and summer, heavy crows like these swayed in the topmost branches of trees, jagged black wads of feathers.

"Your dad's in the rearing house," old Don Swidrak told her as she approached the round pond of specimen salmon and trout. Don sat upon a bentwood bench, both man and bench fixtures for as long as Joanna could remember, sowing dried food on the surface of the water. It was his special pleasure, she knew, to feed by hand these chosen few and dwell dreamily upon the large, silent bodies, slowly switching from one side of the pond to the other.

Not far away, the old man's grandson, in waders, inched along wielding the suction pump that cleaned algae from the pond bottom. Joanna waved. Frank had been a classmate of hers. These days his children, visiting, caught little leopard frogs in the grass and threw them to the largemouth bass, as Joanna herself had often been fascinated to do. The spring of graduation, ten years ago, Frank had taken her to a school dance, an invitation with neither prelude nor postlude. His stiff blue suit had seemed to have no relation to the supple body she had felt moving inside it, and she had known he wished as fervently as she to be back in old clothes, away from the decorated gymnasium, away to the woods. She had imagined the two of them together, scrambling up a hill through brush, laughing. Then that, too, had passed. She had gone off to the city. A few months later he had been married; then, too quickly, a father.

"Daughter," her father said, looking up from his chart, over the tops of his glasses. Above him hung a stuffed and lacquered chinook. Behind him stretched the double rows of cement rearing tanks. There was the constant bubbling sound of old water being exchanged for new.

There had been times as a child, wandering freely on the hatchery grounds and in the woods, when she had experienced a kind of peaceful, suspended existence, like the weightlessness of falling asleep. Even now she sometimes dropped into this welcoming awareness; it was almost like being near her mother again, like being held in a long, secure gestation.

"You're early," her father said. "I might put you to work hosing the floor."

"That's all right," she answered.

When she came up to the house half an hour later to help with dinner, she found her father sitting in the kitchen rocking chair with his shoes off, reading the newspaper. A few pots steamed on the gas range. The room had never been remodeled. The same curtains, printed with cherries, hung at the sink window; the same wood-cased radio had brought the three of them news years ago. He had not remarried. Then there had been two of them, along with the trees, the water, and the company of a million fish.

"She's not going to die, is she?" Sudden knowledge had been in Joanna's words that February night when her father returned from the hospital. Thirteen years old, she had been hunched over her schoolwork in front of the kitchen gas heater. Bright's disease, her father had said, but even the name seemed wrong. For her in her childish self-absorption, the illness until that night had been merely a dark, pervading sense of disorder, eventually to be righted.

Joanna tended the pots and set the table while her father continued to read. From long habit they said very little to each other. Joanna supposed that in the early years she must have tried to bring out his voice to match her own urgent young one, but gradually she had almost stopped yearning for there to be more of him to know. It was almost enough, this steadiness.

"It's ready," she said.

There was a worn plastic cloth on the kitchen table, bare in places of decoration. Joanna watched her father mashing more butter into his potatoes, systematically, every gesture familiar to her.

"Eat up," he said. "You're still too thin."

It was amazing to her sometimes to think that she had come partly from this stubby man with dark circles around his eyes and wiry, graying hair. Every day he did what had to be done, without hurry. After lunch and dinner he took naps on the couch, and when he woke his hair would be standing up, and he would scratch it, all the while wrinkling his forehead and lifting his brows as if to help open his eyes. He spoke to her only of practical things.

Often when he napped in the evening, Joanna would wander along the paths between the long ponds of darting fingerlings, but tonight, still somewhat agitated from her encounter with Morgan, she climbed to the attic of the house with the sudden idea that one or two of the old trunks there might be useful in displaying some of the shawls and sweaters in the shop. She ran up both flights of stairs without stopping. Her legs were no longer weighted with that awful fatigue of her illness; her back no longer ached. Last year at this time she would have had to sit down to rest halfway up the stairs to the city apartment.

She pulled one of the trunks closer to the light of the window and crouched before its contents. Inside was the red paisley shawl her grandmother had said had been bought from an itinerant peddlar a hundred years ago. Joanna draped it around herself; she began to hum, rummaging. Far below, the ponds in a grid of paths reflected the evening sky. It was the hour for flocks of birds to collect in trees. It was the hour when the trees just begin to darken, when boundaries soften.

Wrapped in the shawl, swaying slightly, she turned her face to the window of sky. Unfathomable, she felt, were the forces everywhere at work. Unshakable was what she would like to be, open to these streaming forces but at the same time calm, slightly suspended.

Beneath this twilit sky Morgan slowly paddled his wood and canvas canoe, trolling his fishing line through an upstream dell where his rhythmic sounds were magnified between the shadowed cliffs. At the far end he pulled in his line, swept the boat around, and then stroked with the current toward home. Alone, alert to the water ahead, watchful of the shores, he felt himself to be as strong, as statuesque, as an Indian. He had not shown anyone anything yet. Moments of smallness—fumbling for words, dealing in stores, listening to his ma, facing the town—in the end could be made to shrink away. What had to stay, what he had to keep his mind clear for, was that steady sense of his own towering, natural poise. Clean strokes with the paddle—those were important—and ready eyes and deep breaths.

What was that? He heard a crashing on the far shore and then silence. A scene of war flashed through his memory, but by keeping his eyes open, his mind determined, the lights and noise did not possess him this time; he was learning. He rested his paddle for a moment on the gunwales. No more sound. Had it been deer? Swiftly the river carried him, without his doing anything. By degree after degree the night was coming on of itself. Nighthawks darted out over the water, close to shore.

He could have said to Joanna, "Come anyway. You'll be glad you did." He could have said, "I have something to show you." But he hadn't; he had turned away.

With one skillful angle of his paddle he now brought himself beneath his own willow tree. Ducking its branches, reaching for the grassy bank, he suddenly groaned aloud. The anguish was that no one really knew his stature, what he had started with, what he had managed to put together.

Who was this Rob character Joanna had been talking to on

the telephone? Why hadn't he asked her? Why wasn't he able just to say what he meant?

After she had said good night to her father, Joanna drove back to Spring Street and in appreciation of the soft evening dark, and also in an attitude of vigilance, she sat down on the bottom step of new redwood, where Morgan had been at work that day, and took in a deep breath of fragrant air. The street in its new foliage seemed like a long greenish-black room, with a little skylight here and there. A spotted dog nosed along the sidewalk.

Years ago, Joanna's black Labrador had crept away to the woods to die alone. "Why didn't she let me take care of her?" she had wept to her father.

Now here she was a dozen years later, stretching out her long legs, recognizing what a mercy it could be to find oneself alone and silent at the end of a day. One could sit still, perhaps swaying slightly around a possible core of balance, one's mind vigilant, watching for oneself to become available. . . . The telephones began to ring from the house.

"No," she said aloud, closing her eyes. "No, Rob, please. Not now."

Ring after ring she did not answer. Seven, eight. She got up from the stair, paced down to the street, and then quickly returned up the drive and to her car. The ringing continued in her mind for several minutes as she drove down Spring Street to the south. She turned on the car radio and then turned it off. On the bridge at the edge of town, she slowed almost to a standstill, long enough to see how the Plover was lighter now than the shadowy bank grasses, how a slightly lopsided moon had risen just above the distant fringe of willows at the farthest bend of pale, reflecting water.

After about five miles, she turned onto a county blacktop, angling to the southeast, which she knew generally followed the river, off there invisibly to her left. Up ahead some miles should be the dells. She hadn't been on this stretch of road for years. Here and there rutted lanes led down into the river meadows on the left or into the higher fields on the right. At the top of a hill a line of cows plodded in silhouette, going the same direction, with infinite slowness, as she.

Wasn't that the old quarry road? She stopped and backed up the car. Surely it was. The car climbed for a quarter of a mile, then began a jolting descent around the high western rim of the quarry, mostly obscured by thick brush. Joanna slowed to a cow's pace.

At the bottom of the hill the road stopped. She got out of the car and pushed through brush on a narrow path. In high school, once she and her friends had learned to drive, Joanna had been allowed to come here occasionally in early summer, before the dog days set in and the water was considered unsafe. The June of graduation she had spent a whole day here with her two best girlfriends, wanting and not wanting the attentions of the boys who were performing noisy and daring jumps from the twenty-five-foot-high rim on the other side of the quarry.

Ah—a-ah-a-ah! had been their Tarzan call as they dropped through space. She heard it now in memory, above the tramping of her feet. When she came to the clearing, she stopped, and there she heard the distinctness of a single bullfrog, in his element.

She sat down on the hard rock ledge and drew up her knees, a compact, still shape. Beneath the water was the hard man-made quarrying equipment that she had always been afraid the boys would strike as they plunged from the high rim. But life had gone on; for her, too, it was going on and on. Life was still her element.

Had Morgan really been in already for a swim? Dropping to her stomach, extending herself from the edge, she plunged her hand beneath the surface. If you wanted to swim badly enough, you could stand it, she decided. Her own head and shoulders, extending from the ledge, made an uneasy shadow.

She undressed quickly, crouched to bring up cupped hands of water to wet the insides of her arms and the back of her neck and her stomach and the small of her back in preparation, hesitated for one instant, and then slipped carefully off the ledge, testing with her legs for outcroppings of the rock. Breathy sounds came from her involuntarily. She stroked rapidly out into the bright center and then swam in a wide circle, staying clear of the ledges, immersed now in this liquid mineral, still replenishing itself from the deep springs, which one night long before her own lifetime had burst free and in less than twelve hours, so the story went, submerged steam machinery that could be in a museum now. No light reached it; she could see nothing down below; the distance, she had been told, was nearly a hundred feet.

Man's enterprise had been made featureless in a single night, except that here she was, floating face up now, making a laughing moon of her face, taking on light. Everything, she thought, mattered and exquisitely did not matter.

She felt so easy and free swimming here tonight. Veering from the wide circles she had been making, she swam up and down the length of the quarry several times. Then it was enough. She found an underwater foothold near her clothes and pulled herself up. Well, it had been wonderful; she was very glad she had simply done it, and she was glad now for her body in the moonlight, strengthened, refreshed. She shook her head like a dog and rubbed herself dry with her shirt and dressed in her slacks and sweater. Wonderful.

Back on the county road, having navigated the ascent around the quarry, she hadn't much on her mind but a clean, generalized awareness when suddenly a figure appeared in the beam of her lights, jogging toward her along the edge of the road, a towel around his neck. It was unmistakably Morgan. She blinked her lights, slowed, stopped, then leaned over and rolled down the window as he reached the car.

"Well, look who's here," he said, still breathing rapidly, leaning a forearm on the open window.

"I took your advice and had a swim."

"It's not bad, is it? That's where I'm headed. You wouldn't want to turn around and come in again with me, would you?"

"No, no." She laughed. "I've had enough for one night."

"Well, you only live once."

"So some people say."

"Your hair is pretty wet."

"I know. That's why I'm on my way home."

"Would you want to see my place? You could sit by my stove." He gestured over his right shoulder, toward the river. Standing securely in his own territory, he heard how easily he spoke to her, and for the pleasure of hearing more of that unaccustomed voice, he continued. "I've got the only solar house in Rosedale. Maybe you'd like to see it. You could do something like it off that middle room in the shop, a place for plants."

"All right," she said. "I'd like to take a look. Get in and direct me."

"Straight ahead," he said, a little awkward now that he was actually in the car, "about a quarter of a mile, then turn right. Look sharp, it's just a lane. OK, down we go, a straight line to the river."

"You're going to miss your swim."

"That's OK." He looked over at her as she parked the car beside his truck. "You could have this towel, if you wanted, for your hair." He pulled it off his neck.

"Thanks. Thanks very much." She made a quick turban.

"OK," he said. "Time for the grand tour."

All the while he anxiously scanned first her face, then his kingdom, then again the expression on her face: riverbank, willow tree, canoe, raspberry canes, garden plot. He was sorry he hadn't had time yet for a proper step at the door, now just a concrete block. "This will be a big slab of redwood," he said, "with some planters."

"What a wonderful entrance." She was stepping directly into the solar area, the glassed wall sloping to her right over plants, and to her left was a large room dense with the props of a singular habitation. All indoor activity apparently took place in this one room, for around the central pivot of a woodburning stove were a kitchen area, a quilt-covered bed, a sizable workbench, various shelves and cabinets, and several rocking chairs. Midway between kitchen and sitting areas was a round oak table, with two chairs and a lamp hanging above it. Joanna turned around several times. "You have everything you need. It's wonderful. Now tell me about this greenhouse."

"Those are storm windows." Morgan was moving about turning on a few lights, one of them a small spotlight that beamed upon the plants.

"Really? You're not fooling? How clever." She ran her fingers over a carefully caulked seam.

"Do you like it?" asked Morgan.

She laughed. "Of course I like it. What are those?" She pointed to some heavy double cords that ran at intervals down the window wall, looping around some pulleys at the base.

"Shades," he said. "Look up." He walked over to where the cord ends were cleated from a system of ceiling pulleys to the wall, and, swinging them out toward the center of the room, he began to manipulate the lowering of canvas shades, like a stagehand in a theater. He had a pleased, almost disbelieving expression on his face. "My own design. I lower them on hot days in the summer or at night in the winter."

"How wonderful. But how did you make them?"

"Oh, a friend of mine works for a tent company. I do some woodworking for him, he sews these for me."

"Yes," she said, "that's the best way." But then she immediately reflected that for her he worked for money.

"If you like, I'll make a little fire and you can dry your hair." He pulled a rocking chair closer to the stove. "I've been wanting you to see this place." Again he was surprised at his own voice.

His profile was to her as he knelt on one knee and began to lay the fire with his long, squarish, careful hands. The first jumping flames were reflected in his concentrating eye. He turned to smile at her. His mouth smiled, but his eyes kept their intense, sad, wary disbelief. Deep creases, strange for his age, cut almost vertically down his cheeks. She remembered he had been in the army, and as she pulled the towel from her hair and leaned toward the warmth, she asked, "How was it for you in the army?"

"The army? What made you think of that?" He stared a moment at the fire and then shook himself alert. "I tried not to get too involved," he said in a measured voice, "if you know what I mean. I tried to stay relaxed. When I wasn't out actually doing battle, I was just there, watching the sun come up and the sun go down and the clouds go by, sort of letting myself forget there was a war. I didn't want to focus in on anything in particular, I just wanted to exist."

"Yes, I can picture that," she said, immediately recognizing in herself a similar desire to preserve an inner, unassimilable essence, barely to exist, to stall for time. She drew her fingers slowly outward through her hair.

Now that he was speaking, and with words he had never spoken before to anyone, he did not want to stop. There was more; he had not yet touched on the terribleness, the inescapable terribleness, and now perhaps was the time. "Besides," he said, taking a breath, poking at the fire, "what was going on at home was worse to me than what was going on over there."

"At home? You mean the general lack of public conviction, one way or the other?"

"No. In my family. Haven't you heard about my family?"

"I've been away for nearly ten years," she said.

"Sure. I forgot." He stood up abruptly. "How about something to drink? Here I am, forgetting to offer you something."

He began to pace around the stove, not listening for a reply. Her eyes followed him. She told herself to stay very quiet. He was holding his arms in a strange way, slightly out from his body, with shoulders hunched and hands fisted. His glance toward her was slanting, challenging, showing the whites of his eyes. She waited.

"You must have heard about my father and my uncle. Your dad must have told you when he heard I was working on your place."

"No. My dad's not like that. He just lets people live."

Morgan stopped pacing and faced her.

"What happened, Morgan?" she asked quietly. She had been folding the frayed gray towel carefully and now hung it over the arm of her chair. She folded her hands in her lap. It was her bedtime, she realized, and she did not know where she wanted to be, alone in sleep, or here, waiting for this story, very difficult, apparently, to articulate. Speechless now, Morgan was staring through her, eyes narrowing upon a distress only he could see.

At last he began, and as the story jerked forward, it seemed too old and hopeless even to warrant rehearsing: in the midst of the crude harshness of a country winter an uncle had defrauded a father and there had been what may or may not have been an accident, on the partially frozen river, on a Saturday night. The father drowned, the uncle disappeared, and a burned-out, once-beautiful Norwegian woman, Morgan's mother, still had three children at home.

"But what about her, your mother?" asked Joanna.

"She had already given up on the both of them. So she told me. I am the oldest. I'm the one she talks to."

"So she made do? She had to, didn't she?"

"She said she'd already lost every ounce of respect she'd ever had for my father."

"So she's bitter. But how did she manage?"

"She's a cook. She was already a cook."

"And how old were you, Morgan?" Very quietly Joanna was rocking in her chair, and for whole moments it seemed to her that she was not here at all, but already asleep. Morgan paced and stopped, paced and stopped, delivering his words in spurts.

"I was nineteen. Just been drafted. Ma screamed, but I went. And you know what? For a while I hardly even heard the battles because my ears were so full of all that feuding and wailing back home. I didn't know where I was. Then I said to myself that everything was a mistake, even the war, but I wasn't a mistake. How did I know that? I don't know. But I have good eyesight. I just started seeing real clear and then forgetting, not dwelling on anything, just waiting. I knew there must be some good reason why I was feeling so separate. I knew I wasn't a mistake."

Joanna had stopped rocking. Recognition stilled her. "Yes," she said, "and then you came home and you slept as if you'd never slept before. You were alone."

"That's right! I got myself apprenticed up north. I said to hell with all those mistakes."

"And now you don't know if you should trust anyone the way you trust yourself."

"Listen, nobody in my family is doing what I'm doing. I'm not going to let anybody drag me down."

Joanna stared at the position and height of him against the lighted wall of glass. "But suppose you can't find out everything on your own? Suppose you need other people to teach you what you need to know?"

"Wait a minute." Morgan stopped pacing. He jerked a thumb toward his own chest. "There isn't anybody in the world who knows what I've had to put together in order to come up with this." He gestured around him.

"I suppose not," said Joanna, beginning to rock again. "I'm very impressed with your place here."

"Do you see that bookcase? I've been reading books! I go to the library! Nobody knows all the books I've been reading. I've been going to the libraries all over this county."

"Don't you want to come and sit down by your own fire, Morgan?"

"You're sorry, aren't you? Admit it. You're sorry you came here, and you're sorry you've got a crackpot for a carpenter."

"Are you a crackpot, Morgan?"

"No, I'm not."

"Then I don't have anything to be sorry for, do I? Besides, you're doing a very good job. Don't you think you are?"

"Damn good," he said. He dragged up the second rocker, sat down, and smiled at her uneasily. "You'll probably be glad when I finish with the job and clear out."

"Yes," she said, "but only because I want to be in business. I need to start making money."

"What if you don't?"

"That's a fine way to talk! Why shouldn't I?"

"You'll probably get married," he said. "You'd be better off."

She looked at him steadily from beneath her lashes, not speaking.

"You're not some kind of nun, are you?" he asked.

She began to laugh.

"Well?" he pressed, starting to laugh himself. "What are you?"

"What am I?" She got up and walked out into the cool of the room, beneath the windows. There was now a rasping weariness in her mind. How could she answer any of these men until she knew herself?

"Morgan," she said, "it's really high time I got on home. I've had a long day."

"Now you're mad at me," he said. "You probably don't even want me to come to work on Monday."

She turned to him. "I'm not a nun," she said.

"You probably think I'm some kind of oaf."

She picked up her purse. "Whatever you are you're doing all right. I'll see you on Monday." She let herself out the door and started toward the car.

"Hey!" he called behind her. The door banged, and he loped across the moonlit driveway. He rested both hands on the roof of the car and hung his head to her window. "You're pretty smart, you know that? You're pretty smart to get me to talk that way."

She said nothing, holding her keys in her hand.

He brought his fists down on top of the car. "So now you're going to drive away. You found out what you want to know, and now you're going to go home and make fun of me. You don't care."

She had gone into cold water, she remembered, and felt at home and come up laughing. She smiled at him, steadily. "I like your house," she said.

"You do?"

"Yes, I'm telling you, I like your house. You have good ideas. You're right that a wall like that would work in the middle room of the shop. That's where I wanted to set up the looms and give weaving lessons, and the light would be wonderful."

"What are you saying?"

She reached up and touched his shoulder in a friendly way. "I'm saying that you can trust me with your story. I know a little bit what it's like to come back home and try to build something new. Honestly."

"Why did you come back, anyway?"

She laughed. "Same as you. I wanted to get free of the mistakes."

"Joanna—" He shook his head as if to shake off an old

disbelief. Then he reached down and felt the back of her head. "Your hair got pretty dry."

"Yes," she said. "Thanks for the fire. Will I see you first thing on Monday?"

"I'll be there," he said, and this time he hit the top of the car lightly, like a finishing touch, to send her off.

At dawn the next morning Morgan woke in a surge of well-being, from a dream in which he had stepped onto a stage and spoken resounding words, without even knowing the part. Directly he was aware of being awake, he flung aside the quilt and stepped outside into the multitudinous awakenings of birds. How had he known what to say? He had simply opened his mouth, and everything he needed was there.

He urinated into the grass. A mist still clung to the river; overhead, curdled clouds in shades of dawn looked as if they were being sucked to the rising sun. He stripped off his long underwear beside the canoe and waded into the river, smooth mud between his toes, against his legs a few weeds, a few small fish, his penis afloat now in the fresh current, his eyes at the level where the mist was just lifting, trailing shreds on its underside, from the backwater grasses on the opposite shore, and there he saw the veil being drawn to reveal a great blue heron: lone, balanced, plumed, hunched, savvy in its eye.

Against the current toward the heron Morgan stroked. He, Morgan Peters, was an aborigine at the dawn of an age. He was all of a piece, poised upon a juncture. Everything he needed for the future was available. Closer and closer he was coming to the great bird, one of his brothers. In this new age the species would talk to one another. The great blue heron would open its long yellow beak beneath the canny eye and speak of brotherhood.

At that moment the bird straightened its neck and turned its head to Morgan, lowered its folded leg, took one delicate step, and then, drawing back its head, rose abruptly into the air with an incredible lifting of blue mass, a lingering hoarse cry of alarm.

"It's all right!" shouted Morgan, waving his arm from the surface of the water. "I'm going to be here for a long time, I think."

A STAY BY THE RIVER

I have flown a thousand miles to visit Melanie and Todd. A few minutes ago Melanie and I descended barefoot to the garden, and I watched while she selected the red and pale-green lettuce leaves I am now rinsing one by one in a kitchen that is cut like a windowed cave into the slope on which the house was built—how many years ago, Melanie?

Almost a hundred, she says and opens the screen door to call out to Todd and the children in the gazebo, Shall we eat down there?

Tomorrow I will go to the garden and weed the vegetables; I saw tonight that I could go there regularly by myself and without asking directions find useful and ordinary work. Already I think I can feel my mind easing itself. I am glad for the river at the base of the bluff. From the kitchen window I can see the water glinting in late sun through the trees, but not the train, whose wail I am hearing for the second time since my arrival. My room upstairs has a leaded casement window that I can crank open or shut while sitting in a flowered reading chair. Melanie cranked the window open for me this noon and said they haven't bothered to change the house much from the way Todd's parents had kept it. What else could you do with a house like this? she said. She laughed as if the house doesn't matter to her, or as if she scarcely believes the way she is living.

Alone, pausing at a mirror in the upstairs hallway, I pressed my forefingers beside my eyes and pulled taut the lines of fatigue. I looked from one eye to the other and back again. Without hurry I saw how light entered my eyes and gave back color.

I came downstairs and found Melanie with the children in the sun-room above the kitchen. In spite of myself I thought that if I want a child of my own, I have only a few years left. Melanie's oldest girl sat coloring on a long cushioned window seat. She was keeping her crayons in a matchbox that she slid open and shut each time she chose a new color.

Now Melanie wraps the wet washed lettuce in a towel and takes it out the door to the mossy terrace. I see the balloon of thin white towel circling in the air, spraying waterdrops, as she makes a windmill of her arm. Leaning my hand on the thick stone wall of the doorway, I think of how long these stones have been here, motionless.

Melanie cuts fresh dill and long green onions on a board. I wonder if she is aware of her hands. She is wearing an old white blouse, and I like her brown neck and her long brown switch of hair. I sit idly, luxuriously, in the dark wood breakfast booth, listening to the chicken broiling and watching Melanie's hands. There is a Band-Aid on one of her fingers and on another a silver and turquoise ring.

She is talking about a cottage down the road. We'll walk

down there tonight or tomorrow, she says.

Who did you say he is? I ask.

Burdock, Martin Burdock, she repeats patiently, and for a moment I feel as if I am one of Melanie's children. I wonder what it would be like to be one of Melanie's children, sitting permanently among window seat pillows, choosing colors from the sliding inside of a matchbox.

Melanie is deft. Already she has gotten up a tray with seeded rolls and butter, plates and silverware. She takes wine from the refrigerator. I wonder where she has learned this casual deftness. Mostly I remember her earnestness, and her candor. One of the children begins to cry from the yard, and I see a slight change in Melanie's mouth and down the center of her forehead. Let's go fast, she says, gathering things up, before they all get too tired.

Todd leads me down the steps to a wooden landing high in the trees above the railroad tracks and the river. We are finishing off the wine.

My grandfather built this bench, he says.

A hundred years ago? I ask.

No, not that long. He laughs. We are sitting close and enjoying each other's company. In the gazebo Melanie kissed us both and then took the children up for their baths. You come for the tucking-in, she called back to Todd. The youngest of the three, a boy of two, threw a rock down into the treetops before he followed his mother.

Did you hear it land? asked Todd through the latticework and screens. That's for the train coming, Dad, said the boy. Whatever that means, said Todd to me, winking. He picked up the bottle, and I took our glasses and followed his pale gray shirt down the steps into the darker trees.

Why did your grandfather choose this place? I ask.

Lord knows, he answers. There's an Indian burial ground on the property—did you know?

That's a treasure, I suppose?

Anna's gotten afraid of the ghosts. She's old enough to think about those things.

I drink the light white wine and ask Todd when the next train is due. If this is Saturday, then not until tomorrow morning, he says, stretching out his legs. I like him immensely. He and Melanie were already married twelve years ago when I met her. I liked him then. It gives me pleasure to drink this wine and to sit next to him in the dark trees, knowing we are both twelve years older and still good friends. He leans his ruddy, bearded head toward me and gives me the last few drops from a bottle that in the thick light I can only barely tell is green.

The boatyards are closing down—did Melanie tell you? he asks.

No. Is that bad for you?

Not so bad. If it hadn't been for Dad's death, I probably never would have come back here anyway. It's amazing; we intended to stay a few months to clean up his affairs, and here we are, four years later.

What will you do? I ask.

Oh, there are a few other interests—shipping and storage and so forth, if that's what I want.

Is that what you want?

I'm not much of a businessman, he says. It took months just to understand what my dad had going. He must have thought that he would live forever. His offices were still upstairs at the yards—you can picture it—outside staircase, wooden filing cabinets, dusty windows, dusty ship models, dusty sunshine, and God what a mess of papers! The place still smelled of his pipe. Todd leans forward and lays the empty bottle between his shoes.

I can see it, I say; the historian examining his origins.

Something like that.

And now?

Now the building has been sold and will be torn down this

summer, and I've got to decide whether to keep on with the rest of it or sell out. What would you do?

This place is beautiful. When Melanie wrote that you were moving here, I couldn't quite imagine it, but it's beautiful; the river is marvelous.

I don't think Melanie has quite settled in.

Todd's body makes me think of my own. I see the lightness of his shirt sleeve and his almost invisible hand, and I think of the length of my legs within these soft, loosely fitting slacks.

Todd lets his voice speak on. Sometimes I think I could do nothing more than live off a garden and be with Melanie and the children, he says. We could sell the furniture piece by piece, and then our clothes, piece by piece.

I see Todd and Melanie lying on the carpet of an empty living room, naked in the moonlight of the open French doors.

The shrilling of insects and tree toads seems to be rising in false panic. I try to do nothing but empty my mind and understand those layers of sound, but instead I am thinking about the Indians who are dead and buried someplace on the property. I am thinking that I woke up this morning halfway across the continent. I make a sound, but forget what I had intended to say.

Are you tired? asks Todd. Do you want to come up and say good night to the children?

Sylvie is running up and down the broad, breezy hall in a blue summer nightgown patterned with white butterflies. Light opens out into the hall from the bathroom and bedrooms. My own room, I see, is luminous. Melanie must have come into my room, perhaps with Jonathan naked on her arm, to turn on the light beside my flowered chair. Sylvie follows me and stops at the foot of my bed, twisting the hem of her nightgown in one hand. She allows me to come to her and pick her up, but she is lighter than I supposed, so light that for a moment I feel we could take off from earth on the unused energy of my expectation. Tonight I am relieved to be tethered by a child. She giggles as I press my face against her belly, and I wonder how the vapors of wine must seem to her.

A net has been thrown around this house. It is made of tree branches and shadows and fretted layers of sound. We pass down the hall and through a lighted doorway. I try to think in a simple way about the net of love into which I have slipped for a brief visit. Anna is already asleep with her crayons beside her bed.

Sing to me, says Sylvie, reaching out for her blanket, and I hear myself singing a song I probably haven't thought about for thirty years.

Out in the darkened hallway I find Melanie leaning slackly against the couch, turned toward the puffing curtains of the open window.

I am in the garden, working methodically up and down the rows with a triangular hoe. I have done the radishes, the red lettuce, the green lettuce, and now I bend beside peas supported on horizontal strings. Someone has put collars of straw at the base of the staked tomatoes. When I straighten up again to rest, I see Todd, starting down the road.

He stretches across the front seat of the car. I didn't know anyone else was up, he calls.

I don't think of anything to say. I stand with my hoe, smiling, thinking simply of the early heat of the sun. I wave and he drives away. I think how I would like to be responsible for this garden. I would like to have been the one who carried straw to the tomato plants and tied strings along the rows of peas. Last night Melanie seemed quick and indifferent as she gathered the lettuces and radishes. I marvel at that, now that I am in between the rows myself, slowed down to garden time, cultivating foot by foot and noticing each plant's signs of growth. I think how I could like an entire summer to be measured solely by a garden.

After four more rows Melanie calls me for breakfast. When I come up the slope to the terrace, I see a young woman with hunched, awkward shoulders talking to Melanie. Extra children shout on the swings and beneath the awnings of the sandbox. I look briefly to the river curving out below a point of land some distance along the bluff top, and when I reach the table and am introduced, I am thinking that land coming to a point high above a river would be a naturally chosen burial ground.

The young woman has brought strawberries in a flat pan, small ones that she explains are sweeter and larger ones that are not so sweet. Her voice trembles slightly and she listens solemnly as Melanie tosses off a gay incident of strawberries from her childhood. Melanie is in motion. Some time ago, when I was in the garden, her morning began, and now she is speaking with a force and swiftness that might be called impatience. She glances now and then at the children. Someone cries. She goes to pick up Jonathan and comes back still talking. She is forcing the world away from her with words. The young woman stares down into her coffee cup, tipping the dregs of it from side to side and looking as if she is holding back a helpless pain. I take toast and boiled eggs from a basket and sit quietly eating, stealing my hand out now and then for a strawberry and wondering when the real Melanie will return.

Oh, God, says Melanie, crumpling down full-length on the grass when her visitor has left. That girl is in love with me and I have no idea what to do.

Is that what was going on? I say. I am wondering how Melanie can read such love; how does she know?

I find it exhausting, she says. I'm afraid I do more damage than good. Go on, go on, she urges me. I wish you'd eat every last one of those strawberries. She calls the children over and tells them to eat strawberries, while she herself lies down in the grass alongside a bed of daisies and poppies. Jonathan spits the berries out.

Come here, Jonathan, she calls and catches hold of him, and together they go rolling over and over down the grass. Melanie's laugh is wild and fierce, and the children catch her mood and go rolling over and over. I run inside to get my camera, and as I pound up the stairs I barely hear the trailing sound of the train between their high, rolling cries. Halfway down the hall I stop. I see myself in my apartment, coming out of the darkroom at night, examining a proof sheet of Melanie's life, frame after frame of someone else's life. I turn instead into the bathroom, where I lay a cold cloth over my face, pressing it to my eyes, and then I wipe the garden dirt from my arms and legs. Taking off my shoes and lifting my feet one and then the other to the basin, I wash them in cool water.

Today a dozen moths, some yellow-white like paper and others thicker and mottled brown, that were lured by last night's bathroom light, are clinging, asleep or waiting for death, against the walls. I think of telling Melanie about the stillness of the moths in the growing heat and commotion of the morning, and I hear her saying, pushing back her hair, Todd has been meaning to fix that screen.

As I finish washing my feet, I watch a sluggish lightning bug crawl along the edge of the basin. His back is segmented, the small anterior part touched with red and the lower section long, black, halved, like a stiff frock coat. My own back is a single supple chain of bones; I can feel the nerved complexity of its beginnings at the nape of my skull and at its base the shielding bones of my pelvis and the strong sockets of my legs.

How does Melanie know? I thought last winter with Michael that I knew; now nothing seems to be left. I became critical and bewildered; I resumed my long walks alone. He did nothing to hold me. Why did he do nothing to hold me?

I go downstairs, and Melanie is at the kitchen sink. Jonathan presses into her bare legs, crying. Outside the door Anna shouts something bossily to Sylvie and then rides around the corner of the house on her new two-wheeled bicycle; Sylvie cries and throws a clump of dirt against the screen door.

Stop it, Jonathan. No one can stand to listen to that. Stop it! I wish you would tell me what you want. I don't want to listen to those tears.

Melanie's hands never stop lifting dishes from the soapy water. The announcer on the kitchen radio tells the news. Do you hear me, Jonathan? she says. You've got to stop these scenes and tell me what you need.

We are passing through unmown grasses at the end of the property. I am talking with Anna, holding her by the hand, while Melanie pushes ahead through the heat, straddling Jonathan on one hip. For some minutes Sylvie has been whining to be carried. She will have none of me today. Melanie reaches down finally for her middle child and then struggles on like a beast of burden.

The air is scented with purple clover. We are going to visit Martin Burdock. I brush at the gnats and listen to Anna, who says that fairies leave and reenter their underground homes at the base of trees, where the roots show. She asks me if I have ever been at the equator. She says it is possible to fry an egg on the equator. I ask her what she thinks the equator looks like, and she says it is probably flat, but not very thick. She asks me if I know that Sylvie wants a two-wheeler but can't have one because her legs aren't long enough. I look down at Anna's own gangling legs beneath her faded shorts, her thin chest and urgent face, and my next breath comes quickly, like an ache.

Martin Burdock has retired to a cottage with a garden and a view of the river. Melanie sits on the grass beside his chair with Jonathan asleep across her lap. The girls whisper in their make-believe beneath a flowering hedge. I am not sure what is happening. It seems to me as if Melanie has brought an offering to Martin Burdock, that she has brought herself and the children, even me, into his garden as gifts, as species of blooming flowers. I do not feel like a flower. I am nondescript, my color sucked away. We drink English tea, and I notice that Martin Burdock and his garden are at the same time fastidious and disorderly. He pushes aside a pile of newspapers and fusses a bit at the angle of the sun, adjusting a dilapidated umbrella over the table. We must, it seems, be able to see each other without strain, in the proper light. I see violet and green shadows all along Melanie's skin; her face is flushed and her eyes are gray and yellow.

Martin Burdock is writing a book, and as Melanie sets down her cup and eases her legs beneath Jonathan, I know suddenly that she is using Martin Burdock's eyes. She sees Anna and Sylvie in the shadows, she sees the brilliant river, in a sliding glance she sees me, then the hot heavy head of Jonathan—all through the eyes of Martin Burdock, and then in the next moment as I look at Martin Burdock's aging face, the way its lights and hollows of color incline themselves to Melanie, my breath presses hard in me and I seem to have lost a space of time. Here it is again, I think. Here it is: if I had been Melanie, would I have known? Could I have let it happen?

I am losing track of days. This afternoon a storm brings in cooler air. My mail has been forwarded to me by Edward. My parents are well; they themselves will travel in two weeks. An insurance payment is due on the nineteenth. My brother Julien will stop to see me in August. Genevieve says they're saving most of the proofs for me and that three of the photographs for the catalog had to be retaken. Edward says the city is unbearable; he says my cat mopes but manages a few mouthfuls; he says my avocado plant suffers from the heat, along with everyone else; he says he came across the hall and played my piano the other night, knowing I wouldn't mind; he says, How are you anyway?

I have turned my reading chair away from the room so that

it faces squarely the window bleary with rain in its diamond-shaped panes. In my lap are the letters that verify my reasonable life. When I work, I work very well. I take the time to do my work well. But still, a momentum builds for which there seems no end; I go ahead deliberately, and yet I seem to myself to be racing. No one reaches out to stop me. Michael is a worker too, and when we would come together, it would be because we could no longer work.

Downstairs I find Melanie lying on the living room rug, exercising slowly by the half-open French doors. The storm has subsided into an even rain. Melanie has created a space around herself by the concentrated positions of her body. She smiles at me, but I go away to the sun porch, where I sit on Anna's window seat, just inside the rain. I try to think about nothing much but the rain, another summer storm, and about how everyone has to live somewhere, in some conditions or in others; everyone has a life. I pick up a magazine and read three recipes for blueberries, I think of Melanie's hands cutting green onions and a limp bouquet of feathery dill, I see Todd's shirted back descending through the trees, one hand holding up the wine bottle like a torch.

Melanie comes in and sits down in a wicker lounge, still in her leotard. Are you feeling more rested? she asks. You're beginning to look more rested.

Are the circles going away?

Either that or they're melting into your tan.

This place is beautiful, I say.

You really think so? I notice a careful lightness to her voice.

I do, don't you?

Maybe it's too beautiful. I wake up in the morning and look out the window and I think, God, this place. I look at Todd and the kids and I think, My God, look what has happened. She gestures loosely with her hand, from the wrist, and I see nothing but the perfect repose of her exercised body. There's too much; I'm not equal to it, she says.

Melanie asks me again about my work. I am suddenly suffocated by my work, angry.

I envy you, she goes on.

There's nothing to envy, you don't know what you have.

My words make her stop and regard me. We are afraid we have hurt each other. After a time she nods and says, still cautious with her voice, That's what I meant, I don't understand what I have. And maybe you don't either, she adds.

She tips back her head and we are quiet. Where are the children? I ask.

Jonathan is asleep. The girls are somewhere, the gazebo, I think. I can trust Anna.

I am trying to remember Melanie as I knew her twelve years ago, six years ago.

Do you know what has been happening to me? she says. I have begun remembering all sorts of things. Some days I can barely keep my mind on the present time. Exhaustion, probably. God, but children are exhausting.

What do you remember?

You really want to know? Melanie laughs. All right, this one happened a couple of weeks ago. I was coming downstairs. It was an ordinary day—well, no, rather special because I had been over to talk to Martin the night before. I was coming downstairs and I remembered that when I was twenty-one I had a vision of Christ. Do you think that's possible? she asks without pausing. I was in love with Todd, he had gone away, I had agreed to go out and help at this church group, and there he was one night, Jesus Christ, standing in his robes on the edge of a stream at vespers. I just looked, and he melted away, and I haven't thought about it for thirteen years.

What did you do at the time?

Nothing. I told no one. I just buried it all. I wasn't even going to church at the time. I'm certainly not going to church now. What on earth do you do with something like that?

Melanie is trying to sound humorous, but I see her body is jerking slightly with tremors. She looks very much like Anna just now, six years old, only much older. I feel powerless.

Has anything like that ever happened to you?

No, but I don't think it sounds unlike you, I say.

What do you mean? Do you think I'm a dreamer?

I smile at Melanie, but my eyes are trying to see beyond her black-suited figure to the form of what she means. An experience like that seems to fit in with your intensity, I say.

Intensity! Melanie laughs sharply, and I see she is close to tears. She has tipped back her head once more and is staring at the ceiling, sucking in her lips.

Why are you wanting to cry? I ask, and in a rush I understand that this is the way Edward talks to me; I am almost hearing the inflections of his voice.

There's so much now, says Melanie finally, there's so much at stake now that I find it almost impossible to know the truth of what I'm feeling.

You mean Todd and the children?

All right, if you want to put it that way: Todd and the children. Her voice is abruptly dry, analytical. I don't do anything purely any more, she says. She is looking at me steadily.

I meant what I said about intensity.

Gradually her face softens. Well then, I thank you, she breathes. You see how needy I am, I twist everything about just to get a few crumbs of assurance.

You're being very hard on yourself, I say.

No, you've got it wrong, she says quietly. I haven't been nearly hard enough.

We are at one end of the living room watching a rerun of the day's hearings. Todd has bathed the children and put them to bed, all but Sylvie, who sits stubbornly in his lap, eating graham crackers and letting herself be petted. The living room is airy and pleasant, carefully decorated by the previous generation. Todd wears a pair of threadbare jeans. Melanie is in a soiled robe, intending to bathe but held, as we all are, by the sordid drama, difficult to understand as real. I am sitting on the floor, pulling the drying skin from hoeing blisters on the palms of my hands.

Todd holds the feet of his daughter in one hand, stroking her skin with his thumb. He rubs her back with his other hand. I glance up now and then and see her taking cracker after cracker from the box on her lap until Melanie says, Don't you want a glass of milk, Sylvie? You'll gag on all that dryness.

I want grape juice, says Sylvie contentedly, and I see Melanie and Todd open their eyes to each other above her head, above my head, above the shifting faces on the television.

I can't go to sleep. My head hurts above my eyes, and the back of my neck is tight. My mind rushes repeatedly down a cataract of night and finds itself lodged against the same stones. The pain in my forehead is heavy, my tongue is thick and unwanted, and my heart refuses to lighten itself. I stare at a darkened window. Here is one stone: why should I not have a garden? I had one as a child. What is wrong with me that I don't go someplace where I can have a garden? Another stone, another and another: why can't I learn to read signs, why should I not be able to know the truth about myself, am I impoverished?

I sit in the kitchen booth. Melanie slides me a mug of camomile tea. Stop it, Jonathan, I'm trying to talk, and I don't want to listen to a little boy whining.

She throws up her hands. I'd like to fly away, she says. I could float. She twirls once, her arms above her head. Good-bye, good-bye.

She is talking quickly and laughing. Jonathan has thrown himself on the floor. He cries without conviction and kicks the edge of the booth monotonously with one bare heel.

You'll bruise yourself, Jonathan, says Melanie, and his tears renew themselves.

No, dummy Mama, he cries.

The tyranny of children, says Melanie. I don't know whether to laugh or cry. I'm inadequate.

I think you do fine, I say.

If I were smart, I'd think up something else for him to do besides cry, but my mind is empty. I'm ashamed of him, I'm ashamed of myself. Come here, Jonathan, will you sit on my lap? she says, but as she bends to lift him up, his kicking lands upon her chest. Stop it! she screams, her voice changing, and I sit dully with the settling flowers of my tea as she carries him from the room.

Sometime later she finds me in the garden. He fell asleep, she says as she works along with me, thinning the bean sprouts, some of which are still curled, head bent, while others are holding out new double leaves, like open palms. But he let me talk to him and read to him, she says, so I guess that's something, anyway. Lord! Do you ever want children? Do you mind my asking?

I think I'd like children very much. I just haven't been able to find the right setup yet.

I wish you'd come here more often, she says, straightening up and shading her eyes. I wish a lot of people we've known could be here with us.

I smile. Now that I am bent under the sun, I feel better; the strain of sleeplessness has left my head and passed into a comfortable bone-tiredness. I like the rush of blood in my face as I stoop lower to pull a weed. From my night awake I feel on the edge of my life. The pleasure is intense of sight renewed simply by another day; I could shout aloud with what my eyes are seeing. I tease: I thought you were already suffering from a surfeit.

There's a difference! With enough of the right people around I think I might be freer to be more the way I want to be.

You'll have to enlarge your garden, I say.

You're not taking me seriously.

Actually, I am. I might have said the same thing myself. I stoop again, and the suppleness of my back, the nimbleness of my bony brown plucking fingers, my filthy toes gripping the dirt astound me with their exultant mortality.

Above the forming pea pods there are still some purple blossoms on the upper ends of the vines. The spinach sends up an occasional spike of blossom. Lemon lilies and poppies bloom; an iris clump stands with moist collapsed flowers beside the gazebo, patterned inside with filtered light, littered now with the Sunday paper and the crumbs of our breakfast. Anna is picking clover at the edge of the grass, where the field takes over. Todd and I are in charge. He straddles a tree limb above me, tying a rope for a new swing. All right, there, try it, Sylvie. Two inches lower, I call up, helping Sylvie down.

Get on again, Sylvie, says Todd. Can you do it by yourself?

I want a turn, calls Anna. She comes running up and flings herself on Todd as he climbs down the tree. Take me on your back! She stuffs clover down his shirt and presses her hands over his eyes.

Sylvie hangs from his knees. Throw me around and around, she shrieks.

Don't you want to swing? I ask, but no one hears. Todd is blinded. He pulls them across the lawn, roaring like a monster.

I am the first to hear the screams. They have nothing to do with play. Someone is hurt: Jonathan. I run up to the terrace and around the corner of the house, slipping on the grass of the hill under the silver olive tree. He lies beneath his tricycle on the gravel, bloody on the elbow, inconsolable.

I carry him in through the cool front hall, rarely used, across carpet, past pictures and doors opening onto rooms with chairs, lamps, downstairs to the kitchen. I am thinking that I am simply making myself strong enough to contain his writhing. My ears don't care about the cries. I am thinking simply of running water, of blood diluted and grit washed away. I am more durable than I know. I am holding Melaine's child, and he is a stranger. Some day he will have legs like Todd's, the same thighs, and I will see him stride across a room to shake my hand, perhaps to kiss me, and I will be known as an old friend, from the very early days.

Melanie has shed her shorts and shirt and thrown them in a corner of her bedroom. Now she comes in wearing a white halter dress that doesn't quite hide the garden dirt on her ankles. We are drinking iced wine and soda, companionably. Melanie and I have weeded all the flower beds. We have assembled salads and arranged platters of cheese and sliced meats for the party. I have scooped out too many melon balls to count.

All right? she asks. She holds her hair on the top of her head.

Jewelry, I say.

She rummages and finds an antique brooch of gold with turquoise beads that she clamps into the cotton between her breasts.

That will do, I say. Are you going to wash your feet?

Todd comes to lounge in the doorway. He has been swimming with the children.

Where is everyone? asks Melanie.

Eating watermelon outside, Todd answers.

I look at Todd, looking at Melanie. I look at Todd and think of Melanie coming toward him in a white halter dress.

Are the kids eating my melon balls? I ask.

No, they're not eating your melon balls, says Todd. He grins at me, and I am Todd, straddling a tree, tying a rope, and looking out at the river and down at my three-year-old daughter and at a friend I like so much I don't even bother to entertain her. That friend is myself.

I settle deeper into the chair, enjoying the cold wine and the look of my own sunburnt legs and dusty feet, enjoying this marriage of friends. We have been working in the sun so long that we talk with a burned-out, pleasant incoherence. Today my mind has emptied out, filled up. I told Melanie about the winter, about Michael, and suddenly she began to laugh, and then I laughed. Love: I still have my heart to use; I could lie with Melanie and Todd in this walnut bed inherited from his parents and laugh about love until there is no difference between us.

The evening carries us along. We bathe, but the water cannot wash away the feel of sun. We let the children stick melon balls on their fingers and eat them off one by one. Todd is catching the first of the fireflies when the guests begin to arrive. The feast is simple, but as I lean back on the grass beside a thin man who looks like Zola in Manet's painting, I wonder when bread spread with butter has tasted so good. Speech seems unimportant beside this food. I think of telling my companion how much I am enjoying the pure sight of him, but the words are swallowed along with the last bite of this extraordinary bread and butter. We talk of mulberry trees. I see Melanie weaving among the guests in her white dress. We are talking of trees that attract the birds. My new friend says the mulberries should be ripe soon; he says when he was a child they used to spread old sheets under the trees and shake down ripe berries; he says their juice stains the teeth and hands a reddish blue. I see Melanie and Todd, the children, myself, these few amiable guests shaking down a mulberry tree and crouching around a sheet spotted with reddish-blue stains. Have I ever eaten mulberries? Perhaps once as a child: I seem to remember the house of a friend, a side yard, a driveway of black cinders. Someone laughs from the gazebo, and a moment later the human sound is caught up in the whistle of the train passing below.

The night sweeps us along. We begin to become aware of the full moon. Are you having a good time? whispers Melanie. I have worried this week, she says, that maybe it wasn't worth your while to come all this way; we do so little, we're so dull here in this backwater.

We are standing beside a lounge chair where Anna, all legs and cradling arms, has been overtaken by sleep. What can I give to Melanie? Tonight my sight is perfectly clear; I have countless images to give away. I tell her that the fireflies, again ascending in a mating ritual from the field of clover between here and Martin Burdock's cottage, look to me like a million sparks under water, slower than fire, fluid, phosphorescent.

It's a good thing we looked them up in the encyclopedia, says Melanie; now we know the facts of life.

Todd is organizing an expedition. Roll up your trousers, hold up your dresses, he says, we're going to the point; who's going to the point?

Take Anna to bed first, says Melanie; she'll get chilled with the dew.

I see Todd carrying Anna past a window upstairs. On his way back he passes through the lighted living room to turn up the music—Vivaldi: an expanse of vertical sound that I feel in my spine. I think how all week the bones of my body have extended themselves into a garden hoe. Now I feel myself straightening up, sending up liquid sparks of sensation.

My eyes grow used to the night away from the terrace. We pass single file behind Todd through wet grass. The legs of the man ahead of me are white, with tight knots of muscle at their calves. Melanie has tied her dress around her hips, her bare arms free to pass along the tops of grasses. I try it and come away damp.

We leave the music behind and walk through waves of

moonlight. Then the grass becomes thinner; rocks appear. We are walking on uneven, spongy ground, climbing higher than the trees growing in the shadow of the bluff below. Finally we are on a jut of land above the river, open to the sky, and we disperse ourselves to rest. The moon is magical.

Indians are buried here, says Todd's voice.

The airport wind sock erratically fills, swivels, sags against a heavy sky. Jonathan and Sylvie beg for bubble gum from the clouded glass of a machine. Anna, too, hangs around, looking at the artificially colored balls, her legs twisted, knobby at the knees.

Oh, all right, says Melanie, opening her purse. I suppose it won't kill you.

Todd, in a business suit, paces the waiting room. He stops occasionally to look at the same headlines on the newspaper stand.

Melanie's hair is held up loosely with a barrette. She wears a raincoat over her blue jeans and smokes a rare cigarette.

What's the cigarette for? asks Todd on one of his turns.

Melanie gestures to the metal ashtray stand beside her. I'm responding to my environment, she says.

My plane comes in. We see it land, turn on the minimal runway, and then taxi to the cyclone fence. A few people wait outside in billowing clothes.

Todd pries Jonathan and Sylvie from the window and we go out to the gate. Speaking loudly against the dusty wind, tasting bits of earth with our words, we seem unable to keep our minds upon this leave-taking. The children run in circles, veering with the gusts. Our good-byes are ordinary and quickly blown away. What I see finally are faces, set against a mesh of fence, a magnitude of sky and plowed fields—ancient prairie: I am reminded of how far inland I have come.

THE MILE RUN

When Bernard Hollander watched his son run the mile, no matter how still the hull of his own body might be in the high school bleachers, a vital part of him ran alongside his boy. This phantom runner stretched out from his chest like pure elastic love, marvelously expandable, yet Bernard always breathed more happily when the pulling in his heart relaxed temporarily as Mark would round the flattened circle of the track into a homeward return. This cycle, of course, happened four times during each race—ten times each race before the team had moved to the larger track outside—and it was now toward the end of April. Bernard knew he himself was getting a workout, though of exactly what sort he could not have said. He had been coming to every meet for which he was able to free himself from the shoe company he managed. Making these adjustments in his schedule was a secret joy. The boy was special to him, over and above the blood tie. Out of Mark's natural capacity for harmony he seemed to bear a promise for the resolution of Bernard's many remorses, and being near him was for Bernard a kind of security.

"Hi!" Mark would say to him afterward. "How did my arms look?" or "Did I lay it on too soon at the end?" Sometimes Bernard would have remembered to bring along something for Mark to eat, an orange or an apple or a bag of nuts picked up during his lunch hour, and this he would throw over to him as they walked to the parking lot of one school or another. Bernard had had to learn where a few of these schools were. This was not his native city, but his wife's; the shoe company, also, belonged to her family, and the other children he had helped raise—two girls both nearly grown now and living away from home—were the offspring of her previous marriage. One other child, Rick, Bernard's first son, who had been in the custody of his former wife, two years ago at the age of twenty had disappeared, shortly after his draft papers had arrived. The detective hired by Bernard had found clues suggesting both Mexico and Canada as possible destinations, but nothing came of their follow-up. Lately Bernard had been thinking that if he were to encounter Rick on a street—perhaps on a business trip somewhere—he would recognize him, certainly, but he might not know how to begin to be a father to him.

"You looked pretty good," Bernard said one night to Mark in the car. "All the parts looked as if they were working together. How was your wind?"

"Could have been better," said Mark as he broke into an orange. "I'd like it to be easier, you know? It would be so great if you just never ran out of breath."

"I know the feeling," said Bernard, laughing.

Mark fed his father a few sections of the orange, ate the rest himself, leaned his head back against the seat, and closed his eyes. Beyond his young face was another lane of expressway traffic, then a fence and a tract of houses, then the silhouettes of an army of electric high-tension towers against a western sky of the lingering blue that comes after sunset. There was a softness to the moment that reminded Bernard of his own early boyhood, when at this time of day he had often played in a clump of willow trees by the railroad tracks behind his house. Before and after the trains passed, the sounds would have been mostly of birds settling down and an occasional dog; in spring, peeper frogs had sung in the trees, while down on the ground he had knelt, slapping together mud dams in the creek, sometimes whistling to himself. His father had still been alive then, and the wailing, rushing, hot-and-cold trains had meant merely excitement and forward movement.

Bernard was quiet, and in a few minutes Mark was asleep. It pleased him that he was able to provide his son with this twenty-minute nap—at his age he could probably use every segment of rest he got. Last year, Mark's fifteenth, he had grown four inches; doorways looked startlingly lower above him, and couches, chairs, the stairway by the telephone had become, as it were, draped with arms and legs. When Bernard and Judith took him out for a pizza, which Mark liked much better than fancy food, he would eat twice as much as either of his parents. Every day he fixed himself at least two sandwiches for his lunch, and at night while he did his homework he might drink two or three large glasses of orange juice. Sometimes his legs would ache so much—whether from growing or from the track they weren't sure—that he would be forced from sleep with a sharp cry, which Bernard would register in his own body, somewhere in the center of his chest, as he lay in his bed across the hall.

If a message had come to Bernard that it was necessary for him to die in order for his son to live, he would instantly have surrendered himself, even now, when hope seemed to have renewed her beckoning to him, a man in his forty-eighth year, who had lately been thinking that he might at last have a chance to make good on his life.

Evening was deepening now. Orange sodium-vapor light passed at intervals over Bernard's hands on the wheel and Mark's sleeping face, and by the time they had turned from the highway and entered their own neighborhood it was dark enough for Bernard to be aware that no lights at all had been turned on in their house. Judith might be sleeping. She had caught another cold, her third, maybe even her fourth since Christmas.

Bernard pulled into the driveway and turned off the motor. "We're home, pal," he said. Mark opened his eyes and smiled gently at his father. Was there another child on earth who could go so directly and consistently from sleep to beneficence? Bernard was trying to understand where this sweetness came from. In himself and Judith, personal conflicts between contentment and irritability made each day seem precarious, and yet, together, they had made this boy, who from babyhood had seemed to be drawing on a secret fund of happiness.

Mark, carrying his duffel bag, his tall body loose-limbed and slightly bent in his school jacket, led the way across the yard and to the back door of the dark house. Their dinner hours had been awkward for several weeks because the kitchen was being extensively remodeled. Everything was torn up; even the sink had now been taken out, and for three days they had been carrying their dishes to the basement in laundry baskets. Bernard had overheard Judith exclaiming repeatedly on the telephone that the situation was "extremely inconvenient." Judith's mother, Millicent, had commented to Judith's older sister, Winnie, who had told Judith, who had repeated to Bernard, with nervous laughter, that her mother had said that it did seem to be taking Judith and Bernard a very long time to get their house "properly decorated." Judith's father, Harold, who had hired Bernard seventeen years ago, perhaps with an eye even then to something more than the management of a shoe company, obviously disliked discussions about housekeeping. Everything he didn't want to concern himself with, he hired done. At the shoe company, for instance, he had turned over to Bernard the entire job of working with the architects on the expansion and renovation of their plant at Two Rivers and of the home office and warehouse. Personally, Bernard had never been able to afford hiring everything done, and so in early apartments and houses, and now for the last eight years in this house, he had worked on the fixing-up gradually, doing as much as he could himself, submitting himself and his families to inconvenience.

What Judith could do was limited because she was allergic to dust and paint fumes and all sorts of things. She was, according to her family, susceptible, sensitive, high-strung, easily fatigued, and damaged by her first marriage. She was also, Bernard knew, warmhearted, funny, intuitive, lovable, and misunderstood.

Saving Judith from her family had had the appeal of an inspiration to Bernard in those early years, and he would be the first to admit now that he had not been altogether without the need of new opportunities himself. Over the years, with both her and himself, his patience had taken over when inspiration faltered. More and more, he kept his struggles to himself. He did not want this marriage to be a mistake. He was tired of mistakes. It was something else he was looking for. And then, of course, coming up through this marriage, shining out with apparent self-generation, capable of shaming both of them out of irritability and faintheartedness, had been this last child.

What Mark did when he came home each night was ritualistic: he performed a series of endearments with his dog, Theodore, a shaggy, charcoal-colored mixture of sheep dog and black Labrador. Typically, first came the initial embrace and the scratching of ears; then a kind of mutual prancing, in which they kept each other at bay and Mark pretended to be a second woofing dog; then perhaps another interlude of dissembling in which Mark would kneel down with his head to his knees, whimpering, while Theodore whined and nosed against his ears; then another joyous embrace, with growls and barks, often while they rolled on the floor; then usually a quiet aftermath in which their breathing slowed and Mark petted and Theodore licked and they returned to their original dignity of boy and dog.

Tonight while this reunion was going on, Bernard turned on a few lights and went to look for Judith. She was indeed asleep, breathing through her mouth, in Martha's bed. Martha, the younger daughter, was in college, and Eva had been married less than a year. Bernard had noticed that Judith had been spending more and more time in the girls' rooms. Sometimes she studied or wrote her letters to them at one of the desks; sometimes she got into one of the beds to read when she had trouble sleeping at night, and he would find her there in the morning, with the lamp still on, her reading glasses askew, the book on her chest, her face looking too young to be mother to grown daughters.

Did he love her enough? he sometimes asked himself at moments like these. He wanted to. He wanted to stop having to pay off damages.

"Bernie?" Coming up out of sleep, Judith began immediately to complain about the plumber. It was hard for Bernard to listen to her. When she was upset, she used speech indiscriminately, with numbing effect, which he supposed was at least half the point. At times he could reach her through all those words with a gesture, but tonight he did not want to come too close to her, because of her cold. He sat on the end of the bed and put a hand on the bump of a covered foot and listened. Laughter and barking came from downstairs.

The room was still pretty much the way Martha had left it last fall, when she had gone back to college: pictures and dried corsages on the bulletin board, a few ancient stuffed animal toys among the books in the case, pictures of Chartres cathedral and James Dean on the walls, on the dresser a thick lavender candle, partially burned. Last week Martha had called to wish him happy birthday. She hadn't seemed to want to hang up. Well, how were things going? Bernard had asked her again. Did she want to talk to her mother? No, no, this was a call just for him, she had answered, and she told him a few more things about school. At different times in the conversation she had called him both "Bernard" and "Daddy." After a few minutes her voice had quavered, yet clung to the connection, and Bernard, standing in the kitchen, with his birthday dinner dished up and waiting in the other room, had with words of his own held to her for a little while longer, this child, one of four who were more or less his, whose newest, very important word had been *actually* when he had first met her seventeen years ago.

"It's the inspector who is holding everything up," said Judith in a congested voice. "He can't get here until Monday. Can you believe it? I told Mother, and she absolutely couldn't believe that we'd be left over the weekend without a sink. She said if my father were to get hold of that plumber, he'd probably be so obnoxious the whole thing would get done in a day."

Bernard laughed.

"Well, it's true, Bernard. You know how he operates. He puts the screws on, as he calls it, and pretty soon everyone is doing things his way and sometimes not even knowing what happened. At this point I'm almost ready to ask the tyrant to step in. Don't you find this maddening? Everyone has a threshold for inconvenience—I have a threshold . . ." She sat up, reached for the tissues, and sneezed violently five times. "Oh, these colds are so awful," she said. "Why am I getting so many of them? This whole year—weep, weep, weep. And what about dinner? I came home from class and simply couldn't face the kitchen."

Her left eye was almost completely swollen shut, her short brown hair mussed. She looked boyish, with an almost ageless, delicate quality to her lineaments that seemed all at odds with this anxiety. She looked like Mark, a great deal like Mark. He stared at her. There was a pleasant sensation of fullness, new of late, in the region of his heart. Stop, he wanted to say, don't complain, it's not worth it, there isn't time.

Ashamed of his fastidiousness about her cold, he rose up and moved to sit at the head of the bed, behind her. He put his arms around her and his cheek against her hair. He wanted to be all done with complaint and remorse.

Her words stopped. Perhaps her body was relaxing a little. He covered her hands with his own.

"How was the track meet?" she asked.

"He came in third," said Bernard. "He looked good. He's coming along fine."

"You don't think he's getting too tired out, do you? I worry that he might be growing too fast for all this training."

"I think he's all right," said Bernard, thinking also of himself and the sense he had been having of being in a sort of training. His early morning runs through the streets of spring were only part of his renewed conditioning. It was also possible, he thought, that he might actually be learning how to live. "If Mark weren't doing the track, he might be doing something less worthwhile," he said.

"I suppose so," said Judith. She did seem to be relaxing a little. It was a shame she was so low with this cold. Vitality was right here, in the strength of his arms, in the taut muscles of his abdomen, in the fullness of his heart, yet he didn't know how to make it useful to her.

"How was your class?" he asked, laying a palm on her forehead to test for fever.

"Matisse," she said. "One whole hour of Matisse. It was wonderful. But I've been thinking that I really should be trying for something more useful, like computers. I feel I'm just doing what I was doing twenty-five years ago. Wherever am I going from here? Anyway, I was glad it was dark in there so no one could see how awful I look today. I should have stayed in bed, I suppose, but if I had been here, I would have had to listen to all that noise from the kitchen. And on top of that was the air-hammer work from in front of the Morrisons', and then Billy Morrison came home early for some reason and turned his stereo on full blast, with his bedroom window wide open—I almost called, but how many times can you complain without having it turned against you?"

When the telephone rang, Bernard began to tune in to Mark's voice instead. With his friends, Mark used words like *gross* and *foul* and *shit,* and he complained about the same things his friends complained about. Bernard wanted to tell him that this assumed character with its false language was unnecessary. He wanted to tell his son that in the scheme of things he was more important than he could yet imagine; they were all watching him, listening to him, to see what they could learn.

"Bernie, you won't believe this!" Judith interrupted herself and turned in his arms to face him.

"I won't believe what?"

"Come with me." She got up, took his hand, and led him stealthily down the hallway to Mark's room, over to the bed, lifted a corner of the boy's mattress, and brought out a piece of glossy paper, which she unfolded before his eyes: it was a pornographic centerfold as lewd as any he had ever seen.

"My God," he said as he peered closer.

Quickly she folded and replaced it and pulled him from the room. "I found it when I was changing his sheets," she whispered. In their own bedroom she closed the door behind them. "Can you believe it? Our baby?"

Bernard shook his head and started to change out of his business suit. Judith sat down cross-legged on the bed and pulled a box of tissues to her lap as she continued to talk. "I've heard Gabriella Morrison telling stories about her boys, but I always said to myself, 'That's just what you'd expect from those Morrison boys,' but here we are talking about Mark, and heaven knows how long this has been going on. What does one do or say? It's so private. I mean, we have to let him grow up, but I really would never have expected such bad taste from Mark, of all people. It just seems so totally out of character. Have you noticed anything in him? What does one do or say?"

Bernard zipped up his jeans and reached for a sweater. The picture seemed to him an inconsequential aberration, but also terribly important, in a hot, burdensome way. On one hand, he felt like laughing, as one laughs at the outrageous exuberance of youth, which willy-nilly finds a way to thrust itself forward. On the other hand, he wanted to stop everything and rewind Mark's growing-up to an earlier phase, to give himself some more time to think. Judith's expression, too, was a mixture of merriment and panic.

"I know what you're going to say." She was laughing now. "Boys will be boys—right? You don't have to say a word. I can read it all over you from the way you're flexing your muscles."

It was true: he had been standing in front of her almost unconsciously doing isometric exercises, his mind on Mark, on her, and on the large bed where she was sitting.

"Our baby," repeated Judith. She looked not much older at this instant than she had when Mark was born. Ten years before that, before any husbands or babies, she had been a student of art history, staying away from home. When he had first gathered her and her little girls to him, he had felt grand, glad for new chances, clear-headed for the first time in years, with enough energy, he thought, for himself and everyone else. That was another moment he would have liked to return to, for examination. He told himself that clear vision, once experienced, must then always remain a possibility.

He sat down and put his arms around her.

"You'll catch my cold, Bernie."

"No, I'm not going to catch a cold."

"We've got to eat something," said Judith. "We've got to

get some food into the pubescent boy." She began sneezing again. "My cold is all here," she said, holding a hand over the left side of her face. "The right side feels pretty good."

"Lie down," he said. "I'll go make one of my famous omelets."

Mark, still talking on the telephone, had taken off his shoes and socks and was examining the sole of his right foot as Bernard stepped down to him and the dog, lying side by side on the stair landing.

"I'm sure!" Mark was saying into the receiver. "That's weird, that's really weird." Yet the eyes he rolled up to Bernard bore none of the affectation in his voice, nor did they seem heavy at that moment with sexual questioning. Bernard touched the bare foot and passed on.

In the kitchen he laid out the eggs and the ingredients for a salad. He grated some cheese and while the butter in the omelet pan was melting he beat the eggs. Luckily the stove was still attached, and there was water for cooking from the little bathroom. The setup was inconvenient, but not really "extremely inconvenient." He had taken a beer from the refrigerator but after a few minutes put it away again, untouched, unneeded. The pleasant fullness was returning to his chest, a buoyancy below which the motions of his hands looked simplified and fluid.

He watched his hands pouring the egg mixture into the hot butter. There was light from the stove on his hands, and there must be light on his face, too, as it bent above the steam, and for anyone approaching the house from the back yard there would be light in the window. Say that Rick, returning from his wandering, would look in and, seeing his father's bent face, in an instant would forgive everything: disaffection would fall away; seeing his father, he would see that life was meant to be picked up and passed through yourself, no matter how remote or angry you might feel, and he would see how in turn life caught hold of you and used you, no matter what your shames. Bernard caught up his breath. It was like his own self there at the window, looking in.

After she had eaten some of her dinner, Judith leaned back and said that she felt a little better; food often did that, she said, reduced the symptoms.

"Don't stop now," said Bernard, motioning to her plate, but she continued watching him and their son as they buttered bread and impaled salad with their forks. Mark's third-place ribbon lay in the center of the dining room table where she had asked him to display it. "No big deal," Mark had said, but Bernard saw how the boy's eyes fastened now and then on the white strip of satin.

Bernard was used to having women watch him eat. For his mother, a superlative cook, it had seemed to be a pleasure like food itself, but under the critical, narrowing eyes of his first wife, Patty, his high school sweetheart, he had grown to feel guilty in his eating, as if by the sheer act of maintaining his young life he were also consuming her own vitality. With Judith some of his trust had returned. Her eyes on him had stayed round, carrying old hurts but no grudges. Whenever her speech, weakened by her frustrations, began to enervate him, he would hold to the look in her eyes, which continued to ask one round, innocent question. It was a question he knew she was asking out of her core for both of them, and in response, for both of them, he had been trying to live as gently as possible, trying not to harm. . . .

"This weekend I want to go out to Jeremy's farm," said Mark. "He says I can drive with them to get the new horse. They're working on the new dam, too. I really want to go. Can I go for the whole weekend?"

"Oh, Mark," said Judith. "Saturday is Grandpa's birthday party. Your grandmother would be absolutely crushed if you weren't there. You just have to go."

"Nobody ever knows if I'm there or not," said Mark.

"Oh, they do!" exclaimed Judith. She began to sneeze again, and her eye watered shut. "You don't know. You're the youngest. We'd all miss you. Bernard, tell him."

"Can you go for the horse and still get back in time?" asked Bernard.

"I don't know," said Mark. "I'd have to ask Jeremy." He picked up his ribbon and rolled it tightly around a finger. He looked from one parent to the other, his expression a combination of solicitude and patience, as if he were waiting for them. In his son's gaze, Bernard thought, if they had known how to look, if the three of them could be still long enough, he and Judith might see more of what they themselves were meant to be, but just then Mark said politely, "May I please be excused?" He took his empty plate and glass with him, the dog heaved himself up from under the table and followed, and they were left with each other. Bernard looked down to Judith, who held a wad of tissue beneath her eye.

"When I was his age I was riding horses every weekend," she said. "I find it hard to know what to require of him. You know?"

Bernard nodded, but beyond Judith's voice he was seeing himself at his son's age, already a stock boy in a drugstore after school and on weekends. By that time his father had been dead three years. Everything had changed. Even the trains passing behind their frame house had by then brought forward out of nowhere a new, piercing message. More than once he had closed his eyes at the train's approach, standing as close as he dared to the tracks, and at the moment when his trembling was nearly synchronous with the train's, he would let out his own personal scream.

"There do seem to be a great many compulsory birthday parties," Judith was saying. "I often feel pushed into them myself. I mean, there are just so many nights in a year, and the anniversaries keep rolling around, and if you count up the number of celebrations on my side of the family alone . . .

Bernard? Why are you looking like that?"

Bernard was holding with his fingertips to the edge of the table. Down the polished center of it was a shine, and at the other end sat Judith with a shine all around her that she couldn't see. Stop, he wanted to say to her, there is no time for this, there is something else. But he didn't know what it was.

The telephone rang while they were clearing the table, and when he came back from answering it, still recovering from the boom of his father-in-law's voice, Judith was already at the scrub sinks in the basement with the basket of dishes. She looked small. Everything looked small to him as he stood there on the stairs, small and clear-cut and particular, a delineated, miniature confinement of things and one other person. He stood halfway down the stairs, trying to collect himself. He didn't want to move; he wanted to stand there, studying his basement, his wife, the place where he was.

Judith turned. "Isn't this the craziest way to live?" she asked. "I've been pretending that I am a pioneer woman."

"You are," he said, descending. "Be glad for the running water. Survival is the ticket." He came to stand beside her. "That was your father on the telephone. Word came through this afternoon while I was gone to Mark's meet that the new equipment is being delivered to the Two Rivers plant tomorrow. He wants me to get up there early. That means I've got to go back down to the office tonight and get the revised floor plans and some other things."

"Not all the way down there tonight!" she exclaimed. "Why not tomorrow?"

"There isn't time. Delivery starts at eight."

"Don't go now. Can't you just get up earlier?"

"It's better this way. I'm awake now."

"Don't go," she said in a softer voice. "Stay here."

He stroked the back of her neck. "I'll get going and be right back."

She ducked away from him and flooded water on a plate. "It's crazy. It's bedtime now."

He stayed beside her a few minutes longer and one by one took the clean dishes from her hands. The old sinks were spattered with paint, some from him, some from previous owners. Judith wore her gold wedding band and on her right hand a sapphire surrounded by diamonds that she had inherited from her grandmother. Growing up, she had ridden horses, she had traveled; one night, not long after their own marriage, she had recited for him all the weddings for which she had been an attendant, all the dresses she had worn, all the divorces that had followed. It was crazy the way she had been brought up, she told him, an archaic education, and yet when Eva had been married last summer, dresses had appeared, long dresses, flowers, and a moment of hush during which Bernard had winked at his stepdaughter and pressed her hand, looped through his arm, both he and she members of a particular tribe, set down someplace on earth.

"I'm asking you," said Judith. "Where does all this craziness start?"

"It would be easier for me right now than at five tomorrow morning."

"Why do we live this way?"

He looked at the rings on her fingers and then at her face, her swollen eye, her clipped hair, her delicate bones, her brows and eyes like Mark's. Some of the fullness was still there in his chest, a feeling pushing or being drawn outward. He thought if he could just be still and let it do the work for him, let it push against the confines of their words, he might come to know how it was they were living, and why. But he was tired, also, and between now and morning there was already too little time.

"Then go!" cried Judith, suddenly exasperated. "Don't let me stop you."

"Do you want to come with me?"

"Driving all the way down there is about the last thing I want to do tonight."

"I don't blame you. I'll go and be back as soon as I can. Make a warm place for me." He stood where he was, waiting for her smile.

At last it came, but with it she said, "Bernard, I'm asking you."

"I know you are." He rested his hand for a moment on her shoulder. "I know you are."

Bernard climbed directly up the two flights of stairs to Mark's bedroom. The dog was asleep on the bed. Mark was at his desk, dressed in a sweat suit. Bernard smiled at him. "I've come up to say good night. I've got to go back down to the office for a few things I'll need in Two Rivers tomorrow."

Mark stretched far back in his chair.

"So what's happening in Two Rivers?" he asked.

"New equipment is coming in. Harold wants me up to oversee."

Theodore stirred his shaggy body, resettled himself, and Bernard remembered the centerfold beneath the mattress. Mark at the moment was balancing a pencil above his curled upper lip, where of late he had also occasionally been experimenting with a razor.

"You're a boy of many talents, I see," said Bernard.

"No big deal," said Mark as he tipped his head forward, caught the pencil, and stretched out his long legs. He crossed his arms on his chest and looked at his father. Bernard took a nonchalant stance to cover his absolute pleasure in gazing at his son. He had a wonderful face, not particularly handsome, but wonderful. His eyes laughed; there wasn't a trace of sullenness about his mouth. He looked more intelligent than both of his parents put together.

"I'll drive down with you," said Mark. "I'll be your bodyguard."

Bernard thought he would like to go to sleep in that doorway with his eyes and his thoughts still fixed on his son; he wanted to descend into this love, dead for a time to everything else.

"I'll do the driving," said Mark extravagantly. "I'll be your chauffeur."

Bernard laughed. "You think what I need is an illegal chauffeur?"

"Nobody's watching this time of night."

"Then let's just say you'd better get to bed on time and not break training." Bernard lingered in the doorway. It was as if his own self were stretched out on the desk chair, his own self.

"I knew you'd say that. I knew you were going to say exactly those words," said Mark.

"Then why do you bother to ask?"

"I'm just making you go through the routine," said Mark. "To keep you in shape."

At last Bernard raised a hand in farewell. "Thanks anyway." Then he added, "Good night, son," and turned quickly down the hallway because the fullness burgeoning in the region of his heart was bringing tears to his eyes. Amorphous, almost overwhelming, it made him want to be even more still than he had been in the bleachers that afternoon, until he found a point of clear calm from which he could understand what he was learning from his child.

But he had to look outward now and navigate city streets. And he was very tired. He had to focus, first on the narrow driveway and then on the turns through their quiet neighborhood and then on the suburban commercial street that was taking him back to the expressway. He saw the theater with the movie Mark had been wanting to see. He passed the television repair shop and the figure salon and the shop where he bought most of his clothes. Everything looked very clear to him, falsely clear, he now thought. The sky over the city, the direction in which he was heading, was almost too purple to be believed. Outside were strands of lights, the precise access to the expressway, the determined lanes of traffic, the purple sky. Inside he felt vast and amorphous, uncharted, and what he wanted was to turn around in his mind—he could almost sense what it would be like, this turning—and travel toward himself.

He gripped the wheel and concentrated on staying awake. Traffic was still heavy. The siren of an ambulance cut a path through continuous sound. If you weren't careful, you could think you were in a dream, where nothing mattered because you would continue to sleep and sleep.

Mechanically, he took his exit from the highway and at the top of the ramp was immediately engulfed in the nightlife of the district around the shoe company. Bars and gospel churches, interspersed with boarded-up or grill-protected storefronts, were staggered down the derelict street: Faith Temple, Al and Jan's, Greater New Hope, Tic Tock Tap. By day the streets were almost as strewn with the unemployed as they were by night with various orders of seekers. The grandmothers weren't here at night, though, the ones who managed to step cleanly and miraculously out of dilapidation, in fresh dresses, with hats on their heads and useful bags of some sort in their hands, and often with a child in tow. Bernard felt sure it was they who kept alive the better values of this community. There had been days, driving to and from work, when he had imagined stopping his car and asking one of these matriarchs what words she told herself to make possible this transubstantiation of poverty into pricelessness.

His own mother had been a little like that. The longing in him was sometimes acute to go back to a physical home that no longer existed, to retrace himself, to sit at the kitchen table watching his mother's hands, ready at last to learn what needed to be learned. Before, the experiences just hadn't been there to make him ready. He had been impatient, egotistical. He hadn't known Patty, he hadn't known Judith, he hadn't known Rick, or Eva, or Martha, and he hadn't yet awakened into the special hope inspired by Mark. His desires had been toward escape, toward self-improvement, toward his own independence; he had been powered by appetites, by competition, by the taste of his own strength. My God! The remorse came from the ways he had treated people, he knew that. He slumped forward over the steering wheel, as if he were in an open vehicle trying to ease himself under a low bridge. He wanted to learn better ways to live, but so much time had been used already that he didn't know if there could possibly be enough left.

The red brick warehouse and office of the shoe company were at the end of a darker, more residential block. They had recently purchased and torn down a number of these houses for their warehouse expansion, and so the company buildings at the moment were edged with razed lots. He pulled up near the front door and turned off the motor.

He had first met Judith on this very sidewalk, about this time of year, during a rainy period. She had come to pick up her father. She had been wearing a raincoat and a large silk scarf printed with a design of horses. Martha had been with her, three years old at the time. Bernard had just been hired and given a complete tour and now was being introduced. Harold had been in high spirits, and Bernard had been feeling pretty good himself with the prospect of new, solid chances with an old, solid company. Judith and her daughter had instantly become linked in his mind with this hour of expansiveness; he had never forgotten her look that first evening—quizzical, slightly edgy, hinting at warmths, charmingly distracted by little Martha, who had been pulling at her hand, dancing on the sidewalk, and prefacing almost every sentence with the word *actually*.

Deep in thought, now, and carrying the baggage of weariness, Bernard locked his car and headed for the main door, a well-designed entryway of rounded glass, dating from a 1930s renovation, which Bernard had been fighting this year to retain. The street was on a hill, overlooking an industrial valley, beyond which dark spires and peaked roofs rose up against the purple sky. Key in hand, Bernard paused for this view. He always found it eloquent. It spoke to him of labor, of people living together, of immigration, of cycles of dark ages and light ages.

There was no warning for the hoarse voice that came upon him from behind. "Look man, I don't want to impose. Hell, I *know* I'm imposin', but I got to get to the VA hospital, see, and I don't know the way from nothin'. I just got in from Portland."

Bernard turned toward a liquorish, slope-shouldered man upon whom the general droop of skin and clothing expressed nearly unmitigated discouragement. "I know I'm imposin'," the man repeated. His eyes were somewhat focused on Bernard, but they could have been seeing anything, maybe even a different land.

"You have a ways to go," said Bernard, and he told the man where to catch the bus.

"Do you have fare for the bus?" asked the man. "I don't have nothin' left."

Bernard reached into his pocket and brought out what change there was, even though he hated giving money to tricksters. He felt the line of his mouth tightening. He straightened his own posture, tightened his abdominal muscles. "Take care," he said after the coins had been transferred, and then he turned abruptly away.

"Damn," he said as he let himself into the building. "Damn." His fatigue was now acute, and he knew without a doubt that where he belonged was home in bed, next to Judith, across the hall from Mark, where the debts he could discharge were more nearly his.

With heavy legs he climbed the broad maple staircase to the second floor of offices. He was trying to concentrate on what minimum of action would accomplish his mission and deliver him home again. In his first years here his energy had really been phenomenal. All those pressures he had translated merely as challenges, one after the other, against which he had been glad to measure himself. He had wanted to be established. He had wanted to be valuable. Under his management distribution had increased to a five-state area. He kept a close eye on the shoe lines and quickly weeded out losers. He was firm on quality and taste. In a way, because of his value, he had even learned to manage Harold, and part of this meant knowing when to let the older man have his sway—as, for example, tonight: this craziness, as Judith called it. Well, what could you do? Survival was the ticket, wasn't it?

He turned on just what lights were necessary and gathered up the papers he would need. Some of the drawings were still tacked up on boards from their meeting that morning. He rolled up all these large sheets and slipped them into a cardboard tube, found the order forms for the new equipment, piled up his notebook and appointment book and the newest inventory computer sheets.

He now became aware of a noise from the floor above him, which at the first instant, in his tiredness, caused him no alarm because it sounded so much like the everyday rumbling of the old conveyor belt that ran around the periphery of that warehouse story, a common, faint, background noise. Then he listened to it more specifically. Had it been going all the while he was here? Had someone forgotten to pull down a switch, or had the watchman come for his rounds and pulled the lever by mistake? Bernard wound his way to the back of the office floor, past the alcove where Wilma sat each day with her eye on the shipping docks, up the stairs by the service elevators, into the rich, dry scents of leather and wood. A few single night bulbs burned. And the horizontal conveyor belt was most certainly rolling along, empty as far as he could see, ghost-driven, purposeless. He blinked; his eyes felt dry with weariness.

The pain when it stabbed him from behind was almost not a surprise. It pierced exactly into the region where he had been feeling most vulnerable, most tenderly expansive, but the flash of it was hot, burdensome, harshly confining. There was neither an instant nor an inch left for anything else. He was not even able to turn and meet it. His eyes could not see. His legs would not hold him. I have been stabbed, he thought, I am dying, this is what it is like to be going blindly toward death, this is it; and he was disappointed: it was not the time; he had no strength, nor did he yet know how to make the turn toward his own meaning. Then he pitched forward and was lost to himself.

But he did not die. Much later, days later, when his eyes were again turned outward upon the world, he tried to reconstruct the nonsequential corridors of his unconsciousness, the winds and the breathlessness, the voices and the silence, the darks and colors and the whiteness, but all he could hold to was a memory of an enormous and pressing import, an amorphous and pure content, a timeless entirety that was almost a substance, yet not quite a substance.

He had first opened his eyes upon Mark and Judith, and there had been something simple and clear he had thought he wanted to say, but he had not been able to speak. Judith had taken his hand. Mark had grinned at him. Then speech had again become possible, but with it came difficulty. One day Martha was there, calling him "Daddy," and she held a glass of water so he could sip. Eva came and stood silhouetted against the window, more beautifully than he could ever have said. Harold strode back and forth at the foot of the bed, talking loudly to a doctor, who finally drew him out into the corridor, out of earshot. One night Judith was still there even when the hospital window had been austerely dark for a long time. When she saw his eyes on her, she came to the bed, and when he asked her to lie beside him, she did, without troubling his body, his body and her body stretched quietly and narrowly, their heads close. In that attitude of plain love he fell asleep.

One afternoon as Mark came in the door straight from a

track meet, the boy's energy was such that Bernard felt something newborn in him leap to meet his son. "How did you do?" he asked.

"I came in second," said Mark. "I really did." He held up a red ribbon.

"Listen to that!" said Bernard. "That's terrific. Tell me about it."

While his son talked, and he listened, Bernard felt as if he himself were on the track, both running and watching himself run. The sound of his son's voice was making a track on which he could run, was holding him to it. He watched himself take the far curve and head again toward home, toward himself. Life was still holding him, needing him. He had not yet gone his full distance, and he was glad.

NORTHERN LIGHT

Almost overnight the summer had disappeared. The morning I was to leave for the cottage and meet Karl, there was a damp north wind, and constellations of leaves flattened on the sidewalk two stories below seemed strangely three-dimensional. I wasn't sure if I were staring or looking. I had been thinking about one of my grandmother's sayings, how certain things often happen together, patterns of events, like deaths, births, marriages. My grandmother is often right. Whether her wisdom has come from her own observed nature or from an inherited body of hearsay, it seems all the same to have been useful to her.

Reasons abounded that morning for my susceptibility to an old, fateful voice: the long absences of Karl since he had been put on a project in Houston, the death last spring of his father, the recent separation of good friends, my setting out on the trip. *Mark my words,* I could almost hear Grandma saying in a voice that quavers now with her great age. As I turned from the window to dress and finish preparing the children and the apartment for my departure, what I sensed was the motion of my life, almost a blur of action. I had no time to lose.

Mrs. Bates came as the girls were leaving for school. Karen, bristly with independence, barely suffered me to hug her and quickly wiped off the kiss. Erica wanted to be lifted up so she could wrap her legs around my waist and smooth back my hair and kiss me moistly on both cheeks. I ran down to the vestibule with them and waved as they went out into the gray wind and down the row of brownstones, taking part of me with them. Parenthood is like that, I thought, as I came more slowly back upstairs: it's beyond rationality, it's like stepping out into deep space, or going to the center of the world, or both at once.

In the kitchen Mrs. Bates stood solidly at the sink. I gave her the lists, zipped my duffel bag, remembered Karl's work boots and jacket, and then I was off. It was Thursday, and I wasn't due back to my job in the weaving studio until the following Tuesday. I had until three thirty to drive from Chicago to the Wausau airport to meet Karl's plane from Texas, and we should be at the cottage by suppertime. I had brought along a few provisions, others we could buy in town, but mostly we would be cleaning out the cupboards and preparing his family's cottage for the winter; there was no one else to do it this year.

The sky continued overcast as I drove north out of the city. Gradually the landscape on either side of the road became like an embrace. The green of southern Wisconsin was heavy, the corn that was still standing a laden, drying gold. Dairy herds grazed here and there on hillsides that have been shoved about by aeons of water, liquid and ice. I know the roads well. Once

I saw a formation of migrating ducks, travelers like myself, and occasionally flocks of blackbirds took off from pastures or stubbled fields like unraveling thread, wavering in the wind.

At Fond du Lac I stopped to eat the sandwich I had packed and was glad for the thermos of strong tea. For several weeks I had been fighting an undercurrent of tiredness, as if my soul itself desired gravity. Pregnancy was now a possibility, but I kept telling myself that I had been this late with my period before. I didn't want to be pregnant, I didn't have time to be pregnant. The last few years I had been enjoying my work so much that all I wished for and almost never got from my domestic life was simplicity and regularity.

"Wake up," said Karl. My head was in his lap, and his hand was on my cheek. Immediately I knew where we were by the dips in the road. I lifted my head, and there was the northwoods, flying backwards, and against it Karl's profile, really present. Ahead we were tunneling into trees, going very fast, the illusion was, because of the narrowness of the road and the dips. It was the path to his childhood. He grinned at me. Aspen and poplar leaves covered the road like yellow snow; even in the somber twilight the maples flamed. "Look," he said, "there's Grace Lake," and through a parting in the trees I saw the familiar boggy undergrowth and, pointing up among horizontal strands of mist, feathery tamaracks.

He slowed the car and turned onto the narrower road that curves deeply into the woods to Tomahawk Lake. We were barely moving as a stag leaped across the road in front of us. Karl stopped the car, and to the left, on the edge of a glacial basin, we found the doe, standing frozen broadside among the trees, looking directly at us, beautifully alert. I looked back steadily, leaning across Karl with my hand on the open window and my face in the cold, pine-scented air. "Do you two know each other?" he asked. Then suddenly the doe turned, white-tailed, and was gone into the shadows.

HE WHO CUTS HIS OWN WOOD IS TWICE WARMED, says the sign above the woodbox in the main room. The yellow eyes of the owl andirons glow before a fire. After supper that night, Karl prodded the logs together and added a fresh one to the blaze. When he stood up his head was about level with the gleaming brass kettles and candlesticks on the high mantel. His cheeks were ruddy and his eyes shining. I was slouched as deeply as possible into the old red couch.

"You're not going to sleep again, are you?" he asked. He opened his arms expansively, and I followed his gaze up into pine rafters. "This place!" he exclaimed. "How I love it!"

I stretched out my legs on the table of magazines, the same we had leafed through when we were all at the family reunion in July. Child cousins had gone banging in and out of doors then; the swing on the porch had creaked steadily; there had been captured turtles clunking in buckets, banjo picking, shouts from the dock, the splash of water, the thud of boats, records by Louis and Bix that were originally cut about the same time the cottage itself was built, in the twenties. All the while grief had lapped in our awareness, an underground lake, another dimension. Karl's mother had spent most of the time knitting a sweater for one of the grandchildren. We had taken her on walks and encouraged her to swim, the children cheering as she lowered her blue-veined body into the lake. I had kept my eyes on Karl, too, so much more a perfectionist than his father had been and yet in his good nature so much the same. No one had dreamed his father would die so soon.

Karl came and stood above me. "Have you ever had the opportunity of witnessing the mating signal of the ruffed grouse?" he asked.

"No! How on earth have I missed it?"

"First," he said, shaking out his arms, "he puffs up his chest feathers, like this, then he begins to beat his wings against his chest, like this, slowly and then faster and faster and faster and faster." By now Karl's fingers were pounding his diaphragm in a spasm of sound.

"That is deeply thrilling," I said. "Thank you very much."

"Not at all." He bowed graciously. "Is there anything else you would like demonstrated?"

Once in the middle of the night I woke to the throaty bass horn of the bullfrog in the bay, which made me think dreamily of the surface of the water, of water being inflated mysteriously, sonorously into air. A slow rain was dripping through the pine directly outside the window, against a general downward murmur of the forest. I adjusted my shape to Karl's in the musty bed. We were under three Hudson's Bay blankets. I thought of our children inside their own sleep, far away. A map seemed to be curving down from my closed eyes, and there were no roofs anywhere, just distances. Karl and I, briefly together, lay high up in the north, where the curves began to converge.

In the morning I found myself alone, flushed with waking, remembering a dream about a red bedroom from which I had been carried headfirst by a cataract of water down a conduit to the sea, where the waves churned dangerously between high breakwaters that were like gates to an immense watery space beyond. I hurried to the bathroom and back to the warmth of the covers, feeling drugged. The hour was indeterminate, the day overcast, the bedroom dim anyway from the smallness of its windows and the closeness of the woods. I burrowed into the covers and closed my eyes, too tired even to sit up for meditation. In my next dream I was given a sick baby to hold, its body bloated grotesquely. Trying to save it, I pierced its skin with a needle, but instead of returning to normal size, the baby shrank away altogether; it deflated and disappeared. Stricken, I ran upstairs to a series of white, empty rooms, searching, but there was only a very white, empty light.

I was awake. From the thuds and scrapes sounding through the wall from the big room, I knew Karl was filling the woodbox. The room I was in, where we almost always sleep, is so small as to be nothing more than a room with a bed and a narrow space for stripping or dressing. We spent our honeymoon there. The curtains are red-checked, the light above the bed red-shaded, and the pine outside the window a dark, eternal green. I pulled myself up against the head of the bed, wrapped one of the heavy blankets around my shoulders, and began to meditate, setting out again, taking nothing with me.

Once I heard the door open cautiously; later, when Karl saw I had finished, he came in altogether and sat on the edge of the bed.

"How did you sleep?" he asked pleasantly.

I looked at him objectively. He had brought colder air in with him, an aura of brisk, independent energy.

"What time is it?" I asked.

"Eleven, luxurious lady." He leaned toward me for a kiss, but I stayed him with my hand on his wool shirt. I don't know what I wanted from his face, but I was searching. My body seemed unbelievable.

"I think I'm pregnant," I said.

"So fast?" He laughed, not taking me seriously.

"I might be four weeks along." My voice didn't seem to belong to me. I was remembering how little he and I had actually been together during those four weeks.

"Well, well." His voice changed slightly. He passed a hand over his forehead and eyes and down along his beard. "Four weeks isn't very far. You didn't tell me last night."

"I didn't know last night."

He paused and then his breezy vacation cheerfulness resumed. "You've just had too much sleep. What you need is to get up, girl, up, up, no more of this lying in."

"Stop it!" I said sharply, pushing his hands away. "I haven't had but a fraction of the sleep I actually need, and I know what I know."

He sat back and looked at me carefully, and under his gaze I began to feel less like myself and more like a woman, looking at a man. What I knew seemed only the smallest fraction of what I needed to know.

"Hmm," he said finally. "May I bring you a cup of tea?"

"If you really want to do something, you could get off that horrendous job in Texas and stay home for a change," I burst out. I said a great deal more. Underneath my words I could hear the fire crackling in the other room, with no one to enjoy it. What I said seemed so exaggerated as to have little meaning, except that I meant every word of it. At one point I exclaimed, "How on earth can I attend to my artistic and spiritual life if I have to give myself over to having another baby?"

Karl continued to listen quietly and sympathetically. His comments were thoughtful, reasonable. His face looked robust, concerned, kindly. I threw a pillow at him.

When he left to make the tea, I turned my face to the wall and pulled the covers over my head. The next time I woke the room was much darker and rain filled the windows. I shrugged into a robe and went out to the big room, but it was empty and the fire had died down.

It had been too dark to see much of the lake the night before, and now in the silvery rain the water appeared as an essence beyond the trees. There was no sign of Karl.

The cottage was too cold even for my robe, so I dressed quickly in several layers of wool and then ventured into the kitchen. I felt bony and weak and alone with my questions.

Sylvia, a year before hers and Tom's separation, had gotten an abortion, "the best thing I ever did for myself," she was still insisting to me, and during that period they had often come to our house for long firelit discussions. We had supported their decision. Life had phases, we agreed, and certain activities, such as childbearing, were appropriate only to certain phases. Life went forward; one's creative expressions needed to become more and more subtle. "I've got more in me than babies," Sylvia had declaimed more than once. Our allegiance, ironically, had been to life itself; we had felt that we were holding flames that mustn't go out.

I decided on poached eggs, two of them, with pepper, on toast, and then I ate two more pieces of toast with butter and honey. The tea was delicious too. I ate this breakfast standing in front of the kitchen window that looks out through the screened porch to the lake. The food seemed to be filling and warming empty spaces all over my body, while the rain was so continuous and quiet that my eyes kept losing and regaining focus looking through it.

Sylvia and Tom, Tom and Sylvia: we still couldn't stop talking about them as if they were a couple. Their marriage was parts of ours; our imaginations mingled in a common emotional field that still potently existed. Karl and I for years had talked about Tom and Sylvia almost as much as we talked about ourselves.

What could Karl be doing out in that rain? I was asking myself. The boathouse and the pump house were the only possible dry places. As I stepped out the porch door, the clear laugh of a loon hit me, ascending and descending sharply over the water. I began to run down the path to the boathouse. The lake seemed vast beneath the curtains of rain and the air piercingly fresh. I broke off a shiny leaf of wintergreen, which I was crushing beneath my nose as I pushed open the door.

One of the slip doors was open, and in the interior light Karl was sitting in the metal rowboat, sorting through his father's tackle box. Around him on the benches of the boat were groups of lures and sinkers and bobbers. He looked up at me and then straightened his back.

"I don't think this box has ever been cleaned out," he commented soberly. He poked in one of the rusty tiers and came up with an encrusted clump of hooks, which he threw onto a tangled pile of rejects in the bottom of the boat. "Does this, do you think, represent the inside of my father's mind?"

"Maybe it was the fish he put his attention on, not the box," I suggested as I sat down on the pier inside the ladder posts. The tethered boat rocked on small waves that belonged to the whole of the lake outside.

Karl shook his head in gentle, almost fatherly concern over the humble assortment, which was affecting me, too, by its former intimacy with the dead man. "I hope he had his mind on something." Karl sighed.

"Trees, maybe," I said, "or whether the eagle eggs had hatched or if the rain would hold off long enough for him to work his favorite places."

With my feet resting on the rim of the boat, I was seeing how relaxed my lower legs could be, bobbing with the water.

"Dad liked you," said Karl.

"The feeling was mutual," I answered.

Go ahead, dive in, he had challenged me when Karl first brought me to the cottage, before our marriage. That's just what I did, walking past the other women and diving straight off the dock into the shocking green-brown cold. I am a good swimmer. When I climbed up the ladder, I saw Karl's father's eyes widen briefly with approval and then return to an easy, amiable blandness. Perhaps I had quickened something in him, an old vision. He was a good swimmer himself.

"Here, smell this," I said to Karl as I leaned down toward the boat and held the folded leaf of wintergreen under his nose.

He steadied my hand and breathed deeply. "How are you anyway?" he asked. "Slept out?"

I shrugged. It was not so much a feeling of being slept out, I had been deciding, as of having been marked by sleep. I began to rock the boat a bit with my feet. It was possible to alternate between listening to the rain outside the open door and listening to the enclosed silence of particular sounds, as if a dial could be switched back and forth.

Karl gripped one of my ankles. "I'm glad we're here," he said.

"Have you heard from Tom or Sylvia this week?" Karl called in to me as I was beginning preparations for dinner.

"Yes, both of them. There have been some more problems with the children, as you can imagine."

"What sort of problems?" Karl had come to stand in the doorway of the kitchen.

I was opening and closing cupboards and drawers and feeling vague. Finally I found the rice and began to measure out grains and water. Tom and Sylvia's children had actually spent almost a week in our apartment since Karl had last been home. Almost a month of parenthood, domesticity, privacy, work had accumulated in my mind since we had last been together; it was like an entire civilization that required excavation. There was so much to tell, I didn't know where to begin. I did not, however, want to begin on Tom and Sylvia, or their children, whose sleeping bags and stuffed animals and eating habits and nighttime fears had been cluttering my rooms and my mind so much that I was heartily sick of the drama of Sylvia and Tom, tired of the jargons of liberation, the bitterness of blaming, the canny unruliness of bewildered children; bone-tired.

"Everyone was upset," I said briefly; and then I leaned my forehead against a cupboard door and laughed ruefully. "Do you want to know something?" I said suddenly. "I don't think talking about Tom and Sylvia is good for us. Especially now." I clattered the lid onto the pot of rice and slammed shut a stove drawer.

"But I care about them," protested Karl.

"Long-distance," I retorted before I could help myself.

We ate dinner in near silence that night, our chairs pulled close to the hearth. An anxiety had come over me with the onset of evening, an animal chill inside thin walls on the shore of a lake soon to freeze over. I had put on another sweater and tied a scarf around my head.

Later Karl went out for more wood and reported that the rain was easing. "Tomorrow we'll have to get to work on the closing," he announced. He pulled out the list of chores and over a mug of tea began intoning it to me—swimming ladders up, summer curtains down, winter curtains up, canoe hoisted, boats out, motors drained, porch furniture in, mice poison out, pipes drained, antifreeze in toilets, electricity off, canned goods removed, refrigerator cleaned, blankets stored, beds covered, garbage to dump, tool cabinets locked.

"We have to haul up that dead wood, too," he interrupted himself, "so it can dry out by spring."

I nodded, staring into the fire. Up there winter was very close, the first snowfall probably only weeks away, the deciduous trees already almost skeletal, birds already grouping.

"Tell me more about the children," Karl said as we lay tucked up in bed under blankets that would not have been sufficient had the room been any colder.

"They want to know when you're coming home for good," I answered.

"What did you tell them?"

"I said probably by Christmas."

He sighed. "I hope so. God, I hope so." He rolled onto his back and looked hard at the ceiling. I could see his jaw grinding beneath his cheek. "Blake is getting harder and harder to work with. It's power. Everything is out of proportion. I reminded him that we'd agreed that I'd only stay through the preliminary design, but he wasn't even listening. He's so wrapped up in the politics of it that he's not even thinking about human beings any more. He's scared to death that the second phase of the contract might not come through."

Money, heat, space: I had never been to Texas, but the image I had of it by that time was like an overexposed nightmare of scintillating urban nodes where money changes hands surrounded by blinding space.

I closed my eyes, and then I saw a huge, dark drawer, like the ones in my grandmother's wardrobe, into which I could lay Blake and Houston and the hermetic airplanes into which and from which Karl disappeared and appeared and the third quarter taxes that we hadn't discussed yet and Karen's insomnia and Erica's tantrums and the plumber and the landlord and the mechanic who had cheated me and Tom and Sylvia and Tom and Sylvia's children and all of Karl's clothes and all of my clothes and all our coins; I would push the drawer closed with my foot and walk off into the recesses of the room, which would be dim, like a reddish cave, no walls squared off, the floor a little slippery, the passageways between one room and another like those inside a body, an organ, a heart.

"You're falling asleep again," said Karl.

"No, I'm not."

"Yes, you are, you were snoring."

"I don't snore. Women don't snore."

He laughed and switched off the red-shaded light. "Are you really pregnant?" he said into my ear.

"I don't know, leave me alone," I mumbled because I was already back in the rounded passageways, finding no handholds on the walls, making my way only with difficulty in the darkness, slipping.

When I woke sometime later, Karl was also awake. Two owls were calling to each other, pumping out long series of *whoos* with shivers of sound at the end, owl laughs, back and forth, back and forth. Karl said something as he smoothed back my hair, his hands over my ears, but then I couldn't hear anything; it was like being inside the earth.

All the next morning we worked outside together. Now and then a fine rain would start and stop as soon as we began to think of going indoors. With the chain saw Karl cut fallen trees into manageable lengths, which we shouldered in tandem, carried to the woodpile under the lean-to, and piled in crisscrossed layers. Sometimes we were working on the paths near the lake, sometimes along the road in the woods. Everywhere around us nature appeared to be settling into quietude. Leaves floated on the water and caught along the shoreline like foam or tilted slowly, singly, in the now visible depths of the forest.

It was on our honeymoon that Karl and I had discovered how well we could work together. He had taught me how to split wood, and the pleasures I got from the judicious positioning of the wedges, my own strength, the ring of the sledge, the revealed inner grain of the log were inseparable from all the other pleasures of unhurried daily intimacy. By the time I married, I had known enough of graveyards and train stations and rented rooms and hearts strung out across distances to appreciate the miracle of physical presence in love.

"Let's eat lunch," Karl said.

I had lost count of our trips to the woodpile. All morning in the undecided weather we had put layers of clothing on and off. "I almost feel like a swim," I said.

"You'd freeze your bum off," said Karl.

I went down to the dock anyway, bathed my face, and lay belly and breasts down on my spread poncho above water that was almost opaque. In July, shafts of sunlight angling into the lake had caught on millions of pollen motes, like suspended corn meal, and on schools of minnows flashing in and out of the dock's shadow. I had dived again and again through the layers of cold and then colder watery light. At the bottom of the lake, in the shallows, blobs of sun had trembled on the rocks and sand like the liquid reflections on the boathouse ceiling. Somewhere in between was where we lived, somewhere slightly above the surface of the water.

Rolling onto my back, I came into a view of the high-traveling fronts of protean sky, fringed by pine trees. I breathed in deeply, hands on abdomen.

A seed that is not planted cannot grow, my grandmother had once told me sagely when I asked her about birth control techniques at the turn of the century. The gesture that accompanied this wisdom could well have been a wagging of her finger—at me. The Bible, she said, was a great comfort. Did I pray to God every day? she wanted earnestly to know.

Prayer, knitting needles, sticks, potions, witchcraft, massage: how had it been done in those days? I had never thought to ask. *Product of conception,* I mused, was a cleverly conceived term.

That afternoon, in spite of the fine rain, the chores, the hours closing in toward our departure, we took the boat out for a last long ride, clear to the other side of the lake, where we meandered among islands into labyrinthine swamps, at times almost touching the sharp grasses, now sighting a heron among the cattails, now skirting a vintage beaver dam. We raised the motor and, using the rowboat oars as paddles, slowly dipped down through lily pads and water weeds past lone tamaracks and scrub oaks and stands of bracken against deep backgrounds of forest. The air was lichen-colored.

Airplanes awaited us, more roads, telephone wires, gaping nights, viscissitudinous days, but for the moment I felt washed all around by love. It didn't make any difference to me which turnings we took.

"We could come up here and live all year round, you know," said Karl as we were passing a muskrat house. At least once every time we visit the cottage he says this, as if the words are part of his ritual of communion.

And I said, as I almost always do lately, "Let's get the children educated first." But I smiled at him. Together we had been dropped plumb into this immense moment.

"Did I ever tell you about the time I saw the lynx?" he asked.

I nodded.

"And the bear?"

I nodded again.

"You know I haven't had a bear dream in years. I wonder why."

I shook my head at him. My eyes felt peaceful.

We had come out on the open water now. Near us a loon dove under for a breathlessly long time and finally surfaced some distance away. "Look there!" exclaimed Karl, pointing to a far promontory above which an eagle widely circled and landed on the highest pine. My eyes came back to rest on the spaciousness of the lake. In three clear notes the loon cried out over the water, and in three clear notes the sound returned to us.

The weather cleared and turned much colder that evening. There were stars. Karl aimed another log into the fire, and as the last song on the scratchy Louis Armstrong record began to waver out from the small player, he gripped an imaginary trumpet, widened his grin, and began mouthing the words I had first heard on our honeymoon.

"To spend one night with you
In our old rendezvous
And reminisce with you
That's my desire."

Behind him flames were curling freshly around the underside of the birch log. It was our last fire; the next day we would have to clean beneath the grate and sweep the hearth. Cooled ashes were silken, I was thinking, something to clothe yourself in, to rub on your body like silken powder.

"We'll sip a little glass of wine
I'll gaze into your eyes divine
I'll feel the touch of your chops
All wrapped up amongst mine."

Karl popped his eyes, pursed his lips, and flung himself dramatically beside me on the couch.

"You and Louis are both irresistible," I said. Firelit as his face was, I seemed to see even more of the children in his features: Karen's nose, Erica's lips, the same high forehead on all three of them.

"There ain't nothing can stop that old joy," said Karl.

We watched as the fire settled down into itself, seemed to fuse individual logs into its heart.

"I've been thinking," he said after a time, "about us and the children and how crazy it is for me to be gone. This is no way to live. It's not worth it."

I was silent, careful.

"I'm going to do all I can to bring the rest of the project home," he said.

I nodded, but in spite of my governing, hope leaped up in me like blood, for simple life, animals protected in their den, the ancient pattern of male, female, young.

Suddenly Karl roused himself and rubbed his hands together. "Cold, tomorrow, and *busy,*" he announced, slapping my knee. "You ready for it?"

While he got ready for bed, I stayed by the fire, wrapped in an afghan, lying down alone and not alone with shadows. The demands of motherhood were, I knew, every bit as shocking as reported by honest survivors, and yet I knew now I already loved this possible child, as if I had been holding her close for a long time, for ages and ages, without knowing it.

That night I dreamed that I was betrothed to myself. Two great families were to be united through this match. I went to my bride and bowed to her relatives. I took the chair of her sister. As I looked into her eyes and listened to her talk, I felt my own eyes grow huge with love. Recognition jumped between us. She was more intelligent and I more tender than I had ever dared to hope. It was a perfect match.

Then I was at the bottom of a hill, holding a baby. I stood

before a huge fireplace, like an entrance to a mansion. In my arms the baby had turned to wood, an elongated wooden doll, very precious. I went up to the left-hand wall of the fireplace and opened a door that had on it a carving of the baby; it was like the door to an old coffin. I put my baby in and the door clicked shut, as if two parts had come together. When I took the doll out and held her funny, stiff, primitive form against mine, I thought perhaps she was dead, but, what joy, she began to nurse, and, wonder of wonders, I had milk, I had milk!

Sunday morning was indeed cold, with a clear brilliance into which we squinted with amazement: all that yellow on the forest floor, all that glancing blue of the lake, all those shards of fathomless sky through shifting branches.

"It's always like this," said Karl as he paused in the open door. "The most beautiful day is always the last."

He allowed himself one sigh, and then we burst out of doors and took over the morning. We did the boathouse first, the sounds of wood and metal ringing across the lake, as if in our industry we owned it entirely, our shouted directions to each other filling the spaces between trees and hours. I ran back and forth to the toolhouse several times, stopped once in the kitchen to drink three glasses of water. Doors slammed. Karl banged a finger and swore loudly. We heaved and hauled, cleated pulley ropes, secured doors, and stacked life preservers.

Lunch we ate standing up, making check marks on the chore list as we foraged for remnants of food. I was to do the cupboards, the refrigerator, the hearth.

I rattled the damper and scooped out the ashes and swept clean the sooty cave. Momentarily abstracted from my task, I plunged my hands into the bucket of ashes and began playing with them. Handful after airy handful I squeezed down into finer and finer particles. I am used to working with fibrous materials, of cells linked together, which in my hands seem to want to go in one direction or another, which speak out their most accommodating patterns, but ashes are a wonderment.

Impulsively I brought my hands to my face and smeared my skin with the cool, powdery silk, and then I carried the bucket down the path to the lake and onto the dock, where I slowly shook the dust over the water. I stood above it, staring, as it spread out away from me, and then I knelt down and washed my face in the numbing water.

The blood, when I discovered it in the bathroom, seemed very old, instinctively known, a mother language, both dead and alive, humorous.

Well, well, I thought and went to find Karl. He was loading birch logs into the trunk of the car.

"I'm not pregnant," I announced.

"I thought you weren't," he answered.

"What do you mean, you thought I wasn't?"

"I just know what I know." He smiled as he threw in another log.

"Oh, you're infuriating," I said loudly. "How do we really know anything about each other! We should change places for a year or two, that's what we should do."

"Don't tell me you'd like that," he said.

I threw up my arms.

He caught me before I could go farther. I was laughing and crying. He lifted me up and began turning, and I closed my eyes and didn't touch the ground. When I opened my eyes, the trees were still spinning, all kinds of trees, white pine, poplar, aspen, maple, balsam fir, circling against the sky.

He let me slide to my feet. For a moment my arms were full of him, the way the arms of his parents had once been, the way my parents had once held me and their parents them and how I now encircled my own children, even this latest one, the little one who had slipped away, the minnow I thought I could have followed even farther into love.

Monday at high noon Karl's plane lifted into a nondescript sky, slightly overcast, but with no turbulence predicted. I watched until it was out of sight over the trees. Already this far south the autumn seemed less advanced, and as I drove on alone over Thursday's roads, the colors were again overpowered by green: an amazing color, I decided, so much of it everywhere, so blithely, serenely fecund. Harvesters were at work in a number of fields; cows, the same heavy cows, stood rooted in pasture. Nothing seemed to have changed. It grew dark. Traffic of all kinds multiplied. The city sent out its multifarious signals. The air grew hazy with artificial light.

I wound from the highway into familiar neighborhood streets, lamplit, containing innumerable stoops, doorways, windows into the interior, where the eventful, quotidian work of the heart still waited.

I carried an image: of a day in January, say, the dead of winter, when Tomahawk Lake would be so frozen the deer and rabbits would forage on its islands, when the sun on the precise icy branches of the trees, on the forest filled with snow, on the snowy lake would be brittle and dazzling, when the cottage inside its drawn, stiff white winter curtains might be blue-white, like a cave of snow: it seemed a configuring image, a stillness that wanted to grow, planted in my mind beyond my planning, exacting for its acceptance more than I had ever dreamed of devotion.

RIFFRAFF

When the sun rises above the woods, it explodes into the kitchen like a presence, yet infinitely dispersed. Usually for a few minutes all I am aware of is sunlight. It was about that time yesterday I first noticed those neighbor children running up our lane, a familiar movement across my vision, more like two animals making their customary rounds, surely able in this abundant summertime to fend for themselves. In the warm dazzle I bent again to the sink of berries. Max had been here three days; I was counting them, I couldn't help it.

Truck barked until I unlatched the screen and yelled at him, "Hush up!" "Why don't you untie him?" panted Andy, who was the first to reach the door. "That's why he barks, he sees us and he wants to run." "I haven't been outside yet," I said. I think my voice was pleasant enough; I was just standing there in my bathrobe, screwing my eyes a bit in the sunlight, conscious of the field shimmering up the hill in a parting of the woods. "We'll untie him for you," persisted Andy in the same scrappy, insolent tone that can sometimes raise in me such a choke of anger that I barely know afterward how to treat my own son. "He don't like to watch us running," added Tim. "That's all right," I said, still pleasant, "I'll get him in a few minutes." "Kin we have a drink of water?" asked Tim. "Shelley drank up all the pop last night."

I could feel Max coming to stand behind me. I knew without looking that his arm was resting along the doorjamb above my head. He wasn't touching me, but I felt as if he were. Max has a son too—five years old. Today he went to see him for the first time in six months. Last night, talking about his son, he rolled over and looked at the bedroom ceiling, and I could see tears in his eyes. "Sometimes I need to touch him so badly, just pick him up, that I don't know what to do," he said. "I'm always writing letters to him in my mind that he could maybe read when he's grown."

"Hush up!" I yelled out to Truck again. I could almost hear Orin Ploen saying, "Scum. Dirt. Don't you give them anything, or you'll never get rid of them. You're not to give them anything, do you hear? I don't want them around my buildings, I don't want anything to do with them." God. Orin Ploen can talk for an hour about the hazards of living across the road from such scummy, dirty folk. I think they're mainly why he decided to rent out and move to town. They must have cluttered his view.

"I thought you said your dad was fixing your pump," I said to the boys. "You're not supposed to come here for things, I've told you that." "My dad, he said he needed another part, he said the belt it got worn through." Tim and Andy are the youngest, but they already have taken on that nipped, oblique look of the older children. I think there are nine of them in all, but by the time my counting gets to the teenagers, I seem to fall into a dull-headedness: how to comprehend the evolution of those synthetic chartreuse sweaters and high sharp breasts, those run-over boots and sullen shoulders and jeans bulging with sex. One of the girls has gone to fat, one of the boys has taken to drinking beer with his father on the old car seat in the front yard, but they all merge into one image for me: crude emotion that has somehow found itself in human shape. Screaming needs, I remember saying to myself one day; they all have screaming needs.

Both boys were staring at Max, even though they'd seen him the previous days, talked to him even as he pulled my Jason up and down the lane in the wagon. Their own father is a drunk, their mother too. Both parents pull out early in the morning in a turquoise station wagon to go work at the Harbor Club, and they don't come back until night, sometimes late. She's a cook; I've seen her huge dress emerging miraculously white through that filthy doorway. He's a handyman; this I also know from Lute at the crossroads store. Lute says, "How he can janitor at the club and then come home to a dump like that I can never see. But folks say they do good work. They ever give you any trouble?" he asked me sharply one winter night. "No," I said, but it wasn't long after when I had returned home from work one evening and found Tim and Andy and the youngest girl, Susie, huddled inside my back door on the kitchen steps. Jason had been whining and crying in the car, and I was confused anyway about having to leave him at the daycare center all day; I was worn down generally by the relentless winter; the children said they were out of oil for their space heater, out of wood for the stove, their parents weren't home. I was exhausted with the bleakness of all I had to do by myself. I remember I shouted at them and later I even slapped Jason when he wouldn't sit down in the tub. That was a terrible night—Jason crying, Tim and Andy and Susie pinched together on my couch waiting for their parents to get home. I had thought then of myself, "You're no better than them, you're no damn better," and finally I made the children some cocoa and scrambled eggs, but I still hated myself, hated the ugliness of myself until I felt locked in a prison of unspeakable conditions.

What that family finally did for heat that night, I don't know; maybe they broke up some furniture and burned it in their cookstove. I crawled into my own bed remembering all the reasons why I hadn't been able to live with my husband. A terrible night: everyone, including the weather, was turned bitter side out.

"How come Jason ain't playing out yet?" asked Andy yesterday morning. He kept reaching down and scratching a line of swollen bites that ran up his leg as if a single insect had eaten its way across the boy's sleeping body.

I shuddered. I can barely care for my own child. Sometimes I look at him while he's asleep and it seems to me that I'll never be good enough for what I'm supposed to be doing. And yet the days keep coming. Another one has just passed. Max left at noon today, quietly, his mind already stretching for his son. Yesterday was like a holocaust; maybe it's that I'm expecting something more, after all that drama. I can't fit together everything that has happened. I sit here in my darkened living room, smoking now and then from the pack Max left behind but not really wanting the taste of it, and watching the dull orange of the smoldering heap of rubble across the road.

Anyway, I gave the children a drink. Water you don't refuse. Even Orin Ploen, I suspect, would have fetched them a glassful before he ordered them home. That's what I did; I told them to run along, and the words sounded all right to me yesterday. My mind even rested for a moment on the resilient wildness of those children. I knew they'd scrounge all day for what they needed, warmed by the sun and by unexpected, shrill pleasures, and I knew that sooner or later the turquoise car would return, and sooner or later the pump would have its missing belt. I couldn't imagine then ever seeing anything across the road but a listing porch and torn window shades, and I told myself that lots of people have grown up in houses like that and most of them haven't had country like this to burst out into on a summer morning. You can walk to the lake in half an hour, and there's nothing between here and there but fields of pasture, cherry orchards, and rocky woods. Most of the houses don't amount to much anyway.

We were going into our woods that morning. Jason had been promised, and his anticipation of our picnic, his rumpled pajamas and flushed cheeks, the honeyed toast that he was licking around and around to catch the drips—all seemed to have coalesced to give him an attitude of serene, petted complacency. I thought he looked as if he were contained within a radiant drop of water. Max, too, must have liked the mood because he silently poured our coffee and we sat down close together on the bench, leaning back against the sunny wall and slowly eating cereal and strawberries from bowls held beneath our chins. The simple taste of the grains and fruit seemed to me to reaffirm what we had been trying to make the past three days: a plain friendship, no games if we could help it, more like a searching out. I found myself wishing I'd never get to the bottom of the bowl.

But that salved feeling has never seemed to last, and I feel defenseless against the ugliness that keeps returning. It smolders in me. I never know when it will lick out. There's a dark-haired, heavy woman who also brings her child to the daycare center. One day her step sounded firmer, she seemed to toss her head; her divorce had just come through, she told me. "Thank God I'm free of that asshole," she said. Those words made me imagine how her own thighs must look—hairy, purple around the crotch like a permanent bruise, disfigured with fat. I hated the thought of her. Yet I am a woman too. I cross my outstretched legs at the ankle—swimmer's legs; my feet are bare, this room contains an oak table laden with plants I have potted myself, I have long brown hair that I sometimes braid and wrap around my head. These things do not make me a woman, and yet I am a woman.

One night last month Max called from California. I hadn't seen him in ten years. "Let's see each other," he said. He had combined intuition, need, our few sporadic letters and come up with what seemed to him a brilliant fantasy, only half a continent from accomplishment. "I'm not nineteen any more," I said. "Neither am I," he answered. "Furthermore," I continued, "I have completely stopped wearing makeup." He laughed as if he were touched. Do I want to be touching? Do I want to be touched?

"That's about the way I picture you," he said, and through curiosity of his vision of myself I was seduced. Baths with Jason aside, it had been a year since I had taken off my clothes with another human being—*'ooman bean* is what Jason still says sometimes. Tonight he wanted to know again the difference between fire smoke and tea kettle steam, for the fiftieth time I had to tell him that fires just get started sometimes, and people don't know how, and when there's no water, when a pump isn't working and the trucks use up all they have, then there's nothing left to do but let the flames burn themselves out. He had to know again, and then again, why the trucks had come and gone with two walls still to fall, why the men with water cylinders on their backs had sprayed the scorched grass in a widening fan away from the house, why the turquoise car itself had pulled up and then spun away again soon after with its collected children, blasting the onlookers with a defiant murk of heated dust. And he had to hear repeated the terrible reason why Susie had come screaming up our lane, when our afternoon seemed to contain nothing but the newborn, smoothed-out movements following our afternoon nap, "I can't find them boys, I can't find Tim and Andy, and our whole upstairs is on fire!"

"People can burn, can't they?" Jason said solemnly as I

washed him. "But Tim and Andy didn't burn up, did they?" "No." I tried to reassure him. "But that was why we were all looking so hard; we were worried." "I didn't burn up either, did I? But if I play with matches, then I could burn up because Tim and Andy, they play with matches sometimes but they didn't burn up because they went up the road, but sometimes people play with matches and then they get burned up." I sat with him for a long time before he was ready to go to sleep. I sat with him so long I got beyond my own tiredness, and now I'm simply here, in a house I chose myself, getting used to being alone again.

I think now and then of the telephone, that Max might call and say he has reached the outskirts of the city and is holed up in a faceless motel, waiting for the night to be over so he can go to his son. I wonder if he'll arrive at breakfast time and find the boy in a pool of light, spooning up egg. I keep forgetting that his wife will be there too. I never met her. Max says she has red hair, is beautiful. Valerie. He says she found him impossible, his ideas too strong, apparently. He loves her still, I can tell. Listening to Max, I almost love her myself; what I respond to is the pathos of a man who simply wants to love a woman, but she has become too angry to care any longer. With my husband, Ben, I got so caught up in what I thought it must feel like to be a man that loving, trying to love him and be the sort of woman I as a man would enjoy, was like being a continually disappointed lover of myself. The effort split me right down the middle; I wasn't myself and I wasn't him, nor could I be one way for him and another for myself. It was during this struggle that Ben told me to loosen up; we both needed more experiences, he said, we were unduly limiting ourselves. *Loosen up?* I can hear his voice trailing off like cigarette smoke, what he didn't say dissipating itself into my own confusions. Jason was eighteen months old. For three months, Ben told me, he had been seeing another girl. *Seeing? Girl?* I waited. I watched him with Jason, looking for signs of softening around the eyes or mouth. I needed to know where his love was concentrated, where he would be willing to put himself. But he was distracted, his mind elsewhere; he drove faster than usual, his jaws grinding, and at night he played new records that he let me know were suited particularly to his own expanding tastes. He would take Jason exuberantly in his arms and dance with him while I watched numbly from a doorway, my body locked as if afflicted. I wondered if I had ever loved him.

Then I started swimming again, counting the laps; I took long showers in the locker room of the Y where I submitted my face to the bombardment of water. Features obliterated, I felt stronger: it was there that the flesh began to tatter, pieces of myself spilling out and washing away, even anger sloughing off like deadened skin; my cheeks fell open, as if the sockets of my eyes had grown.

I'm in no hurry, I have been telling myself; wholeness takes time. I am even losing my old idea of wholeness: I begin to picture myself as made up of the same particles as everything else, discreteness at last unmasked. Some days I leave my eyes in the woods, my working limbs and voice in the pool, instructing another generation of swimmers; my breasts I abandon in the garden, hanging over cabbages, my heart beside the face of Jason, napping on his mattress beneath the screened window; my fissured crotch I drop in the field to be washed by rain, maybe to sprout a clump of wild everlasting; my mind lights a lamp at night when the house is quiet and reads another book. I am twelve years old, filling out a questionnaire: *What are your favorite hobbies?* Swimming and reading, that was what I always put; my idea of happiness was to swim all afternoon in the neighborhood pool and then read a book in the ivy-patterned glider swing on our back porch. My father had a grape arbor—he was a banker; my mother was mild and orderly—she taught second grade. Going home is still like drinking a glass of my father's good wine. My parents are lovely, I told a friend last year before I moved up here, and she scowled at me. At least they don't pressure me. If Max calls tonight, I will be glad for his voice; if he doesn't, I will still be here, watching, doing what I can with my life.

Yet the fire across the road persists like a scarred and bloodshot eye. I feel accused. I, too, have screamed and slammed doors, bitten and slapped other bodies, averted my eyes and blinded my heart with pride. I, too, have fingered myself and hidden beneath pillows, have caught my image in bathroom mirrors in the middle of the night and grimaced like a maniac at the disheveled stranger that I am. Last week I ran over a cat on a country road. "Why are you stopping?" asked Jason. "I have to see something," I said. He was eating raisins in the back seat, and I hurried on before he could see. The blood had been almost orange with crushed vitality; that night my menstrual flow began—brownish, diluted with mucus, death out of life. Cats are killed often on country roads and left to birds and animals of prey; those alive hunt mice in the ditches and at night their disembodied eyes reflect headlights like gems.

In bed last night Max and I talked until the horror and banality of the house burning was eased. The neighbors had been grimly, silently jubilant: justice and peace at last, a cancer seared from the countryside, a threat removed, their own sober ways approved once more. Grass and wildflowers would take over before the summer was out, I had been told by one of the congregation on my front lawn. It was a terrible thing, to be sure, but what could you expect and it wasn't the first time, no, only two years ago one of the older boys, that Shelley it was, had set fire to a mattress and the place had been saved only by a passing neighbor, the very husband of my informer, who had rushed up the stairs and thrown the stinking, smoking pad from the window; it was sheer lucky chance, you couldn't expect a neighbor to be on hand every minute, though to be sure her heart had gone out often enough to the youngest ones, that very day she had called out to them, Tim and Andy, and asked them up for a cookie, but they had gone running on like scared rabbits, it hadn't been at all like them, and she had said to herself, they're up to something, but what was she to do, go hobbling up the road after them in her foam rubber slippers?

So yesterday morning as we were about to go picnicking in the woods I gave Tim and Andy a drink of water and told them to run along. We had our breakfast and dressed. Max packed peanut butter and cheese and bread in his knapsack, while I loosened a tray of ice cubes into a container of juice. "Haven't you gone home yet?" I said to the boys as I went out to unchain Truck. "Where are you going with him?" they asked, following me to the doghouse. "Just up the hill for a picnic. Now you go on, who's at your house today?" "Kin we come with you?" they asked, ignoring my question. "No, not today." "You got any soda crackers?" asked Andy. "They'll just make you thirsty again," I said, as Truck jumped, choking at his chain. "Shelley ate up all the chips too," said Tim. "He's gonna get married next week." *Married?* I remember feeling a twinge of panic. "Here," I said hurriedly before we left, and I put some crackers and raisins in their hands. "Now go on home." I looked back often as we climbed up through the field, watching to see that they went down the lane and across the road, half expecting to see Orin Ploen's pickup lurch around the bend before those forbidden children had crossed the boundary.

We carried an old cotton blanket, printed with an Indian design. Truck crashed on ahead. Jason trudged sturdily beside us in his new orange-laced work boots. How come Tim and Andy couldn't come along, he wanted to know, was it because they didn't have their shoes on? Skin kept in the blood, didn't it? Did I think we'd find any more bones in the woods? Jason's voice kept reminding me of the present; ten years ago Max and I had tramped through woods like this one, sometimes with a group of campers from the place where we were both counseling, sometimes alone with a blanket, his sketchbook, my paperback. On duty, I taught swimming and managed a tentful of fourteen-year-old girls; he ran the craft shop and herded groups of adoring teenagers into the sand dunes to sketch tufts of dunegrass, sharp-crested ridges, and shadowed draws. We were both virgins, we confided to each other, but somehow that summer camaraderie was sufficient. He had still thought then it was impossible to love a buddy; he mused on this the other night as we bathed together for the first time. I lay back in the water and wondered if he were going to put me in a category. My face isn't beautiful, I know; I have large round eyes and flat cheeks with freckles; my body is thin and browned; I'm tall; my breasts are small; I don't look as old as I am, though lately I've caught an expression around my eyes that says, *thirty years*. I told him I hadn't been ready either, that lying in the sun and walking had been enough. I remembered liking his curly black hair and heavily lashed eyes and compact body, but I had liked, too, the innocent way we spent our free afternoons—reading and drawing, our feet touching sometimes, one or the other of us joking occasionally.

Now, ten years later, we were being tempered by domesticity; we couldn't escape being a temporary family. Max would sit on the couch reading storybooks aloud while I went on stringing my loom; after Jason was in bed at night we might drink herb tea at the lamplit kitchen table; in the late afternoons we collected salads from the garden while Jason pulled stones up and down the lane in his wagon; one morning Max stripped off his shirt and together we forked year-old manure from the barn floor and wheeled it by turns to the compost pile. Our lovemaking was friendly, almost amused. "Am I a buddy?" I asked. "That's too hard to answer," said Max.

Yesterday was different. I didn't want to leave his side as we walked; he lost his playfulness and looked at me often, straight in the eyes. I showed him the places where I had found wild leeks this spring, covered now by long flattened grasses. Max talked about trees, how they outlive most of us. We commented on the strange porousness of this soil, the unexpected holes beneath hillocks of grass, the sensation of a cavernous world beneath the rock ledges in the clearing where Jason dropped shards of limestone down the cracks and we ate beside a scrubby cedar. Our bodies were getting used to each other: excited by possibility, we wanted more of the good feelings; I felt flowered and hot, ready to slide down hard upon his stem.

Jason had to be carried home; on the last lap, out of the trees, he fell asleep with his body straddling my chest. Far down below the humming fragrant field was the small white house I rent, across the road the dust-colored hovel whose insides I had never seen. Max did later; he ran in while I held Susie and Jason, calling for the boys, making it halfway up the stairs but then being forced down again by smoke—roiling black clouds, he said, hotter than hell—forced back through a litter of garbage and dirty clothes and broken furniture, an unspeakable interior; he was sickened, ready to vomit, sick anyway with dread. One neighbor came, then another and another. They gathered in the road and stood talking or leaning into one another's car windows. Someone saved the television set and the sewing machine; there was nothing else of value. The children had been seen going up the road, perhaps half an hour before. Are you sure, I asked, are you absolutely sure they didn't come back this way? No, someone else had been in his berry patch the whole time, they had only gone one way—up to no good, too. Shush, said a woman, you don't know nothing, anyway it's them parents who's to blame if anybody is. Cedar block houses, said a man, take a long time to burn, this one could go on for days, he'd seen it built, long time ago, seen the way the wood sections were laid atop one another and plastered over. It's a good way, he said—cool in the summer, warm in the winter, a good kind of house—if you take care of it, he added.

I carried Jason easily down the hill, my blood settling into my thighs as we descended. Jason's warmed hair smelled wonderful. "Our little friends are back," said Max. I squinted through the August brilliance and saw two small figures, sitting side by side on our step. We maneuvered the stone wall and entered the back pasture. The gate to the yard hung open as we had left it. I took Jason silently through the house and eased him down on his mattress. Then I came back out to the porch and let loose. "Go on home!" I shouted. "Don't you understand me? I told you this morning to stay over at your own place. Now go on! You're not supposed to be over here."

"Will you give us a drink first?" they asked. "Go get a bucket," I said. I was twitching with annoyance. "We don't got a bucket." "Of course you've got a bucket. You must have a bucket." "We don't have a bucket any more."

I went in, letting the screen slam and brought back two glasses. They drank the water beneath my eyes, set down the glasses on the concrete, and left, scurrying off with a hunched-over, wary posture.

Inside, Max and I worked quickly at each other's clothing. We were new with each other, unabashed with our desire, halfway along already in a process that felt then as inevitable as giving birth. I closed the curtains, and the image of Tim and Andy scuttled across my mind.

The labor of Jason's birth I had accepted with relief: its purpose was unquestioned, I couldn't have stopped it if I had wanted to. I pulled up my knees to my chest as I had been taught, my face strained forward, I took pleasure in thinking of myself as a rounded eloquent shape, a cleaved egg, unanesthetized cunt to the world, its lips parting, ready to speak. For once there was no question of the words, I groaned the way trees groan in a storm. Afterward I lay in a white room, in a clean bed, victorious. Something had happened that could never be taken away. Ben was very busy just then—reports to be written up, the usual late-night sessions in the laboratory; he came to the hospital for hurried visits, bringing the requisite flowers, the prunes I had requested, a fashion magazine that I opened once and then gave away. I explained to myself that he didn't understand what was happening: I had been opened up, turned inside out with effort; I had performed an adult action superbly, and now I was wondering what else this organism called myself could draw itself up to accomplish.

The momentum and purity of childbirth must be duplicated only by death. Into what other actions is one caught so securely, no chance of change or interruption? Every other process seems a confounding of inevitability and possibility. Susie could easily have come banging on our kitchen door the moment before our orgasm, yelling Fire! Fire! and we lovers would have wrenched ourselves apart, stumbling to retrieve our jeans, wincing at the roughness of the cloth. Does adrenaline shrink an erection, I wonder; which is the stronger force? At what moment did the blaze across the road become uncontrollable? Was there a day, a night, an indifferent random gesture that at last rendered irreversible the moral fortunes of that family? Was it my words finally that sent the children whispering, desperately conniving up the wooden staircase to the bedrooms where all those too-familiar bodies had sweated and shivered away season after season of nights?

As it was, Max and I were allowed to have our groaning bliss, our moments of illusory pause. The curtains puffed gently over the bed; I remember watching before I slept the way the light passed over us in this rhythm. Max was dissolving into highlight and shadow; his beard and chest and the caverns of his eyes were of the same stuff as all darkness, the superficial response of our skin to daylight was like that of the bedclothes, the woven wall hanging, the glass of daisies. We, too, could be reduced to the elemental.

Later, I put on a robe and went to the kitchen and brought back buttered bread and mugs of apple juice. Jason woke. We all sat together in the bed, eating and not saying much. Jason had a deck of cards with which he was laying out a symbolic, muttering game. Max and I smiled at each other now and then. I felt experimental, rich, as if I were a stream of water that had just spilled out into new territory. I wondered how long this awareness of myself had been collecting, through what motions of mind my present course had been made ineluctable.

The roof was the first to fall; I suppose most houses burn this way. The walls went one by one, but the fire caused such a roaring that the crumbling of the structure was barely heard. A slight irregularity in the construction of the chimney was discernible at the end, and then it, too, floated piece by piece into the massive blaze. I couldn't tell if Tim and Andy were in the turquoise car; someone said their parents had gone to pick them up at Lute's. I wonder if they'll come back to scavenge, after the coals are cool. If they own the land, they might build again; I never thought of that: would it be possible for that family, even if there were the money, to build a house together? If they should come back, will I still be in the same place?

I get up from the couch to check on Jason. He sleeps uncovered on his side, his feet still look dirty, his cheek is mashed into the pillow, and he is breathing through his mouth—his sleep, my son. I cover him lightly and go out through the kitchen to the back door. Truck whines and comes out of his house as I cross to the shadowy garden. The field is obscured; I can hardly tell the woods from the sky.

This is the hour when telephones are most likely silent. Night has taken over completely, and dark space has become the medium of messages. I'm sending a few of my own. Crushing before my face leaves of basil and mint, I urge my heart—I'm in a hurry after all—to teach itself how to mend and grow; straining my eyes up the hill through the midnight air, shivering suddenly, I ask forgiveness of the trees.

A DAUGHTER'S HEART

The early Saturday morning that Kathleen came home from college for spring vacation, she found her father polishing the brass doorknobs and plates in the front vestibule. "Oh, this is fine," Chris said. He set down the bottle of tarnish remover and the rag and embraced her heartily. He was tall, but only slightly taller than she, and his leanness surprised her; it seemed that before there had been more of him.

"Hello, hello," she exclaimed. She disentangled herself from duffel bag and backpack and hugged her father again, setting them both a little off balance. Her body was stronger than ever from a daily regime of running and exercises, but feelings and gestures were still hard for her to put together without awkwardness. This particular morning, life's potential seemed so vast as to be almost uncontainable; she felt she might fly apart from the inner press of it.

Most of the night on the train she had been awake, talking intensely with the young man who chanced to sit next to her, a divinity student, it turned out, who had had so many of the same questions as she that four hundred miles had seemed insubstantial. Was creation necessary to the Divine? they both wanted to know. Tom, his name had been. Kat had dozed off for only an hour, just before dawn, but she wasn't tired now, not at all. Here was her father, and the moment of reunion was alive with delight.

"May I have a turn?" asked her mother's amused, warm voice. Here were Tina and Carol, too, coming down the stairs, still in their bathrobes. They were all together in the familiar entrance hall, around them the papered walls, the polished banisters, the small desk at the foot of the stairs, the daylight. How clear it seemed! Kat hugged everyone vigorously. She had so much to tell them!

"I think we could have a real breakfast now," said Chris to Miriam. Kat saw the look they gave each other through the excited greetings of their daughters. It was like a note so low and steady she could barely make it out; she only knew it was there.

They had tea and toast and jam and scrambled eggs at the table beside the sunny kitchen window. Quick birds flew now and then to the feeder just outside the glass, built one fall years ago by Chris. The bright air was intermittently snow-flurried, as if with particles of precipitated light. Kat sighed with an upsurge of happiness. Plants flourished in the windows; the large room was fragrant with toast and the cookies her mother was in the midst of baking; the sunlight touched everything, their faces, their hands, the dishes of red and purple jams, the amber tea.

She poured out her life for them—philosophy, French, biology, literature, her runs along the river path, her room in the scholars' house, the repertory symphony, the new good food group, the meditation society, her ideas for travel next summer—and she must hear about them, all the news this minute, entire: Tina's dancing, Carol's editorship of the school paper, her mother's new job in the high school office, her father's counseling and current graduate courses. Hearing their voices was like being inside a familiar piece of music once more; like music their voices reassured her that life was meant to flow inside its forms, to enlarge but not break the heart. Oh, she wanted them to talk and talk until nothing was unsaid that should be said.

"But aren't you exhausted?" her mother finally asked. "Don't you want to nap this morning?"

"I couldn't possibly." Kat laughed, but then the telephone rang, and Carol jumped up; her father said he should be getting on with the paper he was writing; her mother took out the last sheet of cookies and turned off the oven; Tina stretched gracefully back in her chair, long hair loose, lovely slender face fifteen years old now, one small glisten of butter at the corner of her mouth. Breakfast was over.

Kat washed the dishes with her mother. She ran through the cold to the trash can and on her way back crumbled a heel of bread ceremoniously into the feeder. The brilliant fine snow seemed to be whirling out of nowhere, falling, then lifting, as if the center of gravity were everywhere at once. A run to the lake with her father was what she wanted today, just like their jogs of last summer, when they would be out and back in the mornings before anyone else was even awake.

Upstairs in her room Kat unpacked her bags, books mostly, a few bulky sweaters and pairs of blue jeans, a small gray heap of what her mother would probably refer to gently and reprovingly as untidy linen. She laid out the books on her desk and shoved most of the clothes back into the duffel bag in the corner. Clothes were merely an irritant. The largest of the sisters, Kat had simplified her wardrobe when she had gotten away from home to the few garments that felt comfortable on her body—jeans in the winter, gym shorts in the summer, and for concerts a long cotton skirt sewn by her mother.

"Is this all you've got?" Tom had asked her that morning as he had helped her hoist her duffel to her shoulder in the station, and she had been proud of the compactness of her load and the strength of her body. "Only what's necessary," she had said laughing, but then a moment later, turning into the thronging station, she had collided with a hurrying businessman and bumbled onto an upward-moving escalator, when what she really needed was to go down, toward the street and the commuter trains. Gliding back to the level where they had parted, she had looked for Tom, for a young man in a blue down jacket with sand-colored hair and a reddish beard, but he was gone. Streams of strangers had been crossing from one opening or another across the great dusky room, or loitering at the snack bars and newsstand; daylight had appeared only high up, among the grimy clerestories of the vaulted ceiling.

Now in her own bedroom at last, Kat pushed the curtains fully apart and gazed out onto the suburban neighborhood roofs. Her hands shook slightly. Minute tremors passed now and then through her body. The light shivered with snow, turned gray for an instant, and returned to brightness. Here she was. What was her father doing?

His study was at the end of the upstairs hallway; it was a porch, really, overlooking the street, and wherever there weren't windows, he had over the years built shelves for his accumulating books. There were also a large worktable and chair and several filing cabinets and a reading chair of comfortable depth, into which Kat herself had often retreated. This morning, however, the chairs were unused; her father stood at a window, a length of sash cord over his shoulder and various tools and pieces of molding strewn around him. Kat hung quietly in the doorway until he turned around. "Well, here's my girl," he said. "All unpacked?"

She nodded. "Would you like to take a run with me, Father? I've been doing four miles every day at school, faithfully."

"That's discipline!" he exclaimed approvingly. "If I hadn't et so much toast I'd say yes. Later I'll go. Come here a minute, will you, and snake this cord over the pulley to me? All right, that's it, almost . . . there, I've got it. Now hand me that counterweight, please. What a job! Every window in this house suddenly seems to have at least one broken cord."

"Do you always have to take the window apart like that?" asked Kat.

"No other way, tedious as it seems."

"Can't you hire someone to do it?"

Chris laughed shortly as he continued to work. "I can probably do it better and certainly cheaper. Now that army knife, please, and then we'll see if we can get this all back together."

Kat straddled the arm of the chair and handed him tools. Outside the window the reddish maple buds seemed swollen, tossed in the capricious air within the secure limits of their branches' pliancy, unflurried by the drafts of spinning snow. Kat squinted. All this brilliance was almost too much for eyes that were unrested. In summer this porch was a cool shaded bower, as timeless as green repetitive summer days that began and ended with the same sweet sounds, dove calls, other bird calls, coming out of nowhere. There was no way to measure the hours Kat had spent in this chair, enjoying the sweet latent fullness of immobility. It had been a way of putting herself in her father's care, even when he was absent.

"That should do it for this one," said Chris. "One down and eleven to go. Are you going to be my helper or what? You're looking a little tired around the edges."

She looked up at his face. "What's the paper you're writing now?"

"Forster," he said, "and a few of the ones after him who have tussled with India."

"Mmm." Kat's eyes scanned his orderly desk. He still kept his pencils and pens in the marmalade jar. Neat stacks of papers were as usual held in place by some of the glass paperweights he had inherited from his mother, Grandmother Birks, wife of Reverend Birks. The glass collection had been handed down when the manse was dismantled several years ago; for these milky green and pink and yellow plates and pitchers and bowls Chris had built special tiered shelves in front of the dining room windows. He had built the dictionary stand, too, on which the unabridged book now lay open, the printed columns appearing to Kat from where she sat blurred and yet enticingly orderly, all that knowledge so easily contained within two covers.

"Lexicography must be a blissful occupation," her father had said to her one day last summer.

"Then why don't you do it?" she had asked.

"I may, I may yet," he had answered.

Kat slid down into the easy chair and watched as her father gathered up his tools and moved to another window. He always seemed to be busy at something, she mused, but what was it that was strongest in his mind? His work over the past years had been as a guidance counselor in the schools. Now he was back in school himself, as enthusiastic over some of his courses as Kat was with her own.

"Well, what about India? Why do you say 'tussled'?" she demanded.

"Because of the perspective it affords us," he answered, "the extreme perspective, so that there's that much more to integrate."

Kat took a deep breath and plumped herself more heavily into the chair. "Father, may I ask you something?"

"Anything at all."

"Do you remember if you ever used to be afraid of your mind?"

"Afraid of my mind?"

"Yes." Kat found it difficult to continue. She leaned back her head and let her eyes rest on the tossing branches of the maple. Her body tightened as if a sudden electric current had jammed all its connections. "Yes, afraid of where it might take you," she finally said with a shaking voice.

"Of where it might take me?" Chris put down his screwdriver and came to sit near her in the straight desk chair. "Tell me what it feels like," he suggested. He had picked up one of the glass paperweights, and after holding it for a few moments he passed it down to Kat, a magnified pansy that she remembered clearly from her grandparents' house. Its familiar weight felt good in her hand. She rubbed her fingers over the surface.

"It sometimes seems as if my mind has a mind of its own," she said. "A lot of the time I can't concentrate. I daydream too much. I never know what I'm going to think next. Everything seems so much larger than it ever did before. I mean, there's no end to what I could be thinking, is there?

"The time I waste is just incredible!" she blurted out after a pause. "Sometimes I think I'm going to split apart."

"But you've been doing very well," her father protested. "Your record shows that you've put your mind on your work admirably well. You needn't worry about what happens to drift through when you relax a little. Your business is the direction that you're going, isn't it?"

"Yes, but it's as if I'm going in all directions at once. Oh, I don't know!" Kat pressed her eyes shut. She had cried many times with her father before, but today she didn't want to cry. She wanted to be clear. What she saw behind her eyes was herself, a lumbering, long-haired girl sprawled gracelessly in a chair. She opened her eyes and laughed.

"My dear girl," her father said, "if I could make sure of giving you one thing it would be the assurance that the confusions you feel are caused by the wonderful depth of the questions you're asking. You are blessed, my dear, and you have my blessing too, for whatever it may be worth."

Kat looked intently at her father's face. His beard had turned even grayer this year, and his thin face looked tired today. A small amount of money had come to him at the death of his parents, Kat knew, but she wasn't sure how much. An image came to her suddenly, perhaps touched off by the glass weight that she kept passing from one palm to another, of a pair of balance scales, of a pair of chairs like scales, containing her father and herself, she ponderously lower and he above, appearing erect, light, almost transparent in his love. The image troubled her. His provision for her over the years had been so gracious, so natural and seemly, as never to be disquieting. She had never before considered in such a concrete way the possible toll of her life on his, measure for measure of finite energy.

"I've taken up too much of your time!" she said. "You'll never get your paper written."

"It's not every day my girl comes home," said Chris firmly. He was smiling at her. "You make your mother and me very happy, you know, just by letting us watch you grow. We're grateful to you."

In an instant she was up and had her arms around his neck; she kissed him and breathed in his nearness, and in a rush she thought how her well-being still seemed to depend quite literally on his words; without his presence it might happen that she would fall, that she would become in the lapse of time a burden to herself.

The telephone rang a good deal during the day. Two boys and a girl, dressed identically in jeans and flannel shirts and hiking boots, came at noon to pick up Carol for an expedition to the city and stayed long enough, lounging bulkily in the living room, to eat an entire tray of fresh cookies. Kat had broken off from playing the piano and was on the couch, fiddling with a wooden puzzle, one of the many objects—books, magazines, records, games of skill, well-crafted puzzles, the large globe, the piano, the photograph albums—that were on hand to entice the interest. Young people loved this comfortable room; Kat's own friends had often come for a few minutes and stayed for hours. Some of them had told Miriam troubles and questions that would have been unspeakable in their own homes. They had never seemed to mind when Chris quoted poetry to them, or even scriptures. Around her parents they had often become, Kat had observed, more settled in their behavior than was usual and yet at the same time more lively. Gradually over the years she had become aware of what a gift it was her parents had, of what was there for others to receive.

"Fill the tray, will you please, Kathleen?" asked Miriam. She was sitting close by at her sewing machine in the dining room. The ironing board was set up, too, and pressed linens lay piled on the table. A dancing costume was being sewn for Tina, who sat on the floor at her mother's feet with a piece of hand sewing; now and then she artfully changed her posture, so as to give a stretching exercise to one set of muscles or another.

Kathleen plodded to the kitchen and back with the cookie tray. By now she was quite tired indeed but felt held in place by the charming rhythms of family life. She sank deeply into the couch and ate several more cookies. For a blank moment she couldn't even remember what it was she had been hoping to do that day. She knew it involved her father, who was upstairs now in his study, with the door shut.

Carol and her friends took another round of turns on the balance labyrinth box and then surged into the hallway, clumped about finding jackets, and called out high-spirited thanks and farewells. Doors banged. It was a run she had wanted, Kat remembered, out into the open with her father, down through neighborhood streets to the beach, up the shore to the breakwater point, and back again with the victory of exertion.

The sewing machine whirred and clicked beneath Miriam's intent profile. Tina put down her sewing. Her cheeks were flushed. Kat had been told at breakfast how serious the dancing was becoming for Tina now. Encouraged by her teachers, she traveled every Saturday down into the city for additional classes. Perhaps she would go straight from high school to dancing school, who knew? Chris had said. Now Tina rose neatly from the floor, stretched, and floated up the stairs. Kat could hear her stopping to knock at her father's door.

"Kathleen," said Miriam, "what is your clothes situation right now? Do you have anything that needs mending?"

"No. Thank you, Mother."

"What about your underwear, would you like to soak it a bit in some bleach?"

"No, everything is fine, thank you," said Kat as she watched her mother measuring and pinning the hem of the dancing skirt. From upstairs came the murmur of voices.

"And your new room at school?" asked Miriam, looking up at her daughter over the rims of her glasses. "It does sound as if you like it."

"It's lovely to be in a house," Kat agreed. She told her mother about the pine tree outside her window and how the small birds chirped among its branches at sunset; she told her about some of the other girls and about the washing machine in the basement and the cozy kitchen where they could fix snacks whenever they liked.

Miriam's hands efficiently continued with their task. One pin after another was pushed into the soft material; a needle was threaded; daughters were being clothed, readied. She sat almost in the doorway between the two rooms, framed, against a background of colored glass objects and windows of daylight. The spaces around the glass pieces seemed to Kat to pulse with brightness; something inside her was pulsing too, giddily. She rubbed her eyes and then leaned back and closed them. The house was quiet.

"I really do think you should nap for a while, Kathleen. Why don't you just lie down where you are? There's an afghan behind you."

"I don't want to nap."

Miriam laughed. "That's what you've been telling me all your life. Everything will still be here when you wake up, you know."

"Who says?" teased Kat.

Miriam laughed again. "I do," she answered. "I'll keep watch." She dipped her needle over and over into the cloth.

Kat took off her shoes and lay down on the couch. She would read magazines, she decided, while she was waiting for her father to come to a stopping point.

"Are you hungry?" asked Miriam.

"Nothing right now, thanks. I want to run with Father."

"You're going out this afternoon?"

"I guess so." Kat set a pile of magazines on her chest and opened one to an account of a tribal wedding, color photographs from far away in Africa. There were certain things the women did in preparation for the ceremony and certain things the men did. Everyone seemed to be having a good time.

Kat turned another page. "Mother, is Father happy to be back in school?"

"He seems to be."

"Wasn't he happy before?"

"He was dissatisfied. It has been very hard for him to make his job what he wants it to be."

"Will he be getting a new job?"

"We'll see."

"Do you really like your job?"

Miriam laughed. "At my age I'm pleased to have some work." She bit free her sewing thread and held up the finished skirt. "Now there," she said, "how does that look?"

"Very nice," said Kat. "You must be proud of Tina."

"Of course," answered Miriam, "and of you too."

"Don't you ever get tired of being our mother and doing all these things?"

"Sometimes."

"Do you ever want to quit?"

"Goodness, Kathleen!" her mother exclaimed. "This is what God has given me. I do what I can in the time that I have."

"But don't you ever wonder which thing to do next?"

"No, I don't," said Miriam, somewhat impatiently. "I leave that to your father. Why are you asking me all these questions? Do we seem unhappy to you?"

"No," said Kathleen with a sigh. "I was just wondering." She put the magazines away and rolled onto her side, facing her mother, her large-limbed, inert body bent to fit the couch. The comfort of this familiar place seemed to be draining from her whatever energy she had left. She watched her mother stand up and drape the dancing costume on a hanger. She heard the faint ticking of the iron as it began to warm up. Miriam shook out something and hung it over the ironing board. There were footsteps, her father's voice, something about light bulbs.

"Now?" asked Miriam. "You can do that later, can't you?"

"Might as well now," answered Chris.

Kat heard him thud down the basement stairs, and when he returned he was carrying a ladder.

"She's asleep?" he whispered to his wife.

Kat closed her eyes. She heard her parents kissing, then her father clattering up the stairs with the ladder. The ironing board creaked and knocked, like a boat against close moorings, and like a diver heady with gravity, her mind plunged down beneath the surface of the light.

Watch out for the guards, a dream voice babbled, but she couldn't stop to listen.

When she woke up, she was alone, but someone had covered her with the afghan. The laundry and sewing had been put away. A bowl of fruit rested on the table in a pool of its own reflection.

Kat began to cry, very suddenly and without knowing why, and then as suddenly stopped. She stood up unsteadily, alone, it seemed, in the downstairs of the house. No one was in the kitchen, but a piece of red beef stood on the stove ready to cook. The sunlight was on the other side of the house now. The faucet dripped.

A recent picture of her parents was among the many pinned to the bulletin board by the refrigerator. In it they were at a party of some sort, seated at a table with a number of other people, all of the same generation. Kathleen bent closer to peer at the photograph. Many of the other people were overweight and flushed. There were a number of brightly printed clownish garments. Some of the faces looked tan, as if they had traveled to other climates; most were laughing broadly at the camera. Chris and Miriam, however, sat slender and calm and a little pale, with sweet steady smiles and clear eyes.

Kat began to cry again. Through her tears she looked at the other pictures on the board and then she read through the family calendar for the month of April and the grocery list and a list in her father's handwriting of household chores. *To Do,* the paper was headed: *garden seeds, brass hardware, sweep basement, ceiling lights, window sashes, outdoor trim, clean gutters;* the list continued to the bottom of the page in several colors of ink, with some of the items crossed off.

When there was nothing left to examine, Kathleen blew her nose, took a drink of water, and wandered back through the house to the stairs. On her mother's desk in the hallway was a pile of bills, ready to be mailed. There was another photograph, in a frame, which Kat had seen so many times she didn't stop now to look but started on up the stairs. In that photograph three evidently happy children faced the camera, dressed for church, long brown hair braided. They stood on the steps of the house next door to the church where Grandfather and Grandmother Birks had lived for so many years. A lilac tree had bloomed beside that porch, Kat remembered, and it continued to bloom in the photograph on her mother's desk at the foot of the stairs.

The upper hallway was darkened because of the many closed

doors. There were more photographs on these walls, her own graduation face among them, smiling freshly in the dimness, honor student, pride to her family, hope of the future. Kat glanced into this seamless, startling face and quickly turned away. From behind her she heard a murmur of voices in her parents' room and then everything was quiet.

Very quietly in her own room she pulled off her jeans and dressed in her running clothes. She tied back her hair without needing a mirror. She put on her shoes outside the house, sitting on the front steps beneath the maple tree and the windows of her father's study. And then she took off into the late afternoon. No snow remained in the sky or on the ground, but when she reached the lake a last ridge of winter ice rimmed the beach. Whitecaps were giving off sideways spume; deep in the distance, blue-gray water leveled off into purple. Kat ran strongly, without feeling tired. It would be clear tonight. Last night, too, it had been clear during the train ride. She and her new friend had watched the full moon rising. Above the flat agricultural land it had appeared slightly flattened, gigantic, orange, close, oriental. She had looked over her shoulder at it; she had felt it following her; she had seen herself on a plain of earth beneath stars, being called upon to take in the moon, to let herself be overtaken. Tom had watched it too. He had stopped talking, turned out the little reading light above their seat, and leaned across her to get a better view.

Her own heart had felt as full as the moon, enlarged with light, brimming over in waves like music, and yet still miraculously whole, still alive: to be going home! to be containing such a sight! to be rushing along without seeming to move beneath that presence in the sky! Kat took a deep breath and continued running at her own pace all the way to the breakwater point and home.

COMMON HAPPINESS

"You're a good rider, Anders," calls Martin to his younger son, who is shooting along the sidewalk again on the two-wheeled bicycle almost inherited from his brother.

At the base of the porch this older boy, Peter, is kicking at the wooden lattice so hard his foot surely must be aching. The day after tomorrow is the first day of school, and today, one of the last of summer, is the neighborhood street party. "Luckily the cleather is weer and the lomidity huw," pronounces Martin as he casts a look up and down the street of closely set old houses, but Peter pays no attention.

Never mind: Martin likes to be silly with his children. He just wants everyone to be happy. "Ouch!" he cries, pretending to be the porch. "Oh, Peter, stop your kicking." Then in his own voice he says, "I'm going to cut into one of the watermelons, Peter. Would you please call down to Anders?"

Inga is still asleep in their bedroom at the back of the flat. It must be a delicious sleep, the open window shaded by the chestnut tree, the air soft and fresh after the hot spell. In a few minutes he will bring her some breakfast, a surprise. He will tread very lightly toward what he hopes is her good humor. Moving here hasn't been so easy for her. He thinks he understands what she has been trying to say: how he came straight into his new job with the urban development authority, complete with an office, a title, colleagues; while she was displaced, yet again, into domestic derangement.

When he comes back to the porch with the melon and some newspaper and a large knife, Peter is hugging one of the porch pillars, his cheek against the wood; he is hugging the house he had just been kicking. Warm is how the wood must feel, thinks Martin, warm and rough where the paint is peeling. After a summer of wheeling and tearing about, and then moving only two weeks ago to a new city, this boy will be asked to sit still in third grade every day for six hours. Martin thinks he understands about this, too.

He holds out a half-circle of melon, a green smile of rind, luscious red meat. Peter sidles up, one hand slapping along the porch balusters. Anders rides straight up onto the small, dry lawn, throws down the bicycle, and runs up the steps.

"That's still my bicycle," says Peter loudly as he begins to eat.

Well, what to do? One bicycle and two boys is a classic triangle. Should the father repeat the reasoning? Once more:

"Until Peter's new one comes you must share, Anders."

"Dad, Dad, he gets it and then he keeps it and then I don't get any fun."

"It's still mine!" shouts Peter. "You don't even know how to use it."

Martin cuts a large slice for Anders and one for himself. He begins to eat, spitting the seeds over the railing into the yew bushes. There is a choice: more arbitration, silence, or the introduction of a new element. He chooses the last.

"Grandpa grows good melons, doesn't he?" he asks the boys. "We'll cut one up and take it to the street party. When do the games begin? Two o'clock? You'll meet more of the other kids today. Maybe some of them will be in school with you."

"I'm not going to any dumb school," says Peter.

Balancing the breakfast tray, Martin turns the knob of the bedroom door. The air he enters is still consecrated by sleep, and there in the middle of it sprawls Inga, set apart in another realm. In his zone, it is eleven o'clock. He misses her.

"Inga," he says. He sets down the tray on the chest at the end of the bed and goes to sit beside her, holding a letter that has just come.

With her it isn't very safe to kid around these days because he never knows when she will take offense, so he usually tries to play things straight, as far as his nature will allow.

She is waking. "Madam, a letter has come for you."

"Who's it from?" Her voice emerging from that other realm is smooth and sweet, the way he would like it to be always, not pitched by fear or worry.

"Well, let's see." He holds the envelope up to the light, as if to read through paper.

"Oh, give it over," she says, reaching. "It's from Paul. Paul Cornell. He must have gotten our change-of-address card. Yes, listen! 'You've done it again, but I keep hoping that next time you'll see fit to buy that little house across the road from me. It's you, Inga, who should be at work in that garden.' " There is a slight fluttering of her eyelids. She looks up to Martin and then puts the letter back in the envelope. "It's a long letter," she says, as she takes a long, twisting stretch in the bed.

Wishfully, he grasps her arching waist with both hands. He remembers Paul Cornell from the city where they lived two—no, three—moves ago. Paul Cornell has done one of the things he talked about in those days: he has moved to the country. He lives alone with a typewriter, a woodlot, and a woodburning stove. Martin grew up on a farm, in the country of strict toil; he was often impatient with Paul Cornell and his many words. For Martin, the deeper values of a city were just coming clear.

"Madam Sweat-heart, I have brought you breakfast on a tray."

"You're forcing me to get up, that's what you're doing." She has collapsed into fetal position now, her hands beneath her cheek, her eyes fixed on the window.

"Did you get a lot done in the library last night?" he asks.

She shrugs inside one of the old T-shirts she wears to bed these days. Once, she told him that before they married she used to sleep with a dozen or more books in her bed, books with real personalities, she said, who even had the power to protect her. Now she is a student again, and all through this last move of their household she has clung to her books and papers.

"Sit up, lady, and enjoy. This isn't something that happens every day."

From the front of the flat comes the banging of the screen door and the high voices of the boys. Inga pushes herself up. "I have to pee," she says. Without meeting his eyes, she plods past him to the bathroom. Her blond hair is plaited as usual into one thick braid. She is wearing a pair of old gray running shorts that were his in high school. "Beanpole" was what they called him on the track team, because of his lankiness, but he didn't care; he was fast and he was funny, and they called him that because they liked him. Even in those days, what he wanted most was for things to go well, for everyone. Running, he would feel that if he could just work up enough momentum, he could spread out his arms and take the whole world with him, simply by the force of his exhilaration.

When Inga returns, he settles the tray on her lap. From her

look he knows instantly that she wants to be alone. "I'm going to make bread," he says. He kisses her cheek, and as he leaves he hears her taking the letter out of the envelope again.

There are to be games, a potluck supper, and dancing in the street, which has now been barricaded off at either end of the block by the Department of Public Works. Children careen in this new corridor of safety, flanked by trees and wooden porches and a few jutting American flags. Three boisterous fellows are rolling kegs of beer down a plank from a truck. "Easy does it!" one of them shouts.

His hands floury from kneading bread dough, Martin has just stepped out onto the porch to survey the scene. He imagines how at some magical moment the houses will turn inside out, and the facade of privacy will yield to an underlying truth of community. This is one of his dreams.

Some of the neighbors have begun to bring chairs and tables down to the curbs. A flatbed truck has been positioned midway down the block, to serve as a stage. He sees Anders hanging from the edge of it with some other children, but where is Peter?

"Pete?" he shouts. "Hey, Peter!" Well, he has probably gone around the block on the bicycle, out of sight of his brother.

Martin goes back to his bread dough, Swedish rye, sweet with molasses and anise and fennel. He folds and kneads and folds and kneads. Two kinds of bread he provides, bread to eat and money to spend; he likes this thought, and he likes the feel of making both kinds of bread.

Inga is passing through the kitchen on her way to the yard. She stops at the sink for water, and Martin wishes his hands were free to touch her bare back, above the carelessly tied bow of her halter. For several days she has been making attempts to reclaim for gardening the tiny patch of weeds and clay that is the back yard of this duplex. With their purchase they have also inherited Janice and Bernadette, upstairs tenants who dye their hair and come and go at irregular hours. Janice, red-haired of late, wearing purple shorts today, has been sunning herself for the last hour in a metal chair set up on the back section of the driveway, visible from the kitchen window above the sink.

"I think I'll dye my hair red too," says Inga. "Who knows what might open up from there?"

Martin is not alarmed. At the bottom of Inga is a bed of pure and simple goodness; at least he believes there is. The first time he sensed it, before they were married, he wept with happiness beneath a sky that had become expanded, calm, and comprehensible.

"If you do, make sure you get it bright enough," he says, "some indescribable shade between orange and purple." As he says this, he looks deeply into the beautiful natural shades of blond in her long braid.

"You don't think I'd do something like that, do you?" Inga spins around to face him, and there is a brilliancy about her that almost sparks out at him.

He scoops up the mound of elastic dough and holds it under her nose, for her appreciation. "Terrific stuff, eh?" he asks. He wants to bring her back to simpler thoughts.

But she says, "Why don't you think I'd dye my hair? Do you think you know me so well?" There is the slightest narrowing and fluttering of her eyelids, a new mannerism, and he thinks again about the long letter that her old friend Paul Cornell has written to his wife.

"Are you about to give those harlots upstairs a run for their money?" he says jocularly.

"Right," she says, laughing, but not exactly laughing. "It's a free country. It's my own hair. I could dye it any shade in the rainbow."

Martin gives the dough a last punch and then turns it over a few times in the large greased bowl: another splendid batch.

"So how's old Paul Cornell?" he asks as he scrubs his hands.

"I know what you're doing," says Inga. "You're trying to 'introduce a new element.' "

"Well, are you going to fall for it and tell me about Paul, or do you want to keep worrying about your appearance?"

She pretends to sigh at the hopelessness of him. "I think I already fell for you a long time ago, didn't I?"

"It's nice he wrote to you," says Martin. He comes close to her again, hoping this time for a kiss. "You have many admirers, my lady."

They do kiss, but it is not a kiss to calm and set the world to rights; it is a kiss of sparks and questions.

Inga's blue eyes look up at him intently. "While you and I, Martin, have been packing and unpacking boxes and carting away trash, Paul Cornell has been writing an article on post-skeptical intellectuals."

"What's he talking about?" says Martin, kissing her forehead, her eyes.

Inga says, "He seems fascinated and filled with misgiving at the same time."

With his arms around her like this, Martin is sure he knows about at least one time-honored, temporary absolution to misgiving. With a play of lecherousness, he lifts her off her feet.

"You don't care," she says. "You don't care a thing about Paul Cornell and his article."

"I do!" he protests. "He should call me for my opinion. I've got a lot I could say about skost testicle lecteinpuals." He wants to hear her laugh, sheer and sweet, but she sighs again and he sets her down.

"So where are the boys," she asks, "and what time do these wonderful festivities begin?"

At two o'clock in the street a trumpet is sounded, amateurishly, raucously, to announce the games. Outside, everything is beginning. An undefined cheer goes up. Inside the door, husband and wife stand in a stilled moment of concern: Peter has not returned.

Inga presses her fingertips into her forehead. "I've been neglecting my children," she says. "I have, I have."

Almost as a balance to her anxious drama, his love becomes quieter, like a deep thought. Something needs to play itself out. "Peter wouldn't go far today," says Martin.

"I'll take my bicycle around the neighborhood," says Inga. "Oh, I haven't given that child proper attention for days."

Martin watches her pedal off down the street past flags and balloons and picnic tables and people scarcely met, or not at all, new neighbors. She stops at the clutch of men around the beer keg, and he sees her gesticulating her alarm about a little boy in a blue-and-white striped shirt. Almost directly in front of the house, Anders is lining up for a relay race. Anders takes his hand out of his crotch long enough to wave excitedly to Martin, and Martin waves back. Then he sits down on the top step of the porch, staying in one place as someone has to do when someone is lost.

In a few minutes he hears a sound, like an animal scratching, or a child pretending to be an animal, scratching fingernails on wood perhaps, not far away. He knows; in his stillness he has located his son. He goes down the steps and crouches beside the yew bushes, cupping his hands around his eyes so as to see into the dark behind the lattice. "Peter?" he says softly. Martin feels as if he is about to make a double discovery. The child is now crying. "Where is your door?" asks Martin, but he hears only the releasing of suppressed sobs.

On the north side of the house he finds where a segment of lattice has been pulled loose, and while the sounds of outer carnival intensify, he crawls across light-patterned, hardened dirt to the huddled figure.

"Come here now," he says and pulls the boy onto his lap. "What's this all about?" Through the lattice the high-pitched games appear as flashes of color. Martin thinks he knows what the sobbing is about: everything, always changing. As he holds his discovered son, he understands that he is also tending himself, and he prays that as he spreads his arms into the world, he will learn to remain established in this steadiness of love.

Toward the end of the afternoon there is announced a relay race for adults as well as children. "Dad, Dad!" Anders is yelling through the front door. Martin has just run back to the kitchen to take his bread from the oven. Red-haired Janice teeters past the kitchen window to the street; without seeing her feet, Martin knows the sort of high-heeled sandal she must be wearing.

She is balanced on the curb, smoking a cigarette, when Martin follows Anders down the steps. Inga is now sitting on the grass beneath the maple tree with Peter on her lap. Her solution to her self-accused lapse in motherliness and to Peter's grief was to read to him for almost an hour in the big bed at the back of the flat, the shades partly drawn, the street sounds muffled. Martin looked in once or twice but did not interrupt.

Anders is pulling on his hand. Martin winks at Inga. Her hands are flattened on either side of Peter's face, and she looks as if she would like to become a solemn statue of a mother, holding in safety a rescued child.

Each relay team is to be given a burlap bag of clothes, which runners must hastily put on at the beginning and take off at the end of each lap. The directors of the games, the postman in a cotton fishing hat and the woman from the shabby brown house where so many children seem to live, are holding up the outlandish garments one by one: huge, plumed hats, gloves, scarves, men's vests, petticoats, pink leg warmers.

"This one is for me," says Janice, crushing out her cigarette and joining the crowd waiting to be divided into teams. She turns to wave at the second-story porch, where Bernadette is leaning on the railing in a bathing suit that makes Martin think all of a sudden of sausage casings. "Hey, Bernie," shouts Janice.

"Here, here," shouts the postman, waving his hat up to Bernie. "Let's have a few more big people."

Martin holds out his other hand to Inga and Peter. Anders and he and Inga and Peter make a sort of family frieze, almost in linked motion. There, it is happening: Inga kisses Peter and pushes him to his feet; she takes Martin's hand; they all follow Anders into the crowd, where one, two, one, two they find themselves on opposite teams, shouting to one another, lining up, and for a few minutes everything is hilarious. Children are jumping up and down and screaming. On and off people of many shapes and several colors go leg warmers, petticoats, vests, scarves, gloves, theatrical hats.

"Everything has to be put on all the way," shouts the postman. "All the way!"

"Oh, oh," screams Janice as she shimmies into a flounced petticoat. She runs barefoot, her high-heeled sandals tossed off to the curb for any enterprising Prince Charming.

Martin is next on Janice's team, and his heart is knocking with excitement as he fumbles for the garments she is stripping off. Such a roar of human sound! "Dad, Dad, Dad!" he hears Anders screeching behind him.

He finishes his lap just in time to see a good-looking fellow in white trousers setting a large yellow silk hat on Inga's head, and then off she goes for the other team, his long-legged Inga, one hand holding down the hat, the other lifting the petticoat, and she is flushed and laughing, laughing as she returns, laughing as he has not heard her laugh in months, her eyes lit up with an unearthed essence of herself.

"My goodness, wherever did they get those marvelous hats?" she says when the race is done and they are standing by the curb talking with Donald from next door.

"Oh, they would be from Tony Carollo, I'd wager. He's a

tenor with the lyric opera." Thickset, with curly blond hair and a slight Scottish turn to his words, their neighbor points with his pipe to a lawn down the street. "That one in white trousers. He's one of our celebrities."

Inga's eyelids flutter as she locates Tony Carollo. "I hope he sings for us tonight," she says.

"Well, now," says Donald jovially, "and how are you two liking our city?"

Martin has enjoyed his few conversations with ruddy, good-natured Donald, and it was his wife, Maggie, who came next door their first week, only last week, with a dinner of creamed chicken and homemade noodles. Here comes Maggie now, looking very much like her teenage daughters, only rounder, more settled. They have been living in the same house for twenty years; she seems to know everyone. "Come with me," she says, coming right up between Inga and Martin and taking their arms firmly. "I've got all sorts of people I want you to meet."

"Would you have believed such a cast of characters?" exclaims Inga as she stands beside Martin, cutting up fruit for the salad they will be taking to potluck. She sucks up the juice from a slice of pineapple peel.

"A veritable melting pot," agrees Martin. "Sweet land of liberty."

At this he again sees Inga's eyelids come down and just slightly tremble. "Inga, tell me something. Why are you doing that with your eyes?"

"What?"

"This." He tries to imitate her, and for an instant the kitchen trembles and appears immaterial. "You've been doing it for a couple of weeks."

"I'm not conscious of it. Is it unbecoming?" She feeds him a chunk of pineapple.

"I don't understand what it means."

"It must be a survival mechanism," she says. He looks at her and sees thick blond hair, a few freckles, a mouth shaped to be expressive, eyes deep-set, large, lively, at once familiar and remote, discovered and undiscovered. If survival depends on looks, he is about to say, in so many words—first glancing at the clock to see if there is time, time to dive into bed with this exquisite representative of untold aeons of female persistence—if survival so depends, she has only to look at him and he understands what he would do for her, how he would extend himself utterly to win for her one more degree of safe well-being, to win for the world one more tremendous coupling.

He is about to make a gesture to show his submission, his energy, when she lays down her knife, efficiently slides all the parings into the trash basket, and announces, "I think I just have time for a quick shower before the night's doings."

Martin slowly changes his shirt in front of the bedroom bureau mirror. He is so tall he has to stoop to comb his hair. For a long time now he has lived with this attenuated body, this Adam's apple, this high brow, these slightly crooked teeth. He catches his own eye sidelong: is this fellow ridiculous? Appealing? Never mind: that same raucous trumpet is sounding again outside, while just down the hall children of his own flesh, his marriage to the world's other half, are arguing in the bathroom, and Inga herself in a blue-and-white checked sundress appears in the doorway, holding the large blue crockery bowl of fruit.

"Bring the camp stools, will you?" she asks. She looks poised for what is coming. "And how about your bread—are you going to donate a few loaves?"

"Of course," he says. "I intended to. Bread for the multitude."

Tony Carollo praises Martin's bread. Rising from his place

at the end of the picnic table, he lifts up a thick slice as if to propose a toast: "To our new neighbors," he says.

"Here's to Inga and Martin," says Donald.

Maggie smiles upon her husband, two of her daughters, Martin and Inga and the boys, the postman and his wife, and Tony Carollo. Martin feels himself smiled upon, kneaded into the group. They are all eating his bread. Up and down the street at a dozen such tables everyone is eating everyone else's food.

"Here, here!" says the postman in a general sort of way. He is a little drunk. He has pushed his shapeless cotton hat forward to a racy angle, and as Janice and Bernadette pass by with plates of cake he raises his glass. "Enjoy yourselves, girls!"

It doesn't take the children long to finish eating and ask to be excused. They want to watch the sound equipment being set up on the flatbed truck.

"Are you going to sing for us?" Inga asks Tony Carollo.

"Singing is always a pleasure for me," says Tony Carollo with a wide smile for Inga on his right. From the other end of the table Martin sees how she smiles in return, how she shines.

Donald is asking Martin some questions about urban development, and Martin answers warmly, positively. "I've met a great many well-meaning people," he says.

Inga is talking intently to Tony Carollo. What is she talking about? Martin likes to hear her ideas; he is sorry to be missing her intent, animated words.

This is the same woman who last night beat her fist upon a doorjamb until the skin was bruised, until she turned upon him and the fist beat upon his shoulder and the words beat upon him: Soon there will be nothing left of me, she said, and you don't see it; I am being eaten alive. There were more words and more, and always this idea that bit by bit something was being taken from her, like flesh from bones.

Finally, in a flash of anger, he caught her arm and held it tightly: What do you want? And she said, I don't know yet. He said, Right now, what do you want? And she said, Right now

I want to go to the library without a guilty conscience. He said, Go then. She left and came home quietly at one o'clock. With his arm circled around her in the bed, his thoughts, too, completed a journey through difficulties and returned home; they settled upon a recurring conviction, which he then rode into sleep: that strength lies in happiness, happiness held in common; whatever needed to be played out, he would nevertheless hold to that.

"I should say so!" exclaims Tony Carollo to one of Inga's comments. There is an operatic quality to his laugh. Ho-ho! His mouth is rounded, his throat is full of tone.

"Dad, Dad!" Martin hears Anders's voice from somewhere behind him, a voice asking him to turn, but for a moment his eyes have become Inga's; he has lowered his eyelids slightly to look upon Tony Carollo, who is tipping back his head and laughing handsomely at the end of the table, laughing from his depths.

From his depths is also the way Tony Carollo sings when an hour later he stands with his feet widely planted upon the truck and tells them melodically of love with an energy that seems to come straight up through his feet and his white-troused legs, his expanded chest and his bare throat, right out the top of his head. Love! Song in a single lilt is telling an entire story.

Inga, listening raptly, sits beside Martin with her legs crossed and her hands, one on top of the other, held upon her knee. The blue-and-white dress she is wearing is as old as the hills, and Martin has always liked it; she wore it when she was eighteen, under the arbor in her father's garden, and she is wearing it now at thirty, in a street in a city where a few surviving elm trees arch over their heads.

The song hovers over all of them in the dusk. Not a being does not seem adaptable to its power.

"He's very convincing, isn't he?" says Inga as they are clapping.

Now up the ramp of the truck trundle a man and a woman in motorized wheelchairs. Peter stands nearby, eating another ice cream and staring at this parade. The man and the woman, hired for the evening, swing their chairs expertly into position in front of a bank of electronic equipment and announce that the dancing will begin as soon as the rest of these tables and chairs have been moved aside, and there will be something for everyone, they can guarantee that. Their names are Grace and Bob, their business is making sure that everyone has a fine time.

"The war or cerebral palsy or both, do you suppose?" whispers Inga. "My goodness, what courage." Her cheeks are flushed, and she seems to be studying these two people who will never dance on their own feet.

"Here, here!" cries the postman, dancing his way between chairs to the center, still wearing his fishing hat, to which are attached a few gaudy feathered flies. His hands held in the air at about shoulder level, elbows tucked in, his paunch inside the baggy khaki shorts visibly drawn in, his hips shifting, his brown shoes marking time, he beams good-naturedly around, beckons his wife, who refuses—can't he see the large casserole dish she's carrying home?—then beckons Bernadette, who instantly sways forward to meet his outstretched hand. A few people cheer and whistle.

Inga grins at Martin. "Come on," she says. "Are you going to let the postman outdo you?"

"I should say not," says Martin, and he leads her into the movement; he does the best he can, but dancing has never been easy for him. How is it, he wonders, that in running his mind can seem to float above him but in dancing be drawn down repeatedly into awkward reminders of his feet? Never mind: Inga is laughing; she nods to him. "Am I doing all right for a farm boy?" he asks, and Inga nods again. What a treasure she is! With a burst of courage, Martin swings her gallantly around, just as the piece is coming to a close.

The tempo of the next number is much faster. At the first

few beats the teenagers in the crowd shout and surge forward. The postman bravely stays on, not wanting to lose hold of Bernadette, surmises Martin as he leads Inga to the sidelines. "Look." Inga is nudging him. There is Janice, pulling Tony Carollo to his elegant feet, and he laughs as if he is sure of a perpetual audience and willingly follows her, already stepping in rhythm.

"They're very good!" Inga claps her hands.

Martin is watching carefully to see how it is done. Just then Anders darts through the dancing area and pulls his parents by the hands. He wants to be swung; he wants to be whirled; he wants, he wants, and he is getting very tired, Martin can see.

"Come on, then." Inga laughs. "Here we go round. . . ." She catches hold of Martin's other hand, and they start to skip in a circle, now and then lifting Anders high in the air by the arms. Maggie joins them, holding Peter by the hand, and then a few other people, bringing their younger children, until they have a large circle, a nursery school in the midst of the driving beat of rock music. Then—how does it begin?—the teenagers love the idea; they jump into the circle; it becomes huge and misshapen; older sisters and brothers lift little ones shrieking into the air; Tony Carollo and Janice, the postman and Bernadette lend their prestige to the whirling group.

Next, with scarcely a pause, comes a polka. Janice and Bernadette are snapped up by a couple of young men in running shorts. Tony Carollo catches Inga around the waist. She looks startled and then pleased. Martin follows with his eyes as the blue-and-white checked skirt follows the movements of Inga's body. There is a slight, entrancing fraction of delay, he notices, between material and body. No one else at this party knows how long she has had that dress, nor how much of Martin's own history it signifies.

Inga and Tony Carollo continue to dance together through several changes in music. A moment ago the streetlights went on; somewhere in the mechanism of the city clock hands jumped forward, and up and down hundreds of streets the quality of night shifted. Here, the dancers seem to have become more intent.

Martin does not think much about dancing himself. He stands tall on the periphery, drawn up into a sensation of still, gentle transparency. His eyes rest here and then there, gently. He sees that this evening could perhaps be magical enough to transform some of Inga's fear and dissatisfaction, which are unworthy of her. Where all that agitation started he doesn't know. She hasn't always been like this. Why, it was Inga's smile and Inga's kiss that long ago soothed some of his own confusions and confirmed for him the power of happiness.

Janice comes spinning off the floor like a heavenly body needing a breather from dizzy orbiting. She almost lands in Martin's arms.

"Oh! My feet are killing me." She says this, but she continues to sway to the music.

"I find it's a pleasure just to watch the others," says Martin. He is surprised to hear this touch of formality in his own voice.

"It's not enough for me, man," says Janice. "If there's a good time, I want to be right there in the middle of it. Let me tell you, I'm no good at standing around. D'you want to dance?"

She doesn't wait for a reply, but takes his hand and places it around her waist. "You're nice and tall," she says. "I like that."

Flattered in spite of himself, Martin presses his lips together and begins to think about his feet. Inga waves to him over the shoulder of Tony Carollo. Close up, Janice's brightly colored hair is even more unbelievable.

"Dad, Dad!" Anders is dodging toward him through the dancers.

Martin leans down. "What is it, Anders?"

Anders can't say, but he has thrown himself on Martin's leg and is trying to shinny up.

"I've got a little monkey here," apologizes Martin as he lifts the boy to his shoulder.

"You've got real cute kids," says Janice. Her eyes look soft beneath the harsh hair.

"Do you want to take a rest, Anders?" asks Martin. The boy shakes his hot head against Martin's neck. Martin nods to Janice and carries him home anyway, up the porch steps and into their own dwelling.

The separateness of the dim inside rooms is almost a shock. There on the table are Inga's straw hat and work gloves, a few books, an empty glass, and here in the bathroom hang the gray shorts and the T-shirt in which she slept last night. Martin sits on the edge of the bathtub, his head in his hands, and waits while his son urinates.

"I'll lie down with you," he says to Anders. "We'll both have a little rest."

"No, Dad, no," protests Anders, but Martin talks of other things and before long they are lying together in Anders's bed. Suddenly Martin wants the party to be over; he wants to be lying down all alone with Inga; he wants to be reestablished, right in the middle of his own life.

Melody is lost inside the walls of the house; what comes through is the low, pounding, changing beat of the music, one dance after another, which for a time Martin follows, as if he must, because it belongs to life as it is being lived, as it is playing itself, out there on the street. Then abruptly, as Anders breathes of sleep, Martin finds himself released into an even expansiveness, distanced from external sound. Blips of meaning appear from the surface and are submerged. This vastness is full.

When he wakes, it takes him an instant to remember which city he is in, which house, which bed, which hour. He finds the bathroom. Then he stands in the doorway between the hall and the dining room, resting his hands high on the doorjamb, bowing his head, collecting himself. This is the very wood upon which Inga beat her fist; he runs the palm of his own hand up and down over the place.

Outside no one seems to notice him. He is looking for one person only, one blue-and-white dress. From another street not very far away sounds a siren. The sky above the trees is reddish-purple with the collective energy expenditure of the city. Grace and Bob in their wheelchairs look as if they have seen nights like this many times before. The general need for rest is now as discernible over the group as, three hours earlier in the fluid heart of Tony Carollo's song, was the wish for love.

Near one of the rear wheels of the truck Martin sees Peter, who is bent double like a letter *A,* looking at the dancers upside down, through his open legs. Martin crouches and brings his face close to his son's. "Hello, Peter. Have you seen your mother?"

"Dad, try doing this." Peter's face is red, and his fine blond hair fans downward.

Resting his fingertips on the ground, Martin looks through his legs at the dancers. He sees pure pattern, a three-dimensional wonderland, with a vanishing point far down the street, beyond the stop sign at the corner. This momentary land is Peter's discovery.

"Well, Peter, do you like the world better upside down or right side up?" he asks as he straightens himself.

"Dancing is dumb," says Peter.

"What's this, what's this? What's all this silliness about dancing?" Martin swings his son into the air and over his shoulder and down his back, upside down, the sack-of-flour routine that Peter loves. The music is now a waltz. A man Martin has not met is turning slowly by, holding a little girl of about two asleep on his shoulder. Donald, his pipe in his outstretched hand, is dancing with one of his daughters. The postman, with an expression that is a parody of a romancer, has taken into his arms his very own wife. Janice and Bernadette are circling with each other. Martin does not see Tony Carollo.

He shakes Peter by the ankles. "Where's Mom?" he asks again.

"She was just dancing," says Peter.

Martin lets him slide slowly headfirst to the ground. "Come on," he says, taking Peter's hand. "Let's go walking." He starts off into the outer spaces of the party, past clusters of people, bursts of laughter, an overturned chair, an abandoned tricycle, littered paper.

Peter doesn't want his hand held. "Dad," he says when they are midway down the block, "am I having fun?"

Martin stops still. His heart seems to tighten. "You tell me. Are you having a good time?"

"No. This is dumb."

"I saw you playing with some kids."

"They were too dumb."

Martin crouches down. He doesn't know what to say. He wishes with all his heart that he could provide patterns in this real world inside which his son could happily grow.

For the second time tonight Martin is putting a child to bed. This little room in which one child sleeps and another listens to a softly told African tale of the sun and moon personified is at this moment fragile to him, the life in it so precious, so meaningful that he feels he must with devotion and precision shelter it in his mind.

He continues reading in a low voice, calmly, his body stretched out beside his son, but his mind, in a tremendous longing to stablize itself, continually journeys and returns, journeys and returns, asking, What is this life in the center of things, and how can it be safely housed? How can it spread?

Peter is asleep. Anders is asleep. Martin turns out the lamp and goes out to the kitchen. The rest of the bread from today's baking has been put into plastic bags. When did Inga do that? He draws a glass of water.

"Martin?" He hears her voice coming from the back porch. He is so glad at the sound of it he feels like crying.

"What are you doing out here in the dark?" He opens the screen door. She is sitting sideways on a step with her bare feet on a railing, the blue dress high on her thighs. He lifts up her legs, sits down, and puts her feet in his lap. "I wondered where you were. I thought for a while you might have gone dancing off into never-never land with Tony Carollo."

"No, you didn't. That doesn't sound like you."

"I did. I really did."

"Then you must be just as disoriented as the rest of us." She is leaning against the house, one arm resting over her head. "Well, here I am," she says.

He holds onto her feet. "Did you have a good time?" he asks.

"Yes and no. It seemed a little frantic. I'm always bothered by people trying so hard to enjoy themselves."

"You looked great dancing," says Martin. "You're a good dancer."

She is quiet. Her arm is still hooked over her head. The blue of her dress floats between them. In the dark he can just barely see the bruised place on the side of her hand.

"Do you know what Tony Carollo said to me?" she asks.

"No, what did he say?"

"He said he sensed in me great possibilities."

"For what? Great possibilities for him?"

"He didn't say—just great possibilities."

"You made a conquest."

"I don't want to make conquests. That's not my intention. I've got other things on my mind."

Her voice is quiet, localized. All around them are the back porches and windows of other houses.

"I'm worried about Peter," she says.

"Peter will survive."

"Survival isn't quite enough."

"I agree. Completely."

"He's negative about everything. He didn't used to be that way."

"It's up to us," says Martin. "If we're happy then it's sure to make it easier for him. We'll try to make things as good as we can."

Her eyes seem to be narrowed upon a point somewhere beyond him. He turns and peers into the bare tiny yard, from which Inga has removed all the trash and weeds. The chestnut tree is the one good thing in it.

"What are you going to plant out there?" he asks.

"Martin, I don't know what to do."

"About what?"

She takes a huge, uneven breath. "I don't know which things to do first, what to turn to. Nothing seems to belong to me. I feel I'm not even taking proper care of the children. And this time I wanted a big garden. But we didn't find it. Why didn't we find a garden? Did we really look or did we just think we were looking?"

Martin strokes her feet. "It's hard to afford a garden in a city like this," he says, but immediately knows that those words do not make any clearer their bearings.

"Why am I fixed on this?" asks Inga. "Every day here I have wakened in the morning thinking that I might be all right again if I could just go out the door into a big garden."

"Inga!"

"I'm sorry. I'd like to accept things as they are, but I just want to start crying every time I think about it."

"That's not what I meant. Your wish is the best sort of wish. It's just—" He is looking up now into the field of the sky, as if there to find a pattern, a form that would contain these best, these most tender longings. What he returns to is the shape of his own hand, the shape of Inga's bare feet.

"We don't know what's coming next," he says finally. "Maybe we'll find a garden."

At this moment he feels so welded to Inga that he does not know which desires are hers, which are his.

"Martin," she says suddenly, shyly, "do you think I'm pretty?"

SOLILOQUY

Sunday night

Your baby—my sister's grandchild, not mine, I remind you—has been put to bed by Eric. Christa, in her pajamas beside me on the couch by the bay window, is playing with the present I brought her, the wooden box of colored cubes. She is copying the design diagrams from the inside of the lid, turning the pieces this way and that until the painted diagonals align. She reminds me of you at that age, heaven help her. I don't need to tell you how her breathing slows with her concentration, how the frustrations are only barely tolerable, how the tension is released with each completion. She looks to me with smiles of triumph, dumps the cubes into my lap, and begins again. She would not, would not—she stamped her feet—put on her red boots for our walk this afternoon, nor would she agree to ride in the stroller behind Lyda. OK, let's just *go,* said Eric, giving in to her. I like the way he simply got on with the most important thing, which was our walk. Your Eric knows something about action. He doesn't brood, or ask too much all at once.

For half an hour or so he has been practicing his cello in the front half of the living room. I glance up and see through the broad doorway—yes, doesn't he make a picture?—how he lifts his face from a bent listening and turns it ceilingward, eyes closed above a passage. Your absence is here with us tonight. I am reminded how wistfully you once spoke to me of Eric's music, how he can refine it and refine it and pour his heart into it—I am quoting you—without needing to say what it means.

As usual, I didn't know how to respond to the intensity of your probing. It is generally in your absence that I think of words I could be saying, were it not for the cool restraint upon which I landed long ago as a commendable means of intercourse. You could use more of it yourself. Take it easy, pace yourself; you're too intense for your own good, that's what I think, and so was your poor mother. Part of her legacy to me is you; I know that, but set limits to how much I will accept, as all my life I have been careful about how much I would take on of what I understood to be my female inheritance.

Listening to me, with all you have ahead of you, is probably the last thing you should do. Well, I do have my opinions, but I don't give much advice, try not to. No one else's answer, I'm my own question, neither fit nor inclined to be an example. Don't I know only too well what an imposition the admiration of others can be?

So here I am, caring for your children for the week—I repeat, a strict seven days—and only speaking out to you silently in the wake of your emotional leave-taking. Again! exclaims Christa as she turns out the cubes onto my skirt. I look at my watch. Once more, Toots, I say, and then it's off to bed. No, she says challengingly, and I just laugh. I pick up a cube, place it in a corner of the box, and wink at her. She takes it out and changes its position, to her own way.

By now you should have arrived at my apartment. Have you found the little palliations I have deliberately left in store, the custard in the refrigerator, the tin of cookies by the bed, the cashmere shawl and scented soap? Yes, all right, I admit they're small pleasures, but don't undervalue them. And you must sleep, too, before you even think of turning to your work. Now that I am retired, I don't know how I got through all those years on as little sleep as I had. I used to tell myself that what I felt perpetually hanging over my head was ungraded papers, but perhaps it was really just a cloud of fatigue. When I think of all those nights, sitting beneath a lamp, and all those mornings, getting up in the dark, shoveling my own driveway. . . .

Apropos, here comes Eric to carry Christa off to bed. Oh, yes, you are, he says and lifts her up without further ado, grinning at me. He can be charming, your Eric, but he does sweep right along in his own momentum, doesn't he? I find this subtly tiring. Not for you to worry, though; we'll be all right this week. By my age I should have learned enough diplomacy for most any situation.

I smooth out my skirt and take up a magazine. It has been a long day for me, too. Have I ever told you about my friend Madeline, how she spends every Friday in bed, on principle, rain or shine? I like her technique of structured laxity. And she's a sturdy sort, too, not fainthearted.

Let me give another example of what I mean by your overseriousness. This morning: you had just brought in the tea. You sat down opposite me and pressed your fingertips into your forehead. Already I knew I was going to have to find a way to inject a little levity. You were feeling, you said, as if everything you do, each single action, should be by way of preparation, but for what, for what? You looked to me, waiting.

I looked for help to Eric, but he was concentrating on cooking the eggs. Oh, for glory—I laughed—for glory. It was one of those nothings I toss off that have just enough in them to sound like something. It's a way of putting people off when the air gets too thick. I apologize, but actually I was restraining myself; what I really wanted to do was to take you by the shoulders and give you a shake. Then I saw how tired you were. . . .

All action, someone said to me, after a certain age becomes repetitious. Our days do tend to fall into patterns. As a teacher of literature, I should be working out a theory here about points of view, how these are what change, but I'm too tired now myself to get an angle on it, and here comes Eric again, asking me if I am cold, and I realize that I have been clutching my sweater to my throat. At home alone I could have sat like this for an hour, thinking my thoughts, with no one coming across the room to say, Are you cold?

Before dawn

I wake, for an instant amnesic, nowhere, clinging to unawareness, conditionlessness, because, yes, my throat is sore, and I am in a strange bed, a strange room without my comforts. It is only Monday morning. I don't know how I am going to last the week. I must gargle some salt water. How can I gargle without waking Eric and the children? I turn on the light, and your tiny study encloses me, on the walls the map of Boston, the photographs of some people I don't know, of your questionable guru, of your mother and of her mother, who is my mother too, you must remember. My mother. She is sitting on the front porch steps beside some balusters I remember my father turning by hand. Her angular hands are in her lap. What task has she just come from? What of the ten thousand possible things will she do next? I won't think just now of Mother. Boston. Tell me, why do you have a map of Boston on your wall when you are living in Chicago? I feel irritated, funnily enough, that I do not know. And that guru. I frown boldly. I admit I am worried for your mind; to what mass weakness are you giving in?

And I am irritated that now I must steal down a cold hallway to a kitchen not my own, find salt, and perform a gargle as soundlessly as possible. In my own rooms I would turn on the radio at a time like this. I'd turn up the heat, for heaven's sake. I've even forgotten my heating pad, and how am I to rummage for yours at this hour? At least I can take some aspirin. I long for hot tea and toast. I long to rattle about in my own kitchen. It suddenly strikes me that the art of living as I have been cultivating it of late does not so easily transplant. How did I ever travel all over the world in the old days? Were those journeys worth the effort? At the very least I should have learned enough perspective to keep my equanimity in the middle of the night at the age of sixty-seven.

The Chinese, I have read, tolerate their crowded living conditions only by means of the strictest sort of etiquette, manners that become unquestionable out of necessity. I will pretend I am a Chinese grandmother, shuffling down a hallway to my family cell, past family upon family of sleepers. I hear breathing and sighing. I am one small, small piece of human life, a servant of the social order. The game lasts for about two minutes. Here we are, back to the map of Boston. Do you want to know what Boston means to me? It is a dusty path off the Fenway in late summer, where your mother and I once walked, on our only trip together before she married. We had met at the train station, had lunch, seen the museum. Then she took a breath and said that Christian had proposed to Helen, our younger sister. Did I mind terribly? she asked. Did I mind terribly? I remember now the taste of the dust, our summer dresses, perhaps even a terrible happiness, a shocking relief.

This is your room, your Boston, your photographs. I am not your grandmother; I am not your mother; I am not anybody's mother. I am here, let me remind you, not because I have to be. This was a choice, an offering—all right, yes, to your mother too, if you like.

Did you ever hear what Mae West said about marriage? It was something to the effect that marriage was an institution, and she wasn't ready yet for an institution. Ha, ha. And now—good night. Dear.

One more thing. I turn on the light again. Feeling both rational and irrational, I unhook your smiling guru's picture from the wall and slide it into your desk drawer. There. I have asserted myself. Strength of mind presupposes independence, does it not?

Monday noon, time for lunch

Christa will not eat peanut butter, but she will accept avocado. Lyda thumps her feet against the metal high chair, innocently, to be sure, but aggravatingly all the same. We stayed in this morning because of my throat, which I believe I have under control, thank you. If I didn't dislike doctors so much, I probably wouldn't be nearly so adept at doctoring myself.

Eric calls to say he cannot come home for lunch after all and how am I getting along. Oh, cheerfully, I answer, and he tells me again how splendid I am. Perhaps it is his own air of self-sufficiency, but he is one of the few before whose flatteries I do not feel the need to dissemble—through feigned dottiness, deliberate selfishness, anything that will free me from the responsibility of feeding someone else's notions. I've done the same to you on occasion, yes, flaunted my freedom, refused to explain myself. The last thing you should do is to become what others need you to be. Once you start letting yourself be characterized, well, then, you become nothing but a character, I suppose. And you do no good, either, let me assure you.

Thank goodness the questions Christa asks are relatively easy to answer, and Lyda amuses me with her *Da!* as she points to something for which she wants the name. I think I could teach her five hundred new words this week, all from the visible world.

As I carry her off for her nap, my arms simply full of *Lyda,* I am amazed how complete and yet incomplete a child is.

At my age, I know that I am lacking, but it has been a long time since I was naive enough to think that my satisfaction could be found outside myself. Or that I could provide the same to another. How many times have I said, in one way or another, Don't look to me, I'm not what you want, and anyway I'm not what you think?

Lyda reaches for me, and—look—I'm letting her. I let her hands explore the surfaces that make my face. I tell nothing, yet I feel that for this baby I am being told. I relax into a smile. Suddenly, tears are in my eyes.

Tuesday night, bedtime story

All right, you've been wanting some secrets; I'll tell you a story. I must admit that your telephone call tonight unnerved me. I'd had no notion that he'd be trying to call my apartment while you were there. He must have been surprised too. You said it "sounded long-distance." Of course. If you only knew.

I pull up the bedcovers, clasp my hands on my chest, and begin. I am lying as straight and still as a figure on a tomb. My story is an instruction, to myself, given the nature of our earthly end, on remaining singular and clearheaded.

Once upon a time there was a man who worked for a telephone company. As his career progressed, he traveled more and more, often to foreign countries, overseeing new installations, giving seminars to management on new technology, troubleshooting, assessing local labor conditions, etc. Let's call him Stewart; we will make him a character, a voice, crying out long-distance for our attention.

In the small city where Stewart had a home base with a wife and three children also lived a well-traveled, well-read, unmarried teacher very like myself. They met at a camera club, where both enjoyed having an audience for the best photographic slides of their travels. In the middle of a midwestern winter, she would view the foreign marketplaces and hillsides and rivers of her own peregrinations as indirect personal adornments, glimpses in a semi-darkened room by means of which an observer might or might not be able to make inferences about her own experiences of affinity or lack of affinity.

Stewart's wife was not a member of the club. She was, in fact, an invalid, perhaps years ago merely a hypochondriac but now with an impressive list of verified complaints. The children had grown and left home.

When in town, Stewart tended his wife and his garden and spoke to our teacher only in the context of the camera club. When traveling, he began to call her long-distance. From Seoul, Houston, Saigon, Cairo, even an Alaska pipeline outpost came his plaint, telling her that she was beautiful, brilliant, unique, the one person on earth capable of understanding him; his dismay and disgust over what his wife had managed to inflict on herself; his loneliness over the years as the children had turned out noncommunicative, noncooperative; his sensation, in spite of his travels and his responsibility, that he was going nowhere and doing nothing.

He began to send her gifts from these faraway places. When she protested, he implored her to accept them and told her that without her alive in his mind, he would never be able to endure his goings forth and his returns. Often his calls came late at night, and as she sat hunched over the telephone, never quite sure if her poor ears were hearing rightly, she would attempt to dispel her discomfort by reading the titles along the shelves of books beside her and reminding herself of how far she had come, alone, spending not a dollar that she had not earned herself, looking to no other soul for the secrets of her completion. Throughout the conversations, her voice, she told herself, retained its cool, durable note of intelligence. Long before the onset of Stewart, faithful to herself, she had learned to cultivate polite nuances of disinterestedness.

The calls became so repetitious that she could almost listen automatically. Nothing would seem to change except the locality from which the voice said it was sending itself.

Wednesday morning; by now the plot should be thickening

You will be asking, I suppose, why she continued to accept the telephone calls and the gifts—jewelry, books, rugs, even carved totemic figures—when she must have known that in all likelihood, in spite of her careful indifference, they would have to lead somewhere, by the sheer weight of accumulation.

We must pause in this thrilling account, however, to take your children to the park. Stewart does not interest them, nor even the death—not a counterfeit this time—of Stewart's wife at Christmas this last year. Whatever these artless children know about human alliance or misalliance has not yet needed the length of a comic or a tragic view to give it tolerable form, but I suppose the time is not far off when they will begin to search for, or happen upon, resonant parallels to their own drama. For the time being, all three of us are closely engaged in the elaborate ritual, requiring what seems like a hundred small motions, of preparing to go outside. I don't know why I should be so amazed with how children of this age have so little of philosophy or common sense or even time and place awareness. They have to be recalled again and again from the absorbing dream of themselves. And what do we recall them *to?*

Again we encounter the obstacle of the red boots. Without Eric along to swing Christa over the puddles of melting snow, I feel that the boots are a necessity, and I become as stubborn as the child. Lyda is fretful, waiting in her stroller. Upstairs in your apartment dirty dishes and laundry have accumulated. It is a domestic scene in which I am glad I have only a bit part. Toys from yesterday are still strewn throughout the rooms. Last night Eric had a concert and a reception and came home after I was in bed, humming his way up the stairs, into the front room to put away his cello, into the kitchen, into the nursery: a man, a musician, a father coming home. I felt at that instant so distanced by him that I thought he may even have forgotten I was there and that his apparent interest in me is merely a graceful mannerism to hide the intensities of his own purpose. Never mind: I'm doing what I offered to do; his purpose does not dominate mine.

There are four days left.

Back to the boots. As I am already crouched down, with difficulty, I can easily look Christa straight in the eye. I say, firmly, The boots are magic. I point to her feet. With these boots on, I say, you can go anywhere, even through all the puddles; they will take you anywhere.

It works, and although I am slightly ashamed of myself, I feel jaunty as we clop and clunk down the front porch steps and out into the world. I give Lyda a cracker to hold and eat one myself. What am I wearing? My camel's-hair coat and felt hat and cashmere scarf: good clothes; why not, I said to myself years ago; the money is yours, use it.

Christa takes each puddle straight, without swerving. Overhead, a jet airplane bears down with afflictive sound upon our space, heavy with all the possible terrors of life. I hold my head up even more; I refuse to be tyrannized; I refuse to give in to oppression; I will not be humiliated. Some of my friends are afraid these days to walk the streets, but I say to them, Stay mobile, Stay mobile! Keep your mind free! Don't give an inch! Courage!

So I keep walking, although over the years I have more or less detached myself from optimism. I would not be young again for the world, not for this world; I don't know why I try so hard to keep myself in one piece. But you shouldn't be listening to me.

Da! demands Lyda. *Fence,* I say to her. Da! *Tree.* Da! *Wheel.* Christa, jealous, says, Lyda she just a baby, she doesn't talk, she doesn't walk. She's just learning. I say, and you're already good at those things; look how well you're walking. She looks down at the red boots and takes several heroic steps. My heart lurches, and my self-possession falters. Oh, what am I saying! Hearts do not *lurch.*

I catch up her hand as we start across the street to the park. I am by far the oldest person in sight; between Christa and myself there is a distance of nearly sixty-three years; between you, even in your adult, purposeful absence, and me the years are thirty-seven.

Look here, from the grandness of these years of mine, I should supposedly be teaching you a thing or two, but—here I pause beneath a blue sky of swift spring clouds—do I know anything that would be useful to you? It strikes me at this moment how different are the values we are each of us upholding. Weanedness is my specialty; attachment is yours. I feel I would have to bring the sky to earth before I could answer your questions to your satisfaction.

You know that old saying about marriage, don't you—how those outside it long to be in and those inside fear they will never get out? As I said, I keep walking, but with opened eyes.

Sweet-pea is one name I remember being called by my mother when she would at last notice me, among all the other children, when she would have a minute free from exhaustion, and from pain too, at the end. Ten children, thirteen pregnancies, perhaps more. I have already lived—let's see—twenty-five years longer than she did; I could be her mother, for heaven's sake. But, I repeat, I am nobody's mother. No one waits for me to give what I cannot give, to say what I cannot say, to be what I am not.

No, I wouldn't be young again. I feel catastrophe in my bones. Each day when I wake I am actually surprised that my little rooms are still unruined, and I am still waiting for something to happen. . . .

Up-a! Up-a! demands Lyda when she sees the swings. You push *me,* says Christa imperiously. There, you see, is a primary lesson on entropy. Children openly fear what the rest of us desperately conceal with hope: that once love has been split into pieces, the initial creative force dissipated, the power for each of us children, our portion, will be lessened. Look around you; see for yourself.

Nevertheless, I divide my attention equally, scrupulously, between the two swings, the little slatted wooden chair containing your baby and the single, flat, suspended board on which is balanced your earnest, self-important four-year-old. The screaking of a dozen unoiled swings rises above the voices of women, a few of whom pass high, youthful pleasantries to me, which I return in a voice modulated by my well-earned philosophy—not that I mean to dampen any spirits, but of what use is all this nervous, desperate enthusiasm? A lower tone would be more efficient, I think, and less open to disappointment.

But I'm no one to listen to.

Wednesday evening, a sort of party

Eric has decided, with the gusto and finesse of a natural performer, that this shall be "my" night. He came home early, having made a special trip to the fish market for the salmon steaks that are now under the broiler, tidied up a few areas of the apartment superficially, and then bathed and fed the children. Christa screamed in the bath, so loudly that I thought perhaps I should intervene, as you might have done, but then I closed my ears, read my book, and schooled myself yet again in the art of restraint.

We are not drinking spirits, in deference to my delicate stomach, but Eric has concocted an apple juice and sparkling water combination that is quite good. I am dubious, however, about those large, rich salmon steaks. It would have been ungracious of me, I suppose, to have admitted that I would rather have had a boiled egg and a banana with the children at five thirty.

How much of Eric's attentiveness is mere politeness would

be as difficult to assess as the degree to which my apparent enjoyment is dutiful. I do not know, myself. It seems that we are both slightly disappointed in each other and are waiting for something—for the dinner to cook? for you to come home? for the children to grow and prove themselves wonderful? for some form of God to appear in our midst?

I am surprised how genuinely pleased I am when Lyda crawls to my legs—to me—and pulls herself to a standing position. She holds onto my knee and bobs her whole body happily, she is that proud of herself. Are you going to walk to Daddy? I ask her. Show us what you can do. Christa looks up sharply from her blocks on the floor, almost needing to interrupt for attention; then—perhaps her play is too important or the congenial scene itself reassures her—her look softens and she returns quietly to her sprawling creation.

With one hand stretched out in encouragement to Lyda, Eric begins to recount for me last night's concert, how much closer now their quartet is coming to the integration and balance they have been envisioning. Now that they have achieved the necessary marriage, he says, they can go on from there. He goes on talking enthusiastically while I am still uneasy about the discordant words *necessary* and *marriage.*

Shoot! he says, do you know what I should have done? I should have seen that *you* got to that concert. What was I thinking of? We could have gotten a sitter.

Oh, don't think about it another minute, I say. I expected to stay home with the children.

And, you know, it's true, I did not even think last night that I might have been elsewhere than where I was, holding Lyda until she finished her bottle, lying down for a few minutes on Christa's bed after the light had been turned off. The form of this week is taking on for me a forceful, novel simplicity; yes, all right, I have been enjoined by the needs of the children to a *necessary* constancy, perhaps even a temporary sublimity. I am, as they say, "rising to the occasion."

But now Eric has turned to me with the full force of his charm; he is remembering me, determined that it shall be "my" night. How are you holding out? he wants to know. He says he supposes that two children are not much when compared to the household in which I grew up.

Any number of children is considerable, I say, but I am holding up very well, thank you.

Lyda chooses this moment to totter forth from the fortress of my knees, arms held up for balance. Midway between us two adults she begins to laugh, giddily, knowing her accomplishment.

That's it, that's it! cries Eric. Come on, baby, a few more steps. She falls into his outstretched arms and is lifted high. Oh, won't your mama be proud of you!

A baby is crying

Why doesn't someone take care of that baby? Inside my sleep I struggle but cannot escape a leaden stupor. I am dragging up the familiar porch steps of my childhood only to find that inside the old screen with the fan-shaped, wooden, knobbed decoration the doorway itself has been filled with cement. I could break my hand, pounding upon it. This is the old house; here are the balusters; the windows are still curtained with the same lace—but why can I not see through the windows? Why is the doorway filled with cement? I cannot breathe. I am held in a vise between dream and non-dream. The same purple clematis, unchanged for over half a century, sways on the trellis in a breath of wind, but the air is useless to me because I cannot breathe. The baby cries on and on. Oh, someone, I say, someone open this door; I am suffocating. No one comes. Now is the juncture of my death. This is it. I accept it. I am rising rapidly and then falling into the unknown, breathlessly.

No, I am awake. My heart is pounding, like a fist on a door, and I am breathing. The baby is Lyda. From far away I hear footsteps and Eric's low voice. I am not needed.

Crisis, the same night

Intestinal disorder: foulness, discomfort, weakness, boredom: I shall lie so still inside this body that no sensation shall remain. I shall leave off being arms and legs and tortured abdomen. Even the skin over my skull, over my teeth, is now as close to the bone as negation can be stretched. My tongue is dissolving. I shall become nothing but—intelligence; then—nothing.

Abruptly, without an instant of hesitation, I rise and flee toward the bathroom. All is to be revoltingly lost, all that food. Nothing would have been better for me.

In the mirror I recognize in the hollows of my eyes what a cliché is the desire for death. Measured ablutions begin again; water flows.

The hallway is like a cold tunnel. The many voices of myself howl inside my head, but listen to me and you will probably hear nothing. I am clammy and weak, touching cold walls for support as I pass along, my hand held midair as I cross the openings of bedroom doors. The baby is quiet now.

I'm on my own. Where? Two hundred miles away is my own bedroom, the room where you now sleep, but—how strange!—I cannot remember the positions of the furniture, the windows, or the colors. I lie down in your daybed. How strange: it is as if there is a gap in my wits through which I could fall.

Who is it?

At first the pounding seems internal, a violent attack of the heart; then I open my eyes and in the new dawn light see Christa's face a few inches from mine. She is pounding on my chest.

What is it? I ask, and in my voice I hear alarm and also anger at this assault. No one has ever before pounded on my chest as I slept. What d'you want? My words are ragged and coarse. She says nothing, just looking and looking at me. At last her concentration breaks and with an enormous sigh she raises a wadded baby blanket to her cheek. Her eyelids lower slightly. Now I am observing her. Her right thumb is raised to her mouth.

Who makes the first move? She moves; I move; even the light is changing instant by instant so that now I see clearly behind her your desk, your plants, and on the walls shadowy photographed faces. All in a series of small movements it is accomplished that your child is now in bed with me. This smell of hers, warmed, sweet, and yeasty, is like something baking in an oven. Still she has not said a word. She simply came—to *me*.

Sweet-pea, I hear myself saying as I adjust myself to make room for her. The radiant heat of her reminds me of the bricks we used to take to bed in the old house. I slept in the northeast room with your mother and Helen, the corner of the house that took the worst of the winter storms. Do I ever wish the house were still in the family? Eric wanted to know last night. Heavens! I heard my voice rise in a tight spiral of laughter. Heavens, what would I do with *that* old place!

My head rests in the crook of my left arm, arched on the pillow so that what I see of Christa is a minute facial topography, self-contained, safe, and asleep—yet who is she? Other faces are very close to ours.

I could laugh: if this is a comedy, then I should have been laughing, all this epic night.

The real Thursday

At breakfast in a veritable bath of sunlight, Eric and I recount our nocturnal adventures. I minimize my own lingering discomforts and play up the Shakespearean quality of the comings and goings of four evidently enchanted characters. It was all like a Dream of the Vernal Equinox, I laugh, and whatever was the matter with poor Lyda?

I don't know, says Eric, it was a night of general restlessness, I guess. An exhausted, careful patience is folded into the expression on his face. He looks much older, which, I reflect, would make me ancient. Do I feel ancient? No, but if I were at home, I would probably not move for most of the day. Sunk into a chair, peripherally aware of the sun, reading and not reading, letting the day pass and the dusk swarm, not speaking, I would wait for the tide of vitality to return. It always does, doesn't it, even if only to some infinitesimally lessened degree?

I clear my throat. What did you say? asks Eric. Oh, nothing, I say into the void of our fatigue, I wasn't trying to speak.

I'm giving lessons until seven tonight, says Eric. It will be a long day—for you, too.

We'll do all right, won't we, Chicken Little? I say to Christa, my small bed partner. Solemnly, much more subdued than usual, she has been nibbling her toast into shapes.

I look back to catch Eric staring wistfully out the window into the brick wall of the apartment house next door, where in the windows are reflected blue sky and white, blown clouds. Lyda pounds her feet against the metal chair. There is something awful to me about the bareness I have surprised in this moment.

All through the morning of dishes, toys, laundry, picture books I draw myself up and back into the dignity of knowing that in spite of my faults I have almost completed what I was inspired to offer to do. I draw myself up into the reserves of my strength from where I can remind myself of the subtle terribleness of family life: disappointed in each other, we can yet ruin ourselves in the attempt not to be a disappointment.

The story is continued

The afternoon has clouded over, your children are napping, and I have come to your room for my own rest. It is an hour when you might hope for another chapter about our teacher and the problematic Stewart, perhaps even a turning of the plot in the direction of your own pieties. No, no, don't you see, nothing can possibly come of it. . . .

Your judgment of her story as cold and restricted I can nearly predict from others of your heated pronouncements. Do you remember the letter you received from your professor last year just after Lyda's birth? You read parts of it to me over the baby's bald head and your own naked breast—so much skin! I thought; why doesn't she cover herself?—but of your own body and even the baby you seemed to take little notice. The letter had depressed and exasperated you. Your beloved professor proclaimed that he had not much hope left, either for himself or the world; you looked up and said pointedly, sweeping all my disaffections as well into your accusation: the old, you said, have no *right* to say such things to the young. Anyway, you said, your voice almost fierce, what he's doing is just looking at the world through the window of his own bodily infirmities.

My view is that I see both views, yours and his, and I see hers, too, our teacher's: she lifts her face to the photographs on your wall; she takes a deep breath; she wonders if all lives, all stories, are searching for entries into the same security of calm.

She passes over the mysterious map of Boston, over a laughing group of adults and children beneath an elephant-skinned beech tree, over an unknown family in bulky vests somewhere in the mountains, over a serious young man in a fisherman's sweater with light hair and freckles, unlike Eric, until she lands upon the mothers, side by side, forcing herself to look at them thoroughly: your mother, your grandmother, her sister, her mother, who, both of them, proclaiming love, had fathers, husbands, sons, the full male complement, but to her in her solitary vantage their deaths are the spinning out of fatal compromises of intelligence, perhaps, she thinks, the inevitable cost of coupling in an imbalanced world. She breathes again and makes herself look into those eyes that are looking out from inside lives that can no longer be rounded out by anything but the remembrances of others. It seems to her almost impossible that her own eyes should have enough life in them to go freely from one face to the other; why should she be the one to remain? Ah, why should she be the one! All she intended from the very first was a simple personal integrity; she never meant to be the surviving one; she fears she is not worth it, she who knows only too well her own limitations and compromises of heart, after all these years.

By now she is probably unmarriageable. This was what she tried to tell Stewart that appalling night, only last week, when his calls reached their climax. No longer did he need to continue calling long-distance, now that his wife was dead; nevertheless, this call came from Vancouver. He was in a hillside room, his voice told her, looking down upon lights, some of them bobbing because they were on boats. Marry me, he said. The strangeness had to come to an end, he said, how he wanted it to be over, this strangeness that seemed to have been going on for as long as he could remember.

She listened. He had asked a question but gave no room for her to speak; perhaps he, too, was putting off her answer. It was at this hour, in the lamplight of her own rooms, that her long, not pleasurable, not unpleasurable circumspection of this importunate man turned into a fear: harm would be done in any case, she felt, if she listened or did not, accepted or did not. She did not know if she feared more for him or for herself. She felt nearly stifled by dread and guilt. At last she broke in and said that she couldn't speak, she was too overcome, and she felt ill, too; yes, she felt ill, at that moment, and she could not speak; he must understand, she said, and she hung up.

She did then what I am doing now. She took out the blue velvet box of jewelry, scarcely worn, now a fixed point of her distaste and fright—a string of pearls, a thick chain of gold, pearl and gold earrings, a bracelet of jade—all of it valuable, coolly beautiful, but now all she wanted was to be rid of it, yes, to be rid of it. Then his power would be broken; magically the calls would cease, and his proposal would dissolve. She resolved that at the end of the week with your children she would not go directly home; she would make a secret detour deep into the city and find a buyer for these variously meaning jewels. Bemused, unknowing, Stewart would only feel that the connection had been broken.

Now, however, she is beginning to see what might be an even more potent corrective. Leaving the jewelry in a nest of the bed pillow, she paces your study. The furnishings, as in the rest of your apartment, are simple, almost meager: a bookcase, a dresser, a desk, a narrow bed she knows came from your unmarried days, a closet. There is a marmalade jar of pencils, a cyclamen, a quaint bottle of ink, a clock, a stone you must have picked up on the beach. Meditatively, not intending to trespass, she opens the door of the closet, pushes past her own clothes to your faded blue jeans, an old wool bathrobe, your several skirts, a few blouses with pretty bodices that she recognizes to have been your mother's, one of which she raises to her cheek. Her thoughts are collecting. You should have more clothes, she thinks, and jewelry, real jewelry. In your high-mindedness you might scorn these conventional symbols of female worth and think yourself immune from the unfair rules of sexual conflict, but she knows otherwise, and she doesn't like the idea that you might go bare beyond the flush of youth. Your mother, she thinks, would also want to see you adorned, protected, valued.

She closes the closet door and faces the window, a neighborhood of fog. Would the jewels, to her a burden and a threat, be to you a pleasure and a shield? Would the gift be to her a relief, and would she then be free to deliver to Stewart an effective but kindly refusal? Her superstitiousness surprises her; she is face to face with old, old fears.

Closing her eyes, she stands holding to your desk chair, and an image of her father appears, her father asleep on the garden swing after her mother's death—the death of his wife—Aunt Kitty inside with the new, crying baby, the last baby, while she herself, thirteen years old, sits on a rag, shelling peas, sliding her thumb along the inner membrane to loosen the smooth, companionable seeds, almost in a trance of loss and bewildered love, while somehow, in what came to seem to her later to have been incomprehensible, noncommunicative, murderous unawareness, her father sleeps. . . .

Her eyes are pressed tightly shut, her hands grip the chair; then an enormous shudder shakes her, melts her, and in the following softened instant of calm forgiveness and identification she is as if asleep in a rocking swing, under a grape arbor, with peas in a renewable world being shelled into a bowl and the dead living on easily and love having no issue but more of itself.

Friday

Hurry, hurry, into coats, into hats; let all resistances give way. Boots? I begin talking up our coming adventure to the library, and Christa hardly knows I am putting them on. Step ahead, out the door. This is the last full day of my surrogacy, already enclosing the next beginning. Notice the angle of my hat, the firmness of my step.

I woke early this morning to an intimate lucidity, close to myself, energized. What did I see? Myself as a teacher, for over forty years a good, sometimes a very good—yes, an excellent teacher. And I still feel that I stand for what I taught.

Tree! says Lyda. Tree, tree, tree! That's right! I say; it's a long line of trees. Christa, can you count the trees? She begins to count, skipping some numbers, reaching out to touch bark, then running ahead to spread her arms wide around a maple's trunk. Orchard, she pronounces, my orchard, *my* orchard.

At the library she disappears while I am still navigating the stroller through the doors. Once inside, I straighten my hat.

My eyes are alert. The glory, for me, is all those years of encouraging large-mindedness. Think! I'd say to those sixteen-year-olds. Keep going, don't stop there! And, for heaven's sake, I'd scold them, don't whine! Say anything you like, but—please—in your normal voice.

I find Christa on the fringes of a story hour. Go ahead, I whisper, you can find a seat up there. Lyda bounces and strains to be set free. Will she crawl, will she walk? I lift her out of the stroller and set her on her feet. Three steps upright, and then she drops to her knees and heads straight for an area of cushions and toys. Mobiles hang brightly overhead. Below, to a height of about three feet, is a universe of children. I stand beside the empty stroller.

Do I want to die? Listen. I do and I do not. I'm practical. Without my mind, I would best be off on the compost heap. Remember that. I've thought for myself, and my thinking has stood for thinking itself. Someone has to do it, I said to myself years ago. Gradually I saw that I was becoming a sort of antidote to certain varieties of foolishness. I wasn't grasping for anything, wasn't pursuing either ambition or any of the advertised forms of happiness. There's a technique—how shall I describe it?—of living, tranquilly, without exactly dwelling. . . .

No, it's best that you go your own way. Don't listen too hard. We'll see, we'll see.

The picture books for children these days are superb, aren't they? Here is Snow White of the translucent skin, fleeing through an ethereal twilight density of nature, eyes cast backward, transfixed by what comes before and after, the page before, the page after. Whom can she trust?

All right, I admit that even my story has its scenes of love, full-page, both day-lit and moon-lit. Christian was the source of one. I knew it out in the boat, on the lake, in the sun, with voices around us here and there, shouts, laughter, the past and the future calling back and forth across us, and Christian in his navy blue bathing costume, rowing, his hair on his forehead;

but already there was Helen on the shore not far away, taking off her hat and laughing, waving at us, just at the place where if you squinted your eyes the trees seemed to be tilting slightly inward toward a crease in the earth—the river—and I could read what had not even been lived, and what I felt was an earth-dissolving pity for all of us, for our passionate dependence on what we wanted to come next. Something at that moment dissolved in my mind, like a hot afternoon becoming absorbed into a smear of trees and cool water. I cared and I did not care. My long bewilderment cleared a little, and I recognized the legitimacy of calm sight, so full that nothing else at that instant needs to happen. This is all I know to set against a dying world.

And yet: a month ago I did not know I would be here. Out of what feels like nothing, something continues to well up, and if, in the end, it comes to nothing—well, perhaps that is no concern of mine.

I am going to take home a dozen of these books for the children. One way or another, all the stories are useful. Now, my arms laden, let me admit one more thing to you, to myself: I need you to be who you are, as I needed my sisters, for without you, what would be the meaning of my round watching?

It is Saturday: am I glad?

At any moment we expect your footsteps. My bag is packed, my coat hung over the banister; my hat and scarf are worn by Christa, who dances in front of the hallway mirror. In the noon sun Eric plays plangently, drawing you home with each draw of his bow, or so I imagine, though he might be playing for a secret love or, out of fear, to keep us all at bay. If I were the praying kind, I might be praying for both of you.

Lunch is ready; there is a place at the table for you. Now I have one more thing to do. With Lyda crawling at my heels, I enter your study, emptied now of me except for my purse on your desk and, hidden under the leather, the velvet box. I sit down. Lyda chugs up to my chair, pulls herself erect, holding tightly to my skirt, laughing, at the beginning of herself. I take a piece of notepaper and write, quickly, "Dear D., Take these won't you, and do whatever you like with them. Or keep them for the girls. Someday I might tell you the story. Love." Lyda pulls down on my arm as I am signing my name.

Without further ceremony, I secure the note to the velvet box with a rubber band and open the desk drawer. Now, suddenly, two faces are laughing up at me, Lyda's and that of your guru, nearly forgotten: well, yes, I suppose this could all be construed as comical. I don't care, you can laugh if you like. Watch your fingers, Sweetie, I say to the baby, and she says Da! as I substitute the jewelry for the photograph and close the drawer. Then with her clinging to my skirt I take a few steps to replace the photograph on the wall. She is begging to be lifted up, and as I take her in my arms, she reaches for the framed face. He is laughing at both of us. Do you want to know something? I am thinking it just might be better for you if he were a woman. Have you ever considered that?

Heavens! Don't pay me any mind; I'm just an old bundle of bones and contradictions. Go on ahead. Courage!

Lyda touches my cheek. Such a hot, bare hand! She reaches for my earrings—a pair I bought myself in Florence, I'll have you know. Well, it's almost over now—seven days: that's a lot of water over the dam.

FOURTH BROTHER

Sally was being sent to the cellar with a clean shallow pan, blue with white speckles, in which the hunters were to lay the finished birds. Between the clutch of women in the warm kitchen of the farmhouse and the hunters in the old coal room there was a flight of stairs against an interior limestone wall where for an instant she could stop and let loose some of the unwept tears that had been making her throat ache all afternoon. Bit by bit she picked off flakes of whitewash from the wall. On the ledge beside the stairs there were some empty canning jars and an unopened box of mouse poison. She held the enameled pan in the crook of her left arm, against her chest, as she had held her schoolbooks just last spring; only this cool pan was not solid like the books but hollow, an open form over her breast.

Upstairs cold beef from the noon dinner was being sliced,

leftover potatoes were fried, pickles forked into dishes. The gabbing voices sounded from this distance even more like a language she hadn't yet learned. Sally had just set fourteen places at the table in the oak-paneled dining room: for Frank and Maud, her new parents-in-law; for their four sons, George, Herb, Will, her husband, and Luke, the youngest, still not back yet on his motorcycle, even though the wind was reported to have taken a sharp northerly turn; for Kate and Barbara, wives to the two older sons, and their three children; for Rollie, Frank's old father; and for Clara, the sharp-eyed unmarried one who looked after her father; and of course for herself, Sally, the newcomer, the bride, as they called her, who didn't know how to talk to either group, upstairs or downstairs, or to make pickles, or to clean pheasants, or to decode the whine of the metal weatherstripping around the door at six o'clock on a late November night.

From downstairs were coming male voices, laughter, an occasional scuffing or scraping, and smells of limestone, heating oil, outside air, bodies. She took a breath and tried to force back the tears. There was too much feeling in her, that's what, too much feeling that didn't know where to go. Heartsickness at any moment could well up like this. Often she trembled like an animal in danger.

All afternoon, left with the talking women, she had thought about Will's death; over and over she had seen him shot down in stubbled field or mucky swale or in timber, where sight lines would be perilously obscured by multiflora rose. Then what she had done in her mind was to go away with Luke, the youngest, almost her age. They had ridden away together on his motorcycle, her arms around his middle, her face pressed into his brown leather jacket, her eyes closed as she went along to wherever it was that his fierce differentness was taking him. With someone like that, she thought, maybe she could find relief from her own long years of oddity. She could just close her eyes and go along and see what would happen.

So strong had been the impact of her imagined widowhood and her escape that it had been almost a shock after all those hours to hear the other men, alive, pounding home down the outside stairway to the cellar. Their deep voices rushing in had been like an underground wave, and upstairs she had trembled even more, not knowing if she wanted to drown or to be saved.

But Will had not even stuck his head in the doorway to find out how she was. She had just gone on setting places, trying not to cry, moving among the women, making superstitious equations from possible events. She told herself, for instance, that if Will had had no luck as a hunter, if he had been the only one not to kill, then it would mean that their marriage was right and hopeful after all, that Will was recognizing her and making a place for her. But if, on the other hand, her husband was the same as the others, if he had brought down game, and if Luke then came back safely on his motorcycle and seemed to single her out again with his smile and with the questioning, troubled longing in his eyes, it might truly mean that she had missed the right marriage by one brother.

With a fresh grip on the pan, she went down the rest of the stairs and crossed the dim laundry area to the lighted doorway of the adjacent room, whose walls were still blackened by coal dust. In a circle beside the furnace, sitting on stools and crates beneath one bare electric bulb, were three generations of sturdy Haas men, in the central space between their muddy boots a bushel basket and a bucket in which she saw the first layers of feathers, guts, feet, and iridescent heads. The lintel of the doorway was huge and rough-hewn, surrounded by limestone, the threshold nearly a foot wide, sloped in the center from a hundred years of treading.

Will looked up, and before she knew if any of the dead birds were his, or if any of those stretched-out, limp gray rabbits on the cement floor had been stopped in the middle of a bound by one of his bullets, he said to her loudly, publicly, "Heads up, Sally," and he was throwing something to her over old Rollie's stand-up white hair. It was feathers: a chopped-off tail.

"Haw!" said Rollie, turning as she caught it in the pan. "She don't want to get her hands dirty."

Striped black and golden with rusty red at its base, the tail was partially fanned out, as if the cock had been caught at the beginning of a strut.

"Good catch," said Will, but she didn't know whether to be pleased or not. She handed him the pan with the tail still in it.

"Your mother sent me down with this pan for the birds," she said. She said "your mother" because she could not yet say "Mother" or "Mother Haas" or "Maud" out loud, certainly not "Ma," as she was called by her sons and her husband.

"Thanks," said Will, with his public voice, no trace of the tone he used when he wanted to bring her to him, no hint of the promises he had made that together, in secret, they could make something new. His cheeks were ruddy above his beard. He and Luke had the same coloring, lighter than the older boys and their father. Luke hadn't wanted to join the hunting. After the noon dinner he had excused himself almost immediately and hunched out to the garage for his cycle.

"Moody," his mother had said as she had stopped midway between dining room and kitchen, coffeepot in hand. "He's just plumb moody. Where's he off to now?"

Parting the lace curtains on the dining room window, Sally had watched motorcycle and rider leaning around the bend of the driveway, through the open sheep gate, and down the lane, leaving her behind.

Now hours later here she was, asking of the assembled hunters, "Who shot what?"

"George here is the winner," said Frank Haas, indicating his oldest son by a hand slippery with blood. "How many again, George?"

"Three pheasant, one rabbit," said George, almost sheepish

in his pleasure. One of the rabbits he had now taken up on his knees, onto a fold of newspapers, and he was beginning to cut and loosen its skin, then deftly to pull off the fur as one might undress a child. George was the mechanic in the family farm operation. He could fix almost anything if the right part could be found. He lived just across the road from his folks' place, in the midst of a welter of spare parts, machines, hardware.

"Did you get anything, Will?" Sally asked her husband.

"I missed some beauties, but this tail here you caught is from my bird. And I almost got a goose. Can you beat that?"

"Hey, there's a story!" exclaimed old Rollie. "That lone goose comes honking over, and your new hubbie here yells, 'It's mine, it's mine!' and then he goes and shoots and dang if that goose don't set a new course for the southeast at the same minute. I took a shot—"

"I tried for it too," said Frank loudly. "It was a real beauty."

"I couldn't get a bead on it fast enough," said Herb. "That was one fine bird."

Rollie was laughing heartily and slapping his knees. "Dang if we didn't all go wild."

Then all the men seemed to be talking and laughing at once, while Sally still kept watch on a speck of goose in the sky, receding into freedom. Will reached into the gullet of the bird and came out with a lumpy handful of crop and gizzard, which he examined briefly and then dropped with a flick of his hand into the bucket.

Sometimes late at night, Will would confide to her his frustrations with his family, how they didn't take his advice often enough, even though he was the only one so far to have gone through all four years of agriculture school. Herb, the second son, had taken only a bookkeeping course, but he had learned almost as much about the cattle as Frank knew himself. Frank held all the reins now, without much slack, and had the last word on every decision. Even old Rollie—retired to tending sheep, calculating the weather, and watching television in the downstairs bedroom of the original homestead, with Clara tidying every room around him until there was not an inch left to be tidied—even old Rollie let Frank have his blustering way.

When Will was courting Sally so hard she could hardly study or eat or sleep, he had told her that as far as the farms went, he supposed he was willing to bide his time. The seasons kept passing, and Frank was getting older all the time. "As long as I get you, I can wait for everything else," Will had said.

"It's not me you want," she had cried out to him once. "You don't even know who I am!"

He did, he answered; he knew enough. She set up something in him. Before her, he said, he must have been half asleep, hardly knowing what he was thinking.

Before Will, Sally had loved others, awkwardly, inarticulately, and had been disappointed. Even to think of those times now made her hug her arms across her chest and lean a little more against the broad supporting timber of the doorframe. She knew what it was like to begin imagining a whole life with another person, to feel emerging out of friendship a mysterious, secret connection, and then not to have the lofty passion of her heart returned, to receive for all her devoted intensity only incomprehension, avoidance. It was Will's steady exactingness that had made her sway finally in his direction, as if to a destiny she had been too baffled to thwart.

Rollie turned around again in his chair. "How much longer are you women going to give us for these birds?"

"They told me about fifteen more minutes," said Sally, and her own voice sounded to her only faintly audible. "The children are getting pretty hungry."

"And no sign of that Luke yet, I reckon," said Frank. "I'm going to put a monkey wrench into that motorcycle one of these days."

"Haw!" said Rollie. "Don't count on that boy. He's halfway out the door already. I've seen enough like him before."

"Sally, are you cold, girl? Why are you all hunched up like

that?" Will was talking directly to her now, a little less loudly; his hands had even stopped their work.

"No, I'm not cold," she lied. "I just want to watch for a minute."

"It's getting plenty cold outside," said Will. His eyes were on her for another moment, and then he bent to the tail end of his bird. What did he really see, she wondered, when he looked in her direction?

"Didn't I tell you we'd have a stiff wind before night?" declared Rollie.

All the Haas men had a similar way with speech, drawing it out slightly so that their words took on a certain weight, and the listener at first felt that something very important was about to be said.

Sally felt like crying again. She looked over her shoulder into the laundry room and beyond it to the entryroom at the bottom of the outside stairs. Slipping away from the men, she turned toward that outer door. The guns had been propped against the wall at the bottom of the stairs, and beside them from an old coat tree hung the hunting jackets. She took down the one she thought in the dim light looked most like Will's, put herself inside its oversize, unfamiliar shape, and headed up the stairs, her hand sliding along the metal pipe that served as a railing.

The particular feel of the pipe and the sound of her footsteps and the smell of the jacket all seemed cryptically significant to her. And her own hand: how odd and white it looked and what a great distance it was from the swelling throb inside her head. She closed the basement door behind her and, shivering, drew her hands up into the sleeves of the hunting jacket. It was terrifying to think how everything had to be itself; nothing was spared, nothing.

She turned directly north, into the wind, through the gate that led to the orchard. Light from the kitchen windows extended partway beyond the fence, and then abruptly it was very dark. Wheeling around with her back to the wind, she saw Kate near the kitchen window, in front of the sink; then Maud crossed behind her and out of sight; upstairs, lights burned in the bedrooms where the children were playing; the lighted basement half-window was partly obscured by vines, so that the light appeared to be twinkling. In the darkness she was hidden, like Luke, who was somewhere out on these roads now, with the blackness always closing in behind him.

She walked on into the orchard, as far as the crest of the downward slope. From here the house behind could be thought hardly to matter, and the other farm lights out in the distance were so small in comparison to land and sky that it seemed a single blink could make them go away. But they stayed, and she stood still in the orchard, with no one knowing where she was.

Last March, toward the end of her freshman year, on an evening nearly as windy as this, she had stood in the concealment of a lilac bush by the driveway of her history professor's house and thrown little bits of gravel against the window behind which she had thought he must be at his desk. Some of the pieces of gravel were so light they had been blown back in her direction. It had seemed impossible to her that he had not emerged, that he had not been waiting for her signal. The pictures in her mind had been so intense! All the assignments she had done for him had contained hidden messages of her love. She was to have been his link to a greatness impossible without her. Handful after handful of gravel she had thrown against the side of the house and the window, like a scattering of the unspoken sounds that kept catching in her throat.

Nothing had happened. The door had not opened—yet another door had not opened, for the professor had not been her first disappointment, oh no—and now the puzzlement of all those dangling emotions was still with her, even after she had said "yes" to Will Haas, even after she thought she was appeasing life as best she could. For life was huge and angry, she was coming to learn, and you had to trick it; you had to throw sacrifices into it, maybe even pieces of yourself.

At first she had wanted to resist Will and had tried to hide from him, but he had placed himself in her path and refused to go away, no matter how she behaved. "A farm boy named Will Haas wants to marry me," she had finally told her parents, and to her dismay they had seemed relieved. Hadn't it been just one more sign that to them she was so difficult, so odd, that all they wanted was to be rid of her? Early, so early, they had let her know that she wasn't fitting in to their pieties. Something had gone wrong with her, she felt, almost from the start. Inside her, for as long as she could remember, had been this forceful swooshing and thrumming that had no place to go. When was it that she had started to fear that she would never fit in any place at all?

She jammed her hands into the huge pockets of the hunting jacket and faced the wind with tears. Her mind was racing. Then in the depths of the right pocket she touched a dampness from which she instantly recoiled, knowing without being told what it was: the fresh blood of pheasant or rabbit, oozed out just after death. Slowly she felt for it again and touched it slowly, trying to understand. Then she staggered slightly and bent over in the middle as if she had been struck.

Just then from the north came a strong single light on the road, wavering, growing, passing one farm at the crossroads, then the second, then dipping down and heading up the rise: it had to be Luke. She straightened up. "Luke!" she screamed, but of course he couldn't have heard anything but the wind and his own motor. Now he was passing her, passing the house, turning into the driveway, not knowing that she, also, was out here in the wind, alone. "Luke!" she screamed again, and then she began to run.

The big dinner at noon had been a ceremony for the hunt, just as Thanksgiving two days ago had been a celebration of the harvest. Both these observances were very nearly holy in the Haas family, Will had told her that morning in bed. The struggle against time and weather had come to a pause; all the fruits of labor were under shelter; now the snows could fall. She would like winter on the farm, he had told her. There were good times. She wouldn't be alone so much. She'd see: there would be laughter, he said, and warm nights under cover.

Tonight was an extension of the noon dinner; the same food appeared in slightly different form, with the addition of mustard, pickles, cheeses, peanut butter, and jam. It was all right to make a sandwich of the cold beef or of anything else. Rollie stirred a great quantity of strawberry jam into his cottage cheese. His eyes looked pouched and sleepy, and his white hair stood up at all angles. Two cold apple pies had been set out on the sideboard. The men seemed whipped up by excitement and hunger. The story of the goose was told again, in a slightly different version. "That's enough!" someone would say if the children misbehaved, and Sally would see in the small faces a moment of strain and then again mischievous merriment.

Maud and her sister-in-law Clara sat together at the kitchen end of the table, the first woman round, the other spare. Clara was eating a piece of plain bread spread with cheese and drinking black coffee. Years ago, so the story had come to Sally, Clara had gone off to Chicago and sold notions in a large department store. Then she had come home and been reabsorbed into the family and very little was said by her or about her. She always wore long-sleeved blouses, tightly buttoned at the wrists. For twenty-five years she had worked in the hardware store in town, selling cookware and portable fans and gift items of ceramic and wood.

Some of these pieces had been presented to Sally and Will by various family members and friends at the wedding in June: there had been a honey jar in the shape of a beehive, a wooden clock with the signs of the zodiac painted around the border, two ceramic trolls that were actually salt and pepper shakers, a painted figurine of a girl in a long dress, holding a basket of flowers. . . . When she was alone in her little farmhouse with these unaccustomed objects, Sally would move them from place to place, hoping to find the magic combination. The trolls had only laughed at her. During the hot summer, a strong, hot wind had seemed continually to push against her mind, the shrilling of the cicadas had pulsed through the air relentlessly, layer after layer of events, sounds, hours had pushed and shrilled against her. She could have thrown all of herself into the maw of life, she felt, and it would not have changed anything.

On one side of her now sat Will and on the other Barbara, who had done a prodigious job of food preserving that year; everyone had spoken of it—fifty jars of this, seventy jars of that, so many dozens of packages of this or that for the freezer. Now she was about to embark on her holiday baking, more than a hundred little cakes or loaves of bread that would be given to every member of their congregation.

"Isn't she wonderful?" said Maud.

Food passed around and around the table. Clara pressed cheese and jam and bread on Luke. With a fork she lifted a slice of beef from the platter and dropped it without asking on his plate. Luke looked up from his hunched posture and gave his Aunt Clara the furtive glance that perhaps she was looking for, into which could be read every kind of promise or no promises at all. It seemed to satisfy her, this look from her darling among the boys; she took a very small bite of her bread and cheese, she looked sharply around the table at the rest of them. He was her darling, Sally had come to know, because he had gone down and lived with her and Rollie the year Maud had had her operations; because he had been the best-looking of the boys, the one who picked day lilies and asters in the ditches and brought them to her kitchen; because he was criticized, forever being criticized by Frank and Maud and Rollie and those three hulking brothers.

Stealthily, Sally watched the food that was slipped onto

Luke's plate, the glances that passed between Luke and his Aunt Clara, the quick, defiant way Clara shifted her eyes to the rest of the family, and just in time Sally lowered her eyes to her own plate, to the food she was trying to eat.

Run as she would, she hadn't been able to reach Luke before he had swung off his motorcycle and disappeared into the back porch. She had run instead into Will, coming up out of the basement with the bucket of innards.

"Hey!" he had said. "What are you doing, getting some air? Come on out to the pen with me."

Underneath the jiggling barnyard lights, the pigs had been lying on each other in a long row, overlapping like shingles.

"You throw it in," said Will. "Atta way." And again she had not known whether to be pleased or angry. He had put his arm around her and crunched her against him. As they walked back, he had lifted her a little off her feet and said, "Great night, isn't it?" and then he had made her look up into the bare branches of the walnut tree against the huge, blue-black sky through which masses of clouds were being pushed. "It's working up to snow," he had said. "It can come, we're ready."

She had looked and looked, trying to read this sky that her husband knew, under which he had grown up. He had kissed her, there, under the walnut tree. "Winter can come," he had said, and she had felt nearly flattened by his satisfaction.

The meat was the most difficult for Sally to eat. She had taken only a very little, but even that she didn't want now. Most of the others were already on their second helpings, all but Clara, who held only a cup, close to her as if she were guarding it.

"Well, Luke," said Frank suddenly, when his plate was empty and he had reached for a toothpick, "I suppose you think you've done a day's work by burning up some gas." Though he said this offhandedly, around the probings of his toothpick, the effect of his words traveled instantly around the table. In Sally there was a tightening. Beside her Will leaned back and draped an arm around the back of her chair, waiting.

"I did chores," said Luke to his father. Deliberately, it seemed, he kept on eating, in large mouthfuls.

Frank examined the end of his toothpick. "That motorcycle isn't taking you anywhere." A hardness was traveling down the table from father to son. "I've got a mind to lock it up for a while."

"It's mine," said Luke.

Clara had set down her cup and was tensing the fingertips of both hands on the table in front of her barely used plate. Old Rollie looked very sleepy now. He turned in his chair and eyed the dessert.

Luke chewed his food in the midst of his family. "I won't be here much longer anyway," he said.

"What are you talking about?" Now Maud had joined her husband. "Why, you're not even graduated yet."

There was a terrible look on Clara's face, a gray mask contorted by apprehension. To Sally it seemed as if her own future had also been thrust out in front of the group.

Luke took a long drink of milk and set down his glass. "I'm going out to California with Melvin. Next June. Don't worry, I'll graduate."

"California!" Frank broke his toothpick in half and threw the pieces down on his plate. "California is no sort of place."

But now for the other wives and brothers the moment of tension was over. The little children were sliding down out of their chairs. Barbara had gotten up to clear off the table. "You serve up the pies," she whispered to Sally.

Luke and his parents and his Aunt Clara were still bound together at the table.

Sally's hands were shaking as she stood at the sideboard, lifting out wedges of pie. Barbara came to her to carry the full plates to the table. Three young wives were now serving the others. Sally's hands shook and slices of apple kept sliding out of the crust. "I'm not doing very well," she confided to Barbara.

"The taste will be the same," said Barbara, but Sally couldn't tell if she meant it in a kindly way or not.

"California's not the place to teach you how to work," said Frank.

"You don't know," said Luke.

"*You* don't know!" Frank's voice had risen. "You're the one who doesn't know."

Sally came back to her place at the table and saw that Frank had immediately begun to eat his pie, angrily, in huge forkfuls.

"Enough said for now," said Maud.

"No amount is enough with this boy," said Frank with his mouth full. "Nothing sticks."

Sally couldn't swallow much of the pie, either. Just the thought of it oozed of sugar and fat and a dead heaviness. Her throat swelled again with tears. It was terrible, she thought, how the older brothers kept on eating without a word to help the youngest. She was choking with heartsickness.

"What's the matter with your pie?" asked Will in her ear.

"Nothing. I'm just too full."

"It's too good to go begging." He stacked her plate on top of his sticky one and systematically finished off her pie.

"Luke, will you have some more?" asked Clara, who had not accepted a piece herself.

"No more, Aunt Clara." Sally saw him smile sideways at his Aunt Clara, his head turned from his father, and Clara looked helpless as she received his smile.

"Clara, drive me home," said Rollie abruptly, pushing back his chair. "My bones are tired."

"I haven't finished my coffee yet, Dad," said Clara.

"Coffee at night is devil's brew. If you remembered that, you wouldn't be forever walkin' around and around like a spook in the middle of the night." He stood up. "Go get your female things together and let's go."

"If you could still get a license, you could take yourself home."

"Clara! That will be enough," said Frank. "You should be grateful for the roof."

A sick heaviness was in Sally now. This was the kind of talk she had seldom heard when growing up, but it was how her parents might as well have talked to each other. And they might as well have said straight out to her, We don't like you, you're not the right child for us, you're too red and prickly, you cry too much. For she had cried as an infant, they told her; she had cried so much, no matter what they tried to do for her, that they had finally decided she was just an angry baby. And she had just been a baby! It was almost too terrible even to let those thoughts in now.

"Well, I'll be taking off too," said Luke, and he also stood up. "Good cooking," he said nonchalantly to his mother and Aunt Clara, and Sally saw that Luke didn't care any more about pleasing his family; he was doing what he wanted to do and saying what he pleased.

"Where do you think you're going at this hour?" asked Frank.

"A little spin," said Luke, with a particular emphasis on each word, as if each one were a bit of ammunition aimed at his father.

"I wouldn't mind a ride," Sally heard herself saying. "I wouldn't mind a little spin." Her eyes didn't dare now to look at Will. "I've never been on a motorcycle."

A flicker of new expression appeared in Luke's handsome face. He stuck both hands in the hip pockets of his jeans. "It's cold," he said.

"Too cold," said Will's voice beside her. "She doesn't have the jacket for it."

Luke's jaw tightened. "She could always wear one of mine."

"You young ones never know when enough is enough," said Rollie. "It don't make sense to go chasing around at night." He had already gone down to the cellar for his hunting jacket. The cap he was now putting on made his ears stick out even farther. "You should all go home to bed. Mark my words." He brought his pair of gloves down on Clara's shoulder, none too lightly. "My bones are shouting at me, Clara. Thanks for the dinner, ladies."

Luke gestured with his head to Sally. "Come on, then, if you've got a mind to try it."

Sally got up from the table without looking at Will. She followed Luke directly to the back entry, where he handed down his own leather jacket to her.

"But what will you wear?" she asked. Her body had begun shaking all over. One leg trembled so much that she thought it might fly out and kick something.

Luke put on a plaid wool jacket and over that one of the frayed padded jackets that Frank used for chores. "You'll need these, too," he said, and he handed her the scarf and gloves that Maud wore to the chicken house. "All set?" he asked. The nod she gave him felt more like a shudder. Her heart was pounding.

The wind blew the aluminum storm door back against the house. Sally struggled to pull it back. Luke was already halfway out to the motorcycle. One of the barnyard cats jumped onto a dining room window ledge, stretched into a high arch, and then retracted to a rounded shape, its fur ruffling up in the wind. It watched Sally for a minute, and then it turned away and gazed into the lighted room.

"Careful of the exhaust pipe," shouted Luke, too late, at the instant she felt the burn on her ankle. She said nothing. It felt like being branded. She climbed on behind him as all afternoon she had imagined herself doing, and now her fingertips were touching his padded back. She found a place for her feet. Above were the rushing clouds, now moonlit, and the sailing moon, nearly full-faced, all its laughter just a passing reflection.

Luke shouted to her over his shoulder that she was to hold on. She gripped handfuls of his jacket and then as he lifted his own feet off the ground and only acceleration kept them upright and Luke leaned and she leaned around the curve by the toolhouse, she gripped more tightly and in a moment was circling his waist, holding on for life, because they were gaining speed, hardly pausing at the end of the lane, skidding slightly on the gravel that spilled out onto the blacktop, heading north past the house with all its windows alight behind the mulberry trees.

Sally pressed herself against Luke. She hid her face behind him and looked out to the side at the orchard with its little hillcrest, then the valley with the rows of fir trees, then the broad, broad, dark, empty fields where only a few weeks before the combines had been working late into each night behind giant headlights, in a fever to bring in the harvest. Night after night Will had eaten supper and left again and come home at midnight or later, with a heaviness to his collapse into bed that had made her imagine both of them would be sent down through the floors of the house, down through the cellar, down into the earth itself, like heavy, dead lumps fallen from the sky.

It might have been the steady vibration of the motorcycle, or the mile after mile of silent fields, or Luke's acceptance of her once they were under way; somehow her trembling subsided, and there were no more shudders or tremors. She even began to feel a little drowsy and now and then closed her eyes and gave herself over to being taken somewhere. Sheltered by his body and by his jacket around her, she was almost warm. Luke took her on roads where she had never been. They jounced over railroad tracks and crossed a narrow, glimmering river. At the top of the next hill, with an arched iron gate standing up against the sky, was a graveyard, whose particular stones and trees and sprays of bush they passed in the fraction of an instant. They had passed so many hundreds of dark acres that a thrill went through Sally and evened out into a relaxed expansiveness. It was the first time since her marriage that she had been this far from the family farms; riding on the motorcycle was like flying just above what you usually had to labor through, your shoes weighted with mud, your legs leaden.

It was peaceful behind Luke and protected. The sky and earth were securely in their places. She was beginning to feel different from herself, as if her old self had been wrong: life was not angry and omnivorous, no, but gentle and steadying and yielding; if you just got going in the right way, you could fly right through it in safety, maybe even in happiness.

Just as she was hoping that the ride would never end, Luke turned off the road into a grove of trees, beside the lights of a roadhouse, and cut the motor.

"Come on in. I'll buy you something to drink."

Her legs under her were not quite her own. She gave out a laugh.

Luke laughed. "What is it?"

She pointed to her feet. Her whole body seemed to be filled with a slightly new, airier substance, cottony. More laughter bubbled from her.

The roadhouse and the grove of trees were on the banks of a creek. Over to one side of the building a barking dog was tied to the end of an overturned rowboat. There were beer signs in each of the windows of the low building. Inside, the head of a deer had been mounted over the bar.

They sat in a booth near the front because Luke said he wanted to keep an eye on his cycle. He handed her the Coke she had asked for and a long cellophane packet of something that looked at first like licorice.

"What is this?"

"Beef jerky. Haven't you ever had it?"

Her hands began to tremble again as she tried to tear the

cellophane. Luke took it from her and tore it open with his teeth and handed her a strip. "Good stuff," he said.

Obediently, she took a bite and began to chew. Perhaps beef jerky went along with the flying ride and the lightness in her body and the ripples of surprising laughter. Obediently she chewed, even though disgust was beginning to overtake her, disgust was coming up her throat. She felt her eyes grow wider, and before she knew what she was doing, she had spit the whole mess into her hand. There weren't even any napkins. "It's awful!" She looked around her, but the few men in the tavern weren't paying any attention. "It's really awful. How can you eat it?"

Luke swallowed his with a long drink from his beer. "I could live on it."

With her hand cupped around the warm mess, she got up and passed the men at the corner of the bar and made her way down a dim passageway to the only rest room. She had to wait while someone inside coughed and coughed and water ran. Finally, the door opened, and she shrank against the wall to let a huge bald man wheeze past her. She flushed away all the tiny brown pieces and washed her hand and looked at herself in the mirror. She had forgotten to take off Maud's plaid wool chicken-house scarf. Except for that, in Luke's jacket she might look like someone's girlfriend. She took off the scarf and shook out her hair. Then she washed out her mouth several times. In spite of the beef jerky, she still felt pretty much at ease, someone a little bit new to herself, bubbling with newness.

"Sorry about that," said Luke at the table. "I thought you might like it."

"Maybe I will, someday," she said. She drank carefully from her Coke. In the warmth of the room, the exhause-pipe burn on her ankle had begun to throb. She almost liked it there, strong and hot, as a secret sign, connecting her to Luke. "Are you going to get all the way to California on your motorcycle?" she asked him.

One of the men from the bar had gone over to the jukebox. A song began, a drawled plaint, tears and more tears. "Probably," said Luke. He looked out the window to his cycle, visible through the letters of the beer sign, and then tilted his head in such a way that Sally knew he was also looking at himself. He was getting a glimpse of himself in the window of a roadhouse by a creek in a grove of trees where that tied-up dog was probably worn out with barking by now. Probably Luke was sorry he wasn't wearing his own leather jacket so that he would look better, less like the son of some farmer.

Now was the moment to make him turn his face back to her, to show him what was becoming plain to her. "I've thought I might go away myself," she said. "I've thought I might have to go away from here."

"Why would you do that?"

She had his attention now. She took a breath. Great spasms of feeling began racking her. She didn't know if she could get the words out, but she had to; it might be a last chance. She was determined now. This time the sounds would not come back to her in the wind. "I think I have made a terrible mistake," she said carefully. "I think I will probably have to go away from here." She was shaking almost convulsively.

Luke looked at her a moment, sharply, in a way that reminded her of Aunt Clara, and then his eyes slid back to the window, to whatever he was finding there, just to the right of the red and yellow neon letters. Tears, the song was telling, tears and desiring and more tears to come.

"I don't know," said Luke at last, just slightly drawing out his words. "I don't know but that you're better off where you are."

HOUSEHOLD

Here came Nathalie: forty-one, agile of body, angular of face, with large blue eyes under a flap of graying bangs; dressed at the moment in a woolen bathrobe with treadbare piping, she was carrying her firstborn baby, a daughter, down the upstairs hallway for an early morning nursing. There were paint buckets to be skirted, a folded stepladder, a neatened collection of trays and rollers and brushes, for with characteristic productivity Nathalie was making the most of her confinement. It was late February, six fifteen; a frosted light filled the windows.

Once again in the big bed she curved her body around her daughter and bared a nipple. A root was tapped through her to the contented center of the world. Breathing deeply, she closed her eyes beneath the sweep of her mussed hair. Edward turned; she felt his breath, his lips on the crown of her head.

He sighed, groped for a baby foot and thus anchored seemed to be setting off again, into a microscopic pattern of decidua, or a laboratory corridor, perhaps a chain of mountains—how could she know? His body twitched. She could not follow, but she heard him, blowing out dream sounds, this youthful husband who had found her in the fullness of time.

Now she herself was sinking into a whitened space where a single sound produced a peacock, fanning out its splendid iridescent tail. Slowly it pivoted, and Nathalie was drawn down a path between rhododendron and up a hill to a ceremony, a circle of people in white. I can't open my eyes, she apologized; I can't wake up; I am still so tired. With a length of white batiste they swaddled her as she held her baby Caro, swath after swath of fine batiste, at first a glory and then a binding fineness, which lo! at the last moment loosened and released her to the air, a flying mummy, trailing white batiste and cradling her baby.

The alarm from the clock broke open a forest of colors. Edward groaned. Nathalie turned, forgetting the peacock, the rhododendron, the white batiste, and the baby received another breast. A crow screamed across the neighborhood. In the nineteenth-century eaves outside the window pigeons cooed rounded, busy mutterings. What, Nathalie wondered, were those red eyes seeing high above the winter street?

Downstairs she and Edward had to speak softly because of Liza, asleep in the living room beneath the ficus tree on Edward's old couch pulled out to make a bed, a lump of taciturn flesh, one plump bare shoulder just visible above the blanket, one wrinkled hiking boot upright on the floor beside the bed, one tipped on its side. The blinds of the living room were closed and for nearly a week for most of each day had remained tight, in spite of the massings of plants: Liza was sleeping, such protracted sleeps as can pull one through times of deep exhaustion or confusion, though whether healing was actually taking place, Nathalie had not been able to judge. She had not even been told the hurt, only that the child—but for goodness' sake no longer in these last few years a child—of her childhood friend was passing through town and needed a bed for one or two nights, which had been extended into four, now six.

"I'm going to try and reach her mother again today," whispered Nathalie to Edward in the kitchen. She poured boiling water onto tea leaves. The kitchen was the one rescued area of the shabby house, now a glowing of refinished wood and fresh paint and new windows: the heart, they had at once agreed, from which all other renovation would spread—slowly, of course, for there was little time, less money.

Edward nodded and continued out the sliding glass door to the bird feeder with a measure of seeds. Today the air was thick and gray, and there was ice everywhere; a mass of it on a bush looked as if a bucket of cloudy water had been slopped exactly there. Nathalie could make out nothing clearly beyond the first oak and the listing grape arbor, but most certainly Edward, lifting the hinged roof of the feeder, was real, and the baby, strapped into a slanted infant seat on the kitchen counter, flailed arms and legs in pleasure. Caro had learned to smile. She flailed, she smiled; the smiles were evidently connected to the flails. "That's right," said Nathalie softly to the tiny face. "That's my love."

"Murky, but not quite so cold," said Edward, stamping his feet.

"Look, Edward, she's doing it again."

He came to the counter and bent over the baby, who pursed her lips at him and made a sound, miraculous baby.

"Do you hear that?" Edward laughed. "She's trying to talk." He pursed his lips and made an encouraging sound. The baby opened her toothless mouth and smiled. Her feet beat against his thickset chest.

"She's only two months old," said Nathalie. "She can't possibly be talking." But she peered over the top of Edward's head at the infant features that each day were making the smallest, smallest changes.

Edward stood up and put his arms around her. "I'm happy," he said.

The earth, she had discovered, had solid arms after all, need not be conquered or resisted, could answer, concretely. Edward's brown eyes were smiling at her. But was there a slight rasp of weariness in his voice? He was thirty-five. Tenderly she read the crinkles and creases around his eyes and searched into the good-humored lights and wheels of color.

But of course they were both tired; catapulted as they had been into marriage, into parenthood, they had scarcely caught their breaths anyway, and last night Caro had been awake twice past midnight, and Liza had taken to trailing in very late—and though they weren't really responsible, thank heavens, they couldn't help feeling worried—so late last night that Edward had agreed her mother must be reached. What a household, he had said close to Nathalie on the pillow: a newborn infant and an infantile twenty-one-year-old; what a combination. To say nothing of us, Nathalie had returned. And then they had had to smother their laughter against each other, dazed as they were with fatigue and wonder.

In the kitchen, standing firmly together, they swayed in their embrace, and the baby's feet pushed against their thighs.

"What is it?" he asked. "Your forehead's puckering."

Puckering? She put her fingers to her brow. "It's Liza, I suppose. A puzzlement. She's draining me."

"Send her packing," said Edward. "She's had her sleep. She's not ours. You need to get your own strength up if you're going back to work next month."

"The vagueness is irritating me," said Nathalie. "I have this terrible urge to take her by the shoulders and shake her up."

Nathalie seized Edward by the shoulders and shook; then she shook again, surprised at herself. Edward laughed and lifted her off her feet. She swayed in the air against him, and her arms relaxed.

Now he was going away to the windowless chambers of the laboratory where all day his giant's eyes would be focusing on arrested bits and pieces of nature, systematically traveling in among the cells, the parts of cells. The prints he brought home from the electron microscope were to Nathalie like the shots coming home from outer space. A segment of tissue, the surface of a planet: human scale had poured itself into the eye of a microscope, the eye of a camera, and been translated into patterns, aggregations of bits and pieces of nature, held in place by contrary forces, the force for coming together, the force for going apart, gravity, levity. She said good-bye to Edward. She could not follow.

Now all day her arms alone would hold the baby. One could not shake a baby, no. In the unfilled space of that new mind every incoming gesture, every word must count for ten, a thousand, ten thousand. Gently Nathalie carried her daughter past the darkened living room and up the stairs.

"There's my love," she crooned as she bathed this armful. She wrapped her in a towel, she blew into her navel, she gazed closely into her face and made whatever sounds came into her head. No one else was listening. What clock could possibly measure the vastness of each infant moment? "Love," bubbled Nathalie, "Oh, lova-lova-love." Caro squirmed and smiled and clutched at Nathalie's cheek. From no knowledge of each other, in two months they had come to this. "That's right," said Nathalie, kissing the tiny fist, "that's right, lova-love."

In the hallway she almost stumbled over Liza, who was sitting on the floor beside the paint cans, still in long johns and torn satin camisole, examining the valleys between her bare toes.

"Liza! you're awake early."

"I guess I am," admitted Liza, looking up blandly from her round smooth face, her heavy brown fall of hair.

"Well, the bathroom is yours," said Nathalie. "If I had

known you were waiting, I wouldn't have dawdled so long."

"Oh, that's all right," said Liza. "I'm in no hurry."

The shower she took while Nathalie nursed and rocked the baby was indeed unhurried. Gallon after gallon of water funneled down through the pipes of the old house. For a moment or two a piece of plaintive song floated above the water, surprisingly buoyant. On the nursery side of the wall Nathalie continued slowly to rock. Her daughter slept in her arms. She should rouse herself, she thought, and change into her painting clothes. She disliked wasting time. She disliked wasting anything. But the stillness of the child seemed to be holding her still.

What she really must do immediately was to try again to reach Janet before Liza should go off for another afternoon and evening of wandering. Where did she go? Nathalie had finally asked. Oh, around town, Liza had answered; sometimes she talked to people. One night she had come home smelling of beer, unusually cheerful, her heavy body dressed as usual in layers of clothes—trousers, long skirt, shirts, vest, scarves, fur-lined leather hat with flaps dangling, clomping boots. A gypsy, she looked like, or a Bedouin, lost from her tribe. Nathalie, waiting up, making work for herself in the kitchen, had seized the moment. Ah! how had the town been tonight? Pretty good, said Liza; she had been talking to one of the shopkeepers in the arcade; he made jewelry and, look, he had given her this pretty stone. Quartz? wondered Nathalie. Quartz it appeared to be, a piece of quartz; why on earth, she asked herself, but she kept silent. The arcade worried her; the shops, she had heard, were mere fronts.

But here stood Liza. A midnight snack? A cup of tea? she had pressed, a banana, an English muffin slathered in butter? Liza had accepted all three, and while she ate Nathalie had inched closer. Now, what had Liza been saying about her mother; did Janet still have the same job or was she onto something else? Liza licked her fingers; she wasn't sure. Well, did she have the same apartment, the same telephone? Oh, yeah, she still had the same place, Liza had said. And Liza would be going out there before long, was that the plan? What were her plans, anyway? Nathalie had bumbled on, unable to stop herself; why, at Liza's age lots of young women were doing all sorts of interesting things. The possibilities were enormous. What were Liza's ideas? What was going on?

Then the face had closed down again, the heavy hair had obscured half the eyes, half the cheeks, and Nathalie had been saved from saying what was next on her tongue: that at Liza's age she herself had been well along in design school, had held scholarships and part-time jobs, had thought she was learning how to keep herself in hand.

Disastrous, that would have been, a disastrous show of pride, she thought now as she rocked her satisfied baby. Something in Liza's manner had checked her, nothing as extreme as a word, rather an inarticulate arousal, a flicker behind the eyes, but Nathalie had seen it and sensed the source: anger, perhaps even scorn, herself included in the generality of its object, and then something stubborn in herself had risen up in defense of the kitchen, the teapot, the fruit basket, the lithographs on the walls, the woman of forty-one with her baby, her husband, her work, her energy. She had stopped talking. She had put away the butter and begun to turn out the lights. With nothing to hold to but youth itself, Liza had in a flickering of scrutiny silenced Nathalie's hard-won assertiveness.

She continued to hold the baby, rocking slowly. At last the water was turned off; a hair dryer was turned on; the same song was begun again and abruptly broken off.

Nathalie eased Caro down to the crib and stole past the bathroom to their bedroom, still thick with the atmosphere of night. It would be easy to stretch out under the covers and sink down, but instead she made the bed without wasting a motion. She snapped up the window shade, and pigeons fluttered in alarm from the ledges. Briskly she threw Edward's running shoes into the closet and snatched up the dirty clothes. She was quick; she was efficient; she had always been good at sorting out the necessary from the unnecessary. A proper economy was what distinguished her work in graphics too: the right amount of free space, the right concentrations of information, the right shapes for each intention. She had an eye; she was reliable; she cared passionately about the finished piece, the look of it in her hands, the paper, the beautiful, defined letters. Sloth she could not abide, nor carelessness; one might as well be tying a stone around one's neck, so heavy were the effects of these attitudes. There! Six minutes and the room was tidy. She felt re-established.

She pulled the telephone to the bed, lay across the quilt, and dialed the long-distance number she had in this week memorized. Janet was her own age, a friend from grade school days who had married early; who had quickly produced five children—in almost total unconsciousness, she had told Nathalie much later—who had divorced, remarried, divorced, moved here, then there, believed fervently in one after another of various cures of body or spirit.

No answer. Janet had not answered in the evenings; she did not answer in the morning. Nathalie ran her fingers over the blocks of colored fabric on the quilt. She lay back, stretching her body that was now nearly reclaimed from its fantastic expansion into pregnancy. She drummed her fingers on her rigorously flattened abdomen. She was pleased with the firm hold she had been keeping on herself during maternity. Strong-mindedness and sensible habits seemed to be seeing her through with extraordinary smoothness.

Surely it should be easy and reasonable enough to put her arms around this Liza, this child no longer a child, now loose in the world, who had come to lodge in her path and who might have been her own, or even the mother of the baby now asleep down the hall. But what Nathalie wanted to do with the demanding formlessness of the girl was to shake, to shake hard, to rearrange the elements that seemed so irresolutely, so incompetently, held together.

She changed her clothes and filled her hands with paint can and brush and took up where she had left off the afternoon before, the trim around the double window in the upstairs hall, each sill, molding strip, mullion requiring a precise angle of the brush. The paint was white, glossy, steadily redeeming. The view framed was of pine tree, bare oak branches, fog, a suggestion of neighborhood. Liza she could hear now in the kitchen, not clattering, but almost furtively grubbing, rustling. She would let her eat in peace, she decided; she would just finish this window and then go downstairs and casually, mildly inquire into the projected day.

Almost as soon as she had made this resolution of restraint, she set her brush into a jar of solvent, wiped her hands, and went down to the kitchen.

Liza, dressed in Nathalie's dark blue woolen robe, was standing beside the toaster, staring at the slots. For an instant her face looked startled, then slack. Nathalie was both touched and irritated by the free use of the robe.

"All clean?" asked Nathalie. "Your hair looks lovely. Have you found the butter? Do you want to try the new honey? Wonderful stuff. It's local."

"OK," said Liza.

"I see you've boiled water. I'll have another cup of tea with you." Nathalie rolled up the sleeves of her painting shirt and began measuring out tea leaves. "So, you've had a nice shower," she continued. "There's nothing like water. Feeling pretty chipper today?"

"So-so," said Liza.

"You've been tired out."

"Yeah," said Liza. "Real tired out."

"Are you getting rested?"

"I don't know," said Liza. "Maybe."

Nathalie took the teapot to the table near the glass door.

A bird book was wedged in the napkin basket; a candle would be lit again that night; honey glowed in the jar: tokens of their love, hers and Edward's; she felt rich. She poured out tea.

"There's plenty of cereal there, Liza, and more bread in the freezer."

"OK," said Liza. "Do you think it would be OK if I had some of that cottage cheese, too?"

"Of course, of course," urged Nathalie. "Take whatever looks good to you. Those bananas are ripe."

Slowly Liza assembled herself a breakfast and carried it to the table. She dipped honey onto her toast and more onto the concoction in her bowl. She took a sip of tea, sighed, tossed back her hair, and began to work her way through the food.

"Did you know I took care of you once when you were a baby?" asked Nathalie.

"You did? I didn't know that."

"You were a very pretty baby."

"I was?" Liza looked up with her mouth open.

"Yes, you were about a year old, just learning to walk. Janet had come home for her mother's funeral, and I happened to be home, too, from school. Yes, you were adorable. Very pink cheeks, as I remember."

"Were Dick and Hughie there?"

"Oh, yes, I had a workout that afternoon. I think your mother was pregnant then."

"With Jane."

"Yes, it must have been Jane."

"Jane has a baby now."

"That's right. Have you seen Jane's baby?"

"No."

"Well, if you're on your way to see your mother, maybe you could stop at Jane's."

"Maybe."

Liza licked her spoon, pushed her empty cereal bowl away, and began to concentrate on toast.

"More tea?" Nathalie asked brightly. She drummed her fingers on the table. She wanted to get that window upstairs finished before the baby should wake up. She wanted to move on later in the day to the taping of the wallboard in her new attic studio. Clearly before her she saw the finished, readied house. It was her excellence, she knew, to draw out orderliness, to improve the surfaces that came beneath her hands. Neither she nor Edward had ever had a house before. It was still a thrill each morning to reenter the well-proportioned spaces, to see their new life framed through a succession of doorways, windows.

Nathalie followed Liza's gaze into the foggy void of the yard. It would be a day of early twilight. She could see herself turning on lamps, moving from room to room with the baby on her shoulder, listening for Edward, cooking supper; happy.

"So," she said to Liza's soft profile, to her eyes that were the color of the fog, "what are your plans for today?"

"I don't know, Nathalie. I thought maybe I could wash some clothes in your machine."

"Of course. Anything else?"

"I guess I'll go downtown again."

"Goodness, you're going to know more about this town in a week than I've learned in all the time I've been here."

"I like to walk around," said Liza.

"Getting an education?" Nathalie put in and was immediately sorry.

Liza's eyes widened, and in their gray depths Nathalie caught again a flaring up, as if ashes had been stirred. Then the flame dampened. Was it with tears?

Liza said nothing. She smiled faintly and shrugged at Nathalie. Her nose looked red; her full lips were slightly parted.

"Liza, what on earth is going on," said Nathalie as gently as she could. "Are you ill? Are you pregnant?"

"No," said Liza almost inaudibly. "I had some tests."

"Oh, you had tests."

"Yeah." Liza shrugged her shoulders again inside the borrowed robe.

Nathalie took a deep breath and looked out the window; a cardinal, one stroke of red, at that moment alighted on the feeder. "Look there," said Nathalie, "a cardinal."

Liza looked.

"Have you been treated badly, Liza?"

"I don't know."

"Do you want to talk?"

"I don't think so."

"Is there anything you want me to do for you?"

"I thought maybe it might be all right if I stayed here for a few more days."

No, no, not the weekend, Nathalie kept herself from saying. She took a sip of tea. Her head felt too full. "When is your mother expecting you?"

"She doesn't know I might come."

"I thought she was expecting you."

"I haven't made up my mind yet."

"Are you going to call her? Do you want to call her from here? Do you want me to call her?"

Liza's eyes widened again. "Do you want me to go away, Nathalie?"

Nathalie rested her chin in her cupped hands and searched Liza's face, where shadows from the subdued daylight seemed to converge. The mouth hung open. Nathalie felt as if her own intelligence were beginning to falter.

"I'm tired," she said abruptly. "I've got a new baby."

"Yeah, that must be real tiring."

"It is."

"Do you want me to wash these dishes?"

Nathalie flicked her eyes over the two cups, the plate, the single bowl. "That would be very nice," she said to Liza, "especially as I think I hear Caro waking up."

"Sure," said Liza, "I don't mind."

"Liza, I wish you would get in touch with your mother. It's all right if you stay here a bit longer, but I think it would be a good idea if you planned your next step."

"Sure, Nathalie, I'll give her a call."

Good luck, thought Nathalie as she ran up the stairs toward the baby. At the landing she paused and brought her fist down on the newel post. Then she sat down on a step and lowered her forehead to her knees. From the other side of the nursery door came the now angry crying of the baby. Nathalie looked at her own long, capable fingers; she spread them on her knees and pressed their tips hard into the paint-splotched fabric. She slowed her breathing and pushed herself up.

"Baby," she said, opening the door to the red-faced infant, "hello, baby. Did you think nobody was at home?"

Her words in the sparely furnished room seemed loud and strained. The day was almost half over. Methodically, with her lips pressed together, Nathalie peeled sodden layers of cloth from the baby and the crib mattress. Yesterday at this time she had been making almost exactly the same motions, and the day before, almost the same.

In the doorway of the nursery, infant in her arms, she hesitated, listening, in limbo between the possible levels of the house. "Let's look over the attic," she whispered to Caro.

Here, beneath the slanted skylights of the altered dormers, a feasible space was gradually emerging. It was a pleasure simply to ascend to it. Nathalie's hands had been instrumental in every layer of the work. "First the insulation and then the vapor barrier and then the sheetrock and now the tape and the jointing compound," explained Nathalie as she walked about the room, jiggling the restive baby. "The drawing board will go here and the shelves there and the daybed over there, and then your mother can bring home work. What do you say? Say something, you funny baby." She nuzzled her face against the baby's neck. Caro began to cry again. "What? Hungry? Not so soon!"

She lifted her high in the air beneath one of the skylights and shook her gently; she sailed her back and forth, a baby flying, legs dangling, before a backdrop of fog. The crying mounted. "All right then," said Nathalie somewhat fiercely, "here we go again"—and she sank down into a soiled bean-bag chair, a remnant from her own apartment days, and pulled up her shirt—"here we go again—my God," and the baby attached itself to her with ravenous animal pushings. "My God," said Nathalie, closing her eyes, splaying her legs, giving way.

When the baby was finished and lay sated against her thighs, Nathalie bent to study the self-absorbed face. Milk, her milk, trembled on the lower lip; the eyes were half closed beneath the damp brow. Nathalie lapped the tails of her painting shirt over the tiny chest. The baby's breath caught and sighed. I have to stay alive, she thought simply; I have to stay alive long enough to take care of this child. In the air was an anticipatory silence.

Far below the telephone was ringing. "Now we have to answer the telephone," she said aloud. "First one thing and then another."

She reached it simultaneously with Liza. "I have it, thank you, Liza," said Nathalie from the bedroom.

"Sure," said Liza.

"Hello, you two," said Edward. "Hello, Liza. How are you today?"

"Oh, pretty good," said Liza.

"How are you, Nathalie?" he asked.

"Living," said Nathalie. "Right here."

"Say, Nathalie," put in Liza, "what does it mean when the washing machine thumps?"

"It means you should turn it off and rearrange the load. Right away."

"Oh. OK, sure," said Liza. "So I guess I'll hang up now. Nice talking to you, Edward."

"Right," said Edward. "Good to hear your voice."

"Bye, Nathalie," said Liza, "I'll hang up now."

"Right-o," said Nathalie. "Thanks."

"That's OK," said Liza. "Bye." There was a pause, a careful click.

"Well," said Edward, "that was a long conversation."

"Yes, there have been a number of words today."

"Anything definitive?"

"We will most likely have a guest for the weekend."

"Ah-ha," said Edward, as if he weren't completely listening. What were her plans for the evening? he wanted to know. Would it be possible for him to bring someone home to dinner? It was the guy he had mentioned to her last night, the one coming in from the West for an interview. A nice fellow, funny as all get out. She would enjoy him.

"Nathalie?" he said. "Are you there?"

Nathalie had stretched across the bed quilt with Caro on her chest. "Right here," she answered as she slipped her fingers beneath the baby's undershirt and lightly stroked the skin of her back, so smooth as scarcely to seem a barrier.

"This fellow John is a gem, you'll enjoy him. And he knows the rivers. He's been canoeing on some of my old trips."

"Another westerner," said Nathalie.

"He's six-four," said Edward. "You should see him."

"Then we'll need a lot of food."

Edward laughed. "Could you shop? I'll get home in time to help cook."

"All right," she said. "I'll go hunt down food."

"Terrific," said Edward and, hey, how was she anyway—and how was the twerp?

"She's right here on my heart," said Nathalie, "twenty-two inches long, visible to the naked eye, undeniable."

"You sound tired. Could you nap?"

"I should take lessons from Liza and Caro."

"That's a thought," said Edward, but now his attention seemed to have shifted again. She was in a room, on a bed, beneath the delicate, piercing weight of a child whose pulse and breath seemed indistinguishable from her own.

"So," said Edward, "I guess that's all. I'm making good progress today on those slides."

"That's good," she said.

"But I'm having more of that same trouble with Maynard. He's throwing his weight around like crazy. I don't know if it's worth it to put up with the politics around here."

"Isn't there enough glory to go around?"

"In a certain light there is. Depends on the point of view."

"I'm sorry you have to deal with that."

"Right. Who needs it?" Edward sighed. "So much for pure research." Then his voice picked up energy again. " 'Tis but the drama of folly. I'll survive."

Nathalie lay still. She could hear Liza thudding up the basement stairs; otherwise nothing seemed to be moving.

"Edward, I've got to get out for some air. I'll pick up food."

"Right. I'll get home as soon as I can." He paused, as if thoughts were crowding his speech.

She closed her eyes and saw him leaning against the refrigerator in the cluttered office he shared with Maynard; his sleeves would be rolled up; perhaps he would be scratching his chest, or holding a photographic blow-up at arm's length, or running his fingers through his hair. A peacock turned and directed its unwieldly beauty down a rhododendron path. There was a sinking inside the world, then a lifting.

"Edward, I'm falling asleep."

"Go ahead and sleep."

"I'll try to later when Caro takes her real nap."

"Kiss her for me."

"Done. Bye."

"Bye-bye. Nathalie?"

"Edward?"

"No, nothing, I'll tell you later." Now their voices were disconnected.

"Caro," she said, cupping the nearly bald skull with her hand.

"Liza?" she called a few minutes later into the kitchen and then down the stairwell to the basement. "Liza, I'm going to the store. What are your plans? What? I can't hear you. Wait a minute, I'll come down."

With the baby on her hip she went halfway down the steps and found Liza, still dressed in the blue bathrobe, sitting cross-legged on the table in front of the washing machine and reading from a pile of old magazines.

"I'm going to the store," said Nathalie. "Are the machines behaving for you?"

"Pretty good, I guess." Liza stretched and lifted a cascade of hair away from her face.

"You're doing a total cleanup today, aren't you?" asked Nathalie.

"Really. Soap and water, you know, Nathalie?" She gestured to the machine. "Wow."

"Right," said Nathalie. "Nothing like it. So, what are your plans for today, I mean after your clothes are clean?"

"Today? Oh, I'll be going out, don't worry."

"I'm not worried. I mean, you don't have to go out. Look, Liza, why don't you stay here? Or come back for dinner at least. Edward is bringing a fellow over tonight. We'll have a party."

"Oh, that's all right, Nathalie, I won't bother you."

"Liza," said Nathalie slowly, distinctly, hearing her own voice and not yet knowing who this person was, speaking patiently, a baby slung on her hip, "I would like you to be here tonight. I would like you to come home by six o'clock and be here for the evening."

"Yeah?" Liza looked questioningly across the laundry room.

"Yes," said Nathalie. "Definitely by six o'clock, if not before. You can help us cook."

"I could do that, I guess."

"Yes, you could. We'll see you then."

"I'll try to make it."

"Liza, I'm not saying *try to,* I'm saying *do."* Her voice rose slightly. "If you're going to continue to camp out here, then I feel Edward and I ought to be able to say something about what sort of schedule you keep."

"Shall I go away? Do you want me to leave?"

"Liza, the point right now is that I want you here by six o'clock tonight. Tomorrow we'll talk about the rest of it."

Liza had crossed her arms over her chest; her hair fell forwards.

"Liza? All right?"

Liza nodded but kept her head lowered.

The washing machine shifted to a new phase, and water gushed into the scrubbing sink. "Liza?" The person holding the baby now went the rest of the way down the stairs and crossed the room and put her hand on Liza's shoulder.

"Liza? What I'm saying is that I've been thinking about you. Will you please come home tonight?"

Liza covered her face with her hands.

"Do you want to talk?" asked Nathalie. "Come on, let's go upstairs and sit down. Come on." She put an arm around Liza's back.

Liza stayed where she was, but she looked at Nathalie through tears.

"Shall I talk?" said Nathalie. "Do you want me to stand here and tell you what I think? I think you should be where you can get some guidance, I mean month after month. Why aren't you in school? Last time I saw you weren't you in school? Weren't you doing some lovely weaving?"

"I've never gone to a school that was any good," said Liza, half crying.

"Even when you were little?"

"Fifth grade was OK. I liked fifth grade."

Nathalie shifted the baby to her shoulder. If she didn't leave for the store now, Caro might be crying before she could get her home. "You liked fifth grade? I did too. How about high school?"

"Pretty bad."

"And college? You had at least a year, I know."

Liza shrugged. "It was messed up."

"The school was?"

Liza's expression flared up again. "Yeah, Nathalie, even the school was messed up. It was running out of money and the teachers were quitting and most of the time we hardly even had classes, just a lot of meetings. A great big mess."

Nathalie was kissing the downy head of her baby, kissing and tasting and smelling, her body swaying. "I'm sorry," she said.

"Well, it's not as if it's your fault," said Liza.

"Look here, Liza, why don't you put on some clothes and walk to the store with me? We can talk."

"I can't," said Liza with a flash of triumph. "All my things are in the washing machine."

Gypsy layers of cloth, never for a moment still, floated across Nathalie's mind. "Ah, so they are. All right then," she said, more quickly than she intended, and escaped up the stairs, through the empty kitchen, the hallway. The living room was still darkened, the bed unfolded. "Oh, for goodness' sake!" she exclaimed and strode across the room to jerk open the blinds behind the deprived plants. Her heart was pounding.

"What's the matter with me?" she said to Caro in the crook of her arm. "I can't do anything right with that girl."

Silent, Caro watched with large eyes as light from one window after another was let into the room.

"Baby," said Nathalie more calmly, holding her close and swaying in front of the window. "What shall I do?" she whispered, her cheek resting on the baby's head. "What shall I do?" she began to sing softly to a tune that seemed to come from nowhere.

She was still humming as she emerged from the house a

few minutes later, the baby strapped to her chest in a canvas pouch, and as she glanced back from the curving walk to the ice-hung eaves and drooping pine tree, she knew it was Liza's tune that had come to her, the song from the shower. "Well, she's getting to me, all right," she said aloud to the dense air.

Shifting the weight of the baby slightly, she set off with her usual rhythmic, long-legged stride and deep, measured breaths to the market. It wasn't really so cold; isolated drippings could even be heard here and there, as if the crust of winter were prickling open. The damp air felt good on her cheeks.

On the bridge at the foot of the hill she paused and searched the thicketed banks for signs of change. There were yesterday's snow and ice-clotted bushes, today's mist, and this new percolating hint of thaw. It would have done Liza good to come along on the walk, but then it was probably doing her good to be at home performing those lengthy water rites. Nathalie stared down on a darkish opening in the snow that looked as if a small animal had been creeping in and out.

Caro was already making restless snufflings inside the pouch. "Yes, yes," said Nathalie, "It won't be long now," and as she walked on humming to the baby, she began mentally to put together a menu. Usually she was a marvel at planning anything. She saw ahead; she selected; she arranged. Things almost always turned out well under her hands. The feast—fish, new potatoes, small carrots, salad, some sort of fruit dessert—in its accomplished state already had begun to gleam in her mind. Now all she had to do was breeze along through the stores.

"Hush, hush," she said to Caro, "it's not nearly time for you to be hungry." The face in the blue hood was now red with distress and the body pushed against her own.

In the fish store Nathalie drummed her fingers against the glass case and could not make a decision. The fish woman with the cloudy eye suggested sole and lifted limp pieces to the scale.

"Fine," said Nathalie, "perfect," and she hurried on with her package to the fruit and vegetable market. Caro was crying loudly.

"Time for his feed," commented the proprietress.

"Not exactly," said Nathalie.

"Must be colic then."

"Colic?" said Nathalie.

"Three of mine were like that. I'll tell you, I wouldn't want them days again." With her thick hands the woman packed carrots and greens, lemons and grapefruit into the net bag.

"Well, good luck," she said to Nathalie. "Can you carry this? You've got yourself a load now."

"I'll be all right," said Nathalie as she hung the groceries from her shoulder.

"Pretty soon he'll be too big for that pack."

"She," corrected Nathalie, rather loudly. "The baby is a girl."

"She's big for her size. Oh, listen to that, mother, she's getting mad."

"Yes," said Nathalie, "I'll hurry along now."

Outside she stopped to adjust the weights that hung from her. "Hush," she said, "hush." By the time she was climbing the hill to home, she felt numbed from the baby's almost incessant crying and her own tiredness.

The blinds in the living room had been closed again and what appeared to be the humped form of Liza lay beneath a disorderly mound of blankets. In the kitchen peanut butter and jelly jars sat open on the counter beside an opened magazine. The water faucet dripped. Nathalie, still dressed in her winter jacket, the baby strapped to her chest, stooped in front of the refrigerator to put away the groceries. She stood, dizzy. Across the room the breakfast table seemed remote. She felt taken aback by this strange, hourless midday.

At first Caro seemed eager to nurse, but then she twisted away and began again to cry. "Hush-a-baby," said Nathalie, "now stop, now stop. That's enough," but the crying did not stop. Nathalie paced the braided nursery rug. Exactly below, Liza was asleep or perhaps pretending to sleep. Pine tree and oak outside the nursery window were motionless in the somber light.

"Hush, hush, my little baby," she sang. The monotonous crying had no direction. Little mallet blows of sound beat into Nathalie's mind, holding her in place. She didn't know what to do.

"Stop it now," she said, no longer singing. She lifted the baby in the air and shook her gently and then not so gently. "Stop, stop, stop," she said, "this is ridiculous."

Caro now weighed eleven and one-half pounds. Her eyes, squeezed together, did not seem to see anything, even Nathalie. The veins in the small neck and forehead protruded. Her delicate fingers were splayed out rigidly in the air, as if she were an amphibian in the midst of a leap.

Nathalie caught her down tightly to her chest. If she could, she would have swallowed her, to keep her quiet, to keep her safe.

She laid the baby down and undressed her and put on a clean diaper and then she carried her down the hallway and plopped the screaming, nearly naked form in the middle of the big bed. Then she took off all her own clothes, leaving them where they fell, and opened the covers and drew the baby in against her skin. Nathalie pulled the covers high up over their heads until they were in a soft cave. Caro's angry feet beat against her belly.

"Do you want milk?" whispered Nathalie. "Here." But this time as the baby twisted away from the suction of nursing, she kept the tip of the nipple between her gums.

The pain was intense; it went straight to Natalie's navel. She leaped out of bed. "That's it! That's enough!" she shouted down at the baby in the covers. For an instant only, Caro was startled into silence; then the crying resumed with fury. Naked, shaken, surprised at herself, Nathalie walked back and forth at the foot of the bed. "You're wasting a lot of time," she said. "Do you hear me? This is ridiculous." She crossed her arms across her chest and hunched her shoulders. "I've got a lot of other things I should be doing. Do you hear me?"

The chill of the room finally drove her back under the covers. "All right, this is it, baby." She rolled Caro over, curved her own body around and began to rub the small bare back. The shoulder blades, like unfinished wings, were scarcely the distance apart of Nathalie's forefinger. The baby made the tremendous effort again and again of rearing her head; finally the exhausted crying became muffled by the mattress.

Up the bumpy runnel of the back the mother's fingers traveled, up behind the ears, over the skull to the throbbing fontanel, back down the complicated topography of the spine, up and down. Nathalie closed her eyes. The crying continued, gradually at a distance. She herself was being drawn back into an earthly crevice, down past different realms of light, down to a deep glowing quarry, opened for her—was it possible?—by the birth of the baby. She thought she had been shown how to go to the heart, once and for all, if she could just remember the inward way, but now she began to ride higher up on a sea of sleep, salty, noisy, agitated, which suddenly gave way to a new phase, smooth, like the calmest water, easy to navigate, quiet.

When she woke, the room was nearly dark and Caro was stirring. "Here," she whispered and adjusted their bodies until the baby could nurse. For a while there was no other sound. Nathalie lay still, because of the baby, and because she felt there was something she might remember if she could be still enough.

The front door slammed; voices were in the downstairs hallway: Edward's voice, the voice of the guest, Liza's voice. Nathalie began to smile. Now in what disheveled state, exactly, had Liza been found?

Nathalie stretched, yawned comfortably, propped the baby up beside her to be burped, and felt no desire to move an inch from this fullness. The evening could go ahead quite well without her or, if it chose, come and circle around her in this place.

The voices, however, continued on through the downstairs hallway to the kitchen. There was laughter, even Liza's. The sound carried energy, shape, rising and falling, sometimes merging. Water was turned on; ice trays rattled. In her childhood she had often listened like this, from one room into another, in anticipation. Now she was on the verge of getting up.

The voice of Edward separated itself; his footsteps rose, entered; the bedside light was turned on; he was present. "Here you are!" he said.

"Here I am."

He lifted the covers. "What's this I see—flesh?"

"Flesh."

He slid in beside them. "It is a pleasure to find you like this."

"We slept."

He pressed himself close and drew a shirted arm over both her and the baby. "I feel overdressed."

"I like you any way. What's going on downstairs?"

"I've put them to work."

"What about Liza—is she presentable?"

"She has her outfit on, yes. She looks better tonight. What did you do for her today?"

"Nothing, I've done nothing all day long."

"True?"

"No, untrue. Plenty of nothing, I don't know. What time is it?"

He kissed her. "I wish it were ten o'clock and everyone else were in bed."

"But it's not."

"We could pretend."

"All right. The cows have been milked, the ship is moored, the town is quiet."

"And here we are, kissing and keeping the world safe."

"Is that true?"

"Absolutely."

"How do you know?"

"My research for the day," he said. "I know, I know." He lifted the baby over to his own chest. "Now then, kid, what do you have to tell us tonight?"

Caro arched her back and threshed with arms and legs as if she were swimming in place, fastened to her father at her navel. She made sounds; she smiled; she drooled. "Wonderful," said Edward. "Now what else?"

The baby squealed, then growled.

"Listen, will you?" he said proudly. "Has she ever done that before?"

"Not exactly. Actually, today she has been crying quite a bit."

"Crying? Why crying?" demanded Edward of the baby, rocking her on his chest. "Why crying?" He burrowed his face into her.

Nathalie lay on her side. With one eye she saw two close head shapes in the lamplight, an almost abstract eyeful of loving, and she, too, must be held within the pale of light, she thought. Downstairs dinner was being cooked by strangers, or near strangers. A year ago she and Edward had only just met, at the arboretum, on cross-country skis, one bright Sunday of new snow. . . .

"Edward, we should go downstairs and be with our guests."

"That's right," he answered, without moving.

"What about poor Liza?"

"Poor Liza seemed to be having a fine time making a salad. John is scraping carrots."

"But then what?"

He sighed contentedly. "Then I suppose we must appear." He flourished the baby at arm's length above him. "And the wine will be opened and we will eat and drink to happiness."

Instantly, with a surge of good feeling, Nathalie stretched her body in a long, flat-bellied twist. "Ah!" she exclaimed. "I've had a good nap."

Edward put the baby to bed, but as it turned out, the baby did not want to be put to bed. Nathalie had no sooner dressed and made her kitchen entrance and begun laying out fish fillets than the message from upstairs became acute. Nathalie paused, her fingers wet.

"This must be a new stage," she said. "Where has my good little girl gone?"

"I'll go get her, shall I?" offered Liza. The blue bathrobe had been replaced by a long cotton skirt and a blouse, now clean but unironed, and the same quilted vest. She had brushed back her hair. Her cheeks were flushed.

"Wonderful," said Nathalie. "Would you please?"

Edward stood beside Nathalie slicing lemons; their shoulders brushed; close together, their hands skimmed and touched down over the variously colored food.

In front of them John paced before the island counter, talking, gesticulating, lifting and eating on the spot shreds of lettuce from the salad. He was indeed as tall as Edward had described, lean, bearded, younger than she had imagined, energetically jolly. "We were flown and then it was downstream all the way," he continued. "Man alive, the fishing was incredible."

"Much whitewater?" asked Edward.

"Enough to give us something to brag about. What a trip."

"Here," said Nathalie, handing him a knife, "why don't you slice the bread."

"I've been eyeing that loaf," said John. "If you think I haven't eaten all day, you're right. Too busy." He sliced off the heel of the loaf and stuffed it into his mouth. "You've got a great place here. I like old houses. How is it having a kid? One of these days I might get married and have a kid."

"So far having a kid is different around every bend, and you never know when the whitewater is coming," said Edward.

Nathalie laughed. Glancing up, she saw the bright nucleus of the room reflected in the new windows opposite; in motion were herself, Edward, the tall guest, and now here came Liza, carrying a surprising length of baby on her shoulder; it looked as if the little one had grown even in the last hour. The house, for a time, held them all.

"Shall I take her?" asked Nathalie, wiping her hands.

"Oh, that's all right, Nathalie. I haven't had her much."

Nathalie's eyes grew larger; she turned and slid the fish into the oven; she straightened up, a woman who had lived a certain number of years, who was now cooking food in a warmly lit room of younger people. She no longer knew how to begin to measure herself, she thought, or anyone.

When the baby had been newly born, she had been placed for a few moments on Nathalie's abdomen and, feeling the new weight, Nathalie had raised her head and marveled with some shock that this complete and thrusting creature, still umbilically connected but now with a once-vital layer of nature's protection withdrawn, had actually been carried inside her body; there couldn't have been space for all of that, she had felt, and what had been set in motion seemed then, as now, larger than she had known she had room for.

Edward had begun, with ceremonial flourishes, to open the wine.

"This bread," said John, "is absolutely fabulous. I could eat the loaf."

"Are your parents still living out West?" she asked.

"Nope," he answered, his mouth still full. "They died ten years ago. One day they were there"—he waved his hands—"and the next day they weren't. A small plane went down."

"Oh, I'm so sorry," said Nathalie.

Liza come closer with the baby. "What did you do then?" she asked.

"Then I lived with my uncle's family."

"Were they nice to you?" Liza pressed on.

"Oh, they were all right," he answered, "but what really made the difference was a biology teacher I had. He got me started."

"Like what do you mean?" asked Liza. She shifted the baby casually, expertly, to the crook of her arm.

"Nathalie?" said Edward, nudging her hand. "Wine?"

She accepted the glass and found him smiling at her, one smile at the forefront of countless others; a smile it had been a year ago that had looped her in and stayed her heart where it could freely grow.

"I mean," said John, "that he knew where he was and he could open the door for others. It didn't take much, just a few words here and there."

"You were lucky," said Liza.

"Something just clicked and off I went."

By now the baking fish had begun to yield up its fragrances of deep seas and melting butter. Nathalie tested the carrots and potatoes that steamed on top of the stove, earth scents. From behind her came the unfretful baby sounds, gurglings, blowings, then testings in a higher register. Each of the other voices had its own compass, within which it ranged experimentally. Sounds lifted off into thin air.

She turned. It was delicious how light she felt, how spacious.

"Liza," she said, "listen to how happy the baby is with you."

BOILING RIVER

The graffiti were scrawled and multicolored, from pens and pencils of various sorts, makeup sticks, maybe even blood. Anne peered at one brownish-red name, THELMA. Near the mirror a smaller, penciled message read DIANE LOVES GOD; a trucker's wife she might have been, one of those who takes turns with him driving and sleeping, this woman in a double rapture. FUCK ME had been lettered with another hurried hand on the mirror itself in a lipstick that was almost purple.

A volley of male laughter collided with her emergence from the ladies' room, in a gas station somewhere near Cheyenne was all Anne knew. She had been asleep in the car, having given in at last to those uncharted regions when the maps on her lap began to blur, only waking as Tony had tried to ease himself out from under her head. She had looked up and seen a line of gas pumps and a pickup with three dusty, wind-whipped children in the back, holding back a brown dog, which had been barking at something, straining to get up and over the battered metal edge. Then the man in the driver's seat had yelled a few harsh words, the truck had pulled away fast, and all four of them, the children and the dog, had fallen back and out of sight, where she hoped there had been straw or blankets or something.

The laughing men, Tony among them, were in front of the cash register. Embarrassed, she glanced at the front of her blouse and then at the back of her jeans and at her shoes. Four days only they had been married, and there was no map for this territory either.

Away from the men was a doorway to which she stepped, waiting out the guffaws. Before her was a garage with an oil-stained dirt floor, littered with equipment, and a broad outer opening that gave onto land that was here too high and dry to be called prairie at all. That belonged to yesterday, to Nebraska, to the sweet grasses and Russian olive trees and to the moment in the state capital in the quiet center of the prairie wind, when she had paid secret homage to a calm bust of Willa Cather, who had said that the history of every country begins in the heart of a man or a woman.

No one was at work in the unlit garage; only a small bird at the far bright opening seemed caught in a fluttering between inside and outside. "Yessir, there are strange talents in these here parts," said one voice behind her, and the laughter burst out again. When it had subsided, Anne turned toward the group, a knot of smoke and hats and shirts under an animal's head mounted on the wall, a large rabbit, it looked like, but with antlers. Tony, no hat on his curly hair, was reaching out for his change, and when they were back in the car it would be her job to write down the expenditure in a new small notebook. She went straight for him because he was her entrance into this knot; once beside him, she took a long look up at the antlered head, with its short gray fur that grew in sworls here and there and its glass eyes.

"Bet you've never seen a jackalope before, little lady," said the man at the register. When she said no, she hadn't, a few of the men sniggered, but by now the group was dispersing and the joke, whatever it had been, had lost its force. On the way out she noticed a worn chair and a shelf of paperback books beside the front window, a smudged sign tacked onto the case that read TRUCKERS LIBRARY TAKE ONE LEAVE ONE, and, beyond that, down at the end of the room in a dark alcove, a couple of teenage boys in western hats, playing high-beeping video war games.

Outside in the June morning they bent step by step into the strong wind, into the west, where a crescent moon was still faintly visible. For an instant it seemed to her possible that she could rise from her toes with the wind and return lightly to earth. Tony was now pulling her close with an arm around her waist, drawing her along with him exuberantly.

"So what about the jackalope?" she asked when they were out of the wind. Tony started up the motor with an extra roaring, laughing to himself, and she gave his shoulder a punch, starting to laugh herself, and said, "It's your job to tell me."

"Why, a jackalope is what comes of a jack rabbit mating with an antelope, of course."

"Really?"

"You've never seen one before?" He was turned from her now, gauging his mergence onto the interstate. He had a fine, imposing head, with dark hair in tight curls, a head that had first reminded her of old coins or sculptures, its most characteristic pose slightly tilted, and he often stood with his graceful body in an S-curve, which had impressed upon her when they met a strange, almost vexing familiarity. Her love for him, too, was almost like the longing of homesickness, but not the confused homesickness she had sometimes felt for Tennessee during her years away at college; it was more personal, more fateful. Recognition of it one rainy Wisconsin day last November had given her an extraordinary hour in a transformed world, where every last object for that brief time had reflected the dawning, unifying radiance of her knowledge. It was as if a solemn mark had been pressed on her forehead but then had penetrated out of sight, out of ordinary reach, so that now she would need to spend a lifetime in recollection of an ideal joy so serious and simple and elemental that it almost seemed unwarranted by their two elaborately youthful selves.

"That's impossible," she finally pronounced. "In order to do that a rabbit would have to be a super-jack."

At this Tony whooped and pounded the steering wheel, saying, "I love it, I love it!"

It had happened again: she had been had; she folded her arms across her chest and kept her eyes straight ahead upon the reddish, sparsely vegetated onrush of Wyoming. With Tony, she never knew when the joke might be on her.

"Tell me one thing," she said. "Did you tell those men we had just gotten married?"

"No, of course not. Certainly not. Why would I do that?"

"What was all that laughing about?"

"Hell," he said, "it was just a dirty joke, not something that even bears repeating, and not something that touches us, all right? Those men were just tired of driving."

Anne heard the laughter all over again. She looked behind her at the empty back seat of the car and the receding highway.

"Hey," said Tony, placing a firm hand on her knee, "we're together now, remember."

"I know that," she said. She took out the black notebook and asked how much the gas was. Her numbers were small and careful markings. Outside, the landscape rose and fell around them as they wound between reddish mesas through grassland where this year's new green had not yet overtaken the old colors of sereness. The grass grew in clumps; between them was just earth. Every now and then would appear a cluster of buildings, a node of habitation. "Winter out here would really be something," she remarked.

"I wonder how close we are to the missile sites."

"Are they really here?" she said. "It's hard to imagine them."

"They're here, all right. We're on top of a time bomb." His jaw as he spoke tightened and jutted. "There is probably enough stored in these very silos to vaporize all of us. One hour is about all it would take, I've heard. And computers could do it all, the whole shebang."

"How can you talk about it in that tone of voice?"

"What tone am I using?"

"Objective. Informed." She turned sideways in her seat to scrutinize him. He had tricked her with that silly jackalope business, and now she felt the need to argue, to right a balance. From deep inside she listened to the two of them skirmishing, maneuvering, and it almost frightened her how young they seemed, how ordinary. "But you don't *look* objective," she continued. "You look emotional. Your jaw looks emotional."

"I try to think straight," said Tony. "I try to save my emotions for the appropriate things."

"And what is it appropriate to be emotional about?"

"You." He laughed. "You and you and you."

"You'd be a psychological cripple if you really meant what you were saying."

"Listen," he said. "Seriously. First of all you have to look calmly. If you start reacting to something right away, you'll never get the facts straight. Don't you agree?"

"Yes and no. With something like nuclear war, I think maybe it's better to start with as much horror and disgust as you can bear and then let everything you find out factually be colored by your feelings. I mean, facts can be manipulated, but the heart can't."

"Hmm," he said. "Let me think about that a minute."

"I hear these politicians and bureaucrats talking about

strengths and weaknesses until I want to scream. War is war, right? It is a dishonor and a shame, and anything that fuels it, even verbally, is a dishonor and a shame."

"All war?" asked Tony calmly.

"Yes, all war." By now her cheeks were burning. She had a strong desire to punch Tony in the shoulder again or to sink her teeth into him. The light on the hood of the car looked harsh and unrelenting, and you couldn't argue with it any more than you could argue with the tumbleweed that rolled and bounced across the highway and up against a fence. There were tears in her eyes, and it seemed to her that the world had always been and would always be out of balance. Armies rose up from the grassland, relentlessly.

Then she forgot about talking to Tony because one of the warriors was coming home. He had come home before; he had come home again and again in the refuge of her imagination where for as long as she could remember she had tried on life as one might try on garments. The warrior was an adventurer, an Odysseus, a leader of mythical proportion; she too was the best of her sex, an essence materialized. On the bed she had prepared, a platform built into the landing of a gigantic castle stairway—below was water for bathing in a torch-lit grotto; above was the great hall, hung with silk, the air pierced by birds—on this bed were heaped the finest of the blankets she had woven, miracles of lightness and warmth. The embraces of this epic couple were also miracles, for through them, over and over again, the world was woven back together.

It was an old story, which had become her own. Anne's face grew even warmer as she contemplated the honed and silky gestures that passed between these lovers.

"Sleepy again?" asked Tony.

She looked at him without speaking. Her imagination at this moment seemed as much a betrayal as an instruction. Hero and heroine he and she were not—no, most certainly not. She took a deep breath.

"Well?" asked Tony. He was unwrapping a stick of chewing gum with one hand. "You know, it's funny how you can get all warmed up on some subject and then just let it drift off into nothing."

"Is it?" She was barely able to speak. She felt almost fainthearted to think how with each other they might be forced to fight for their lives, word by word, touch by touch. Old, very old, was how she felt, thinking of how young she was.

West of Cody that night in the dusk of the mountains they had a flat tire while Anne was driving. "Oh, I'm sorry!" she exclaimed.

"Shit!" said Tony, and he got out and slammed the car door.

Anne's hands were still shaking on the wheel. They were on a narrow shoulder of road at the base of a dark, forested mountainside. In near silence they had been traveling, both of them now very tired.

The air she stepped into was as cold as cold water, and it was full of the sound of water, the rushing of the swollen Shoshone, which they had been following for miles, on the other side of the road. The trouble was with the right rear wheel. She took up the flashlight and aimed it as Tony fitted in the jack and pried off the hubcap. Without a word, she hunkered beside him, shivering, holding out the cap like a dish for the nuts. A few cars went by, but not many. For the last hour the road had been climbing, and there would be snow in Sylvan Pass, they had heard, almost three feet of it left from the heavy winter.

"Damn." Tony grunted as he struggled with a tight nut.

"Damn it!" he exclaimed when he had taken all the luggage from the trunk and discovered that the spare, too, was flat. "How in the hell did that happen?" In disgust he flung the tire down on the rock shoulder.

She pressed her lips together and said nothing. A car climbed past them but did not stop. The sky still held a little light. In silence she began to help him put all the luggage back in the trunk. Their bodies worked closely together, meshing without touching. She was aware of everything he did, as if she were developing a new sense just for that purpose, to be aware of him.

"What a mess," he said. "Who needs it."

All this while the constant tone of the river had been going steadily through her.

"There was a gas station at that motel some ways back, wasn't there?" he asked.

"I'm pretty sure," she answered.

"I could take one of the tires and hitch a ride and get them to fix it and bring me back." She had stuffed her hands up the sleeves of her wool jacket as he scrutinized her. "But what are we going to do about you?" he continued. "I don't like taking you with me, and I don't like leaving you here."

"Do you realize this is our First Flat Tire?" she said.

"I suppose you'd like me to have it bronzed."

"Sure. We could use it for a front-yard planter."

"You're some kid," he said, suddenly in better spirits, lifting her off her feet. "You'd better come with me and keep me out of trouble."

They put one of the tires back on the car, lowered the jack and locked it away, and then ran across the road with a tire and the flashlight to wave down a car. Below them the Shoshone silvered the last of the light. She realized she was happy to be standing beside Tony in the middle of nowhere, waiting for car lights to come around a bend.

"This isn't exactly what I had in mind for tonight," said Tony.

"It's all right," she said. "I like it."

"You're shaking all over."

"I'm not really cold," she said. "It's just excitement. Maybe I'm frightened."

Their hitched ride, as it turned out, was both innocuous and dreadful. Using their new passengers as an audience, a man and a woman continued an argument that seemed merely a recrudescence of a chronic, vitiating dispute. Tony had wedged the tire between the seats and was now sitting close to Anne. They held hands, breathed a foulness of cigarette smoke, and were forced to witness the petty feud, which they themselves several hours later in bed, in a giddiness of fatigue and the relief of being moored for the night at last, began to mimic.

"Seven hours is much longer than it took last time," said Tony in a false voice.

"It isn't," she fired back at him, overenunciating each word. "If my memory serves me correctly—and it almost always does—it took us at least this long, and that is why I wanted to leave earlier today."

"No, it was longer this time," intoned Tony, "much longer. Last time we ate dinner in Cody."

"I don't know where your mind was, my dear," she said. She lit up an imaginary cigarette and blew the smoke into his face. "Last time we ate dinner at the Lake Hotel. I remember distinctly. I had the trout."

"My bride," said Tony to the imaginary passengers, who had been themselves, "is a college graduate, unlike myself, but whether she knows it or not, it is still possible for her to make mistakes."

They were sitting side by side in bed with the remains of a picnic supper in their laps: apple peelings, cheese rind, half a bag of sunflower seeds and raisins, a carton of milk. Under the covers she crossed a bare leg over his and said in a saddened voice. "That was the strangest part to me, Tony, how he called her his 'bride.' They must have been sixty."

"I've heard men say that before," he said. "I think it's meant as a chivalric expression."

"Chivalry, my foot. He was trying to humiliate her. They were trying to humiliate each other. Is there any milk left?" She drank from the quart carton and then lay back with a sigh and a kind of shuddering.

"What's that?" asked Tony. "What's all that shaking about?"

"I don't know. I'm not really cold." She turned her face into the pillow. She felt him gathering up the bits of food and paper and then returning with all his weight to the bed. She was falling and falling into the valley made by his body; roads and mountains slid through her mind; the journey still going on, the continual movement.

"Are you sleeping?" asked Tony. His hands were moving on her.

"No, I'm hearing you," she said, but what she was seeing were three dusty children, upset back into the bed of a truck, jounced off into an interior called Wyoming. The truck became nothing more than a distant point in space to her watchfulness, and yet at the same time she was one of the children, lying low to keep out of the wind, crying out beneath sheer velocity and enormity.

When she woke, time had passed, the light had been turned out, and Tony was asleep beside her. For a moment all was still in their room and in the corridor outside and above and below them in the old hotel on Yellowstone Lake and outside their window, at whose sill she had knelt after their midnight arrival, trying in the fresh blackness to make out lake and mountains. She touched his solid chest. They were together, at the moment almost as still as two mountain ranges: the royal pair, learning to take on a quality of mountains, together. But she had scarcely begun to sink into this thought when he woke and began shifting toward her, and though her arms were open, her body moving, she was still trying to embroider the ideal story.

Straight from sleep, tumescent, instinctive, he was traveling to meet her, and toward him she was also tending, arching, but an incompleteness was pulling her back, the need to go deeper before she could go forward.

"Wait," she said, but her word was like a single overpowered bird cry in the face of a tremendous sea. He kept moving.

She bit him, hard, on his left shoulder.

In an instant with a shout he had leaped from the bed and was standing at its foot, thoroughly alive, completely naked, as young as he would ever be again. The bed covers had been flung aside.

"I did it," she said.

"You're damn right you did!"

"I've never done that before."

"Well, how did you like it? My God!" He came back to the bed. "What did I do? Was I hurting you?"

"No, you weren't hurting me."

"You've got to promise not to do that again. What a shocker."

"I can't promise," she said. "I didn't know I was going to do it until I did it."

"My God," he said, suddenly laughing and clamping the palm of his hand over her mouth, "I've married a madwoman."

They began again, slowly, from the beginning.

"Do I need to gag you?" asked Tony.

"No," she answered sweetly. "I feel disarmed already. For the moment."

Gradually dawn was coming on, like an enormous slow breath of light that made the air look grainy, as if atoms themselves were being formed.

"Wait. Listen. Did you hear that?" asked Tony. "Stop moving." Still rooted in her, he reared up from her breast, and she made herself be still and watched his face and tried to hear what he was hearing. "Ducks," he said. "I think those are ducks taking off from the lake." His face was nearly ecstatic. "It's so incredibly quiet up here you can hear everything. I think that's the sound of their wings and feet on the surface of the water."

She listened into the new space of day and heard a swift flurring, fanning, slapping that made the whole unseen lake immediately more real; for an instant she felt who she and he were, their human position, their long task, and then without moving, without their needing to move, because what they wanted was as close as the next breath, deep pulsations released them into ineluctable connectedness.

The whole of that day passed over the lake, and of it they saw only what could be seen from the large windows of an old-fashioned room. The sky was nearly faultless, but they did not seem to feel—or at least did not express to each other—any lack in not standing clear beneath it. Several times from the depths of the old claw-footed bathtub, large enough for both of them, their private lake, they gazed up into framed azure for all the world as if they themselves, just as they were, made up an entire universe, a sufficiency.

They ate the rest of the apples, four of them, the remainder of seeds and raisins, and several cellophane packets of saltine crackers and melba toast Anne had filched from a Nebraska truck stop. Everyone on earth, she said, sitting in the open window wrapped in Tony's striped robe, everyone should have the opportunity to come, with a love, to such a room, high above a lake, with one pine tree almost within touching, and in the distance a ring of mountains still in snow. She gestured sweepingly with an apple core. Think of all those torrents of water melting off those heights, she said, all of it, all those processes going on without their help—they were doing nothing but staying in this room—and yet. . . .

And yet—what? asked Tony. He was shaking out the last of the sunflower seeds into his palm, even the gray seed dust from the bottom of the bag.

He wasn't to laugh at what she was about to say, she warned.

He? Laugh? He licked his palm, then sat up straight in imitation of a model child and promised that she could trust him, she could tell him anything.

She had the feeling, she said, that in their being together they were doing more than being together—did that make any sense? Clearly now in her mind emerged the heroic couple approaching their embrace, but she did not dare bring them to his attention, for surely they were laughable; even to her they were also laughable.

In what way? he asked.

Well, she said, she had this new feeling that the world depended on lovers, as if each time there was an act of love, all of nature was a little happier, a little more harmonious.

Walt Disney style? Tony wanted to know, and he whistled a happy trill and made his hands into friendly, hovering birds.

Never mind, she said. She bit her lips and looked out the window. Laughter and tears both seemed possible.

He apologized. He came over to the window and knelt beside her and put his head in her lap. She was good, he said; he felt her goodness, and he was sorry when he wasn't able to say the right things.

Good? *Good?* She pondered the word, with her eyes still on the mountains. She remembered how good it had felt to bite him, an eternity, though not so many hours ago. She was glad she had done it. No, she wasn't. Yes, she was.

"Bullshit," she said.

Hunger, finally, about six o'clock in the evening drove them out. It felt odd to put on clothes; strange, unsteadying to step out into a long public hallway, like passengers disembarking. In the old elevator, operated by a college girl only slightly younger than themselves, they were silent. A German family behind them were discussing something or other energetically. Tony stood with his hands clasped low in front of him, his eyes on the roof of the cage, his chin jutted self-consciously. Anne lowered her gaze. A slight flutter went through her, of anticipation or panic she couldn't say.

In the lobby Japanese was also being spoken. A string quartet played not far from the huge fireplace.

"That's real class," said Tony, and she felt embarrassed for both of them, as if they had left behind some important pieces of clothing. It seemed to her that they were both walking awkwardly, not knowing what to do with the newly attached extra feet and hands, which were, of course, each other.

"Two," said Tony to the hostess, but it was clear to Anne as they made their way across the humming dining room that not two creatures but rather a single, barely emerged, barely evolved, perhaps monstrous and doomed hybrid was about to be seated and fed.

She looked at Tony over the top of her menu and in a voice that deliberately took on the inflections of the unfortunate woman in the car the night before said, "I think I'll have the trout." At this they smiled at each other, then began to laugh, saved for the moment from their uncertainties, their own brief shared history affirmed.

Their exceptional hunger, too—and the reason for it—was a secret bond; surely they must be the hungriest people in the room; they were on the verge of being etherealized by emptiness. Soups and salads were placed before them, rolls, then on request more rolls, more butter, large baked potatoes, broiled fish, green peas, strawberry torte with whipped cream. "My goodness," said Anne at the end of it all, "I'm feeling very thick."

"We should walk," said Tony. "Let's go down the road and try to find that place where they rent out boats."

"I want to know something," said Anne when they were outside, taking a backward look from the end of the entrance drive at the yellow hotel in its setting of trees and lake and mountains. "Do you think we can really afford all these lodgings?"

"Brides are supposed to enjoy, not worry," said Tony.

"Answer me."

"The answer is yes and no, depending on how you look at it. You know our situation as well as I do. We decided to do this. We wanted it, right? Besides, there's something I haven't told you."

"Well, tell me, for heaven's sake."

"Your father gave me some more money just as we were leaving."

"He did? How much?"

"Three hundred dollars."

"Three hundred dollars! Buy why didn't you tell me?"

"I don't know. Maybe I was waiting for the time when you would start frowning and asking me if we could really afford this trip."

"Am I frowning? I must look awful. But you should tell me these things."

Suddenly she stopped beside the road and stamped her foot.

"Damn it, I'm not a child. I don't like this: my father gives *you* money and neither of you says a word to me. What do you think that makes me feel like?"

"He was just trying to be nice to both of us."

"Then why didn't you tell me so I could start feeling good?"

"I don't know."

"Listen," she said. "Do you know how emotional I feel? I feel so emotional that I am also thinking very, very hard. Do you know what happens in India sometimes?"

"No, what happens in India sometimes?"

"Listen carefully. Brides are sometimes murdered or driven to suicide, often by immolation, by their in-laws so that the son can marry again and get another dowry."

"What connection are you making? India is an impoverished country. A lot of people are desperate."

"A lot of people are desperate all over the world."

"I thought you liked India. I thought you said it was one of the most spiritual places in the world."

"Right. I'm just telling you this as an example of some of the absolutely awful attitudes that are rampant all over. Bride-burning is blatant, but there are innumerable subtler degrees of the same thing, which all boils down to using up another person for your own selfish ends."

"Now you listen to me," he said, and he sounded a little heated himself. "What you're saying isn't logical, it doesn't follow. Just because your father gives us a gift doesn't mean you're being sold off and it doesn't mean I'm about to use up the money and then conspire against you. That's trash. Where do you get these trashy ideas? This is a civilized country." He paused and then added dramatically, as if wanting to change the whole thing into a joke, "This is America."

"Ha, ha," she said, "very funny."

"What is this?" he asked, spreading out his hands. "What have I done? All I'm trying to do is get myself married and then get on back to medical school so I can grow up to be a responsible person."

She sighed. "We both have a lot we want to do, don't we?"

"You're damn right. We both have to think straight. Take you: if you're going to study history, then it seems to me you've got to think positively or otherwise you'll just get pulled into all the negative parts of the past. You could get lost." He swirled a forefinger to make a whirlpool of air in front of her nose. He brought his face in close to hers. "You could get lost in a fascination with wrongheadedness."

"I'm not pessimistic by nature," she said, straight into his eyes. "You know that. I'm only trying to point something out to you."

He backed away. "But why this gigantic complaint? Why this accusation?"

"But you're complaining too. You're complaining that I'm taking you away from your work."

"When did I say that? I'm doing what I want to do. I'm trying to do what you want, too. I don't want to be told that just because some guy in India is a dirty rat that implies I'm going to be. This is here. This is now."

"You're right," she said. "This is here and now."

He was shaking his head as if to clear it, and she felt sorry for both of them. They had walked a long way down the road without paying much attention to anything but the clamor of their own voices, rising and falling in the air in front of them like two contentious birds. Where they were was beautiful, she was ashamed to see: evergreen, spring green, lake blue, sky blue—all intensified by the evening sun of middle June.

She took a deep breath and said no more. She listened to their footsteps crunching through the pine needles and gravel on the edge of the road; she listened to their breathing. She thought about where she was, beside him, and then she began thinking about thinking.

"There's the fleet," exclaimed Tony when they came in sight of the harbor. "Would my father ever have a great time here! Let's reserve one for early in the morning. How early can you get up?"

"That depends on both of us." Even as she said the words there was a shifting in her mind, and now she was looking at the boats and thinking about desire, about her body and its journey, about the rumpled bed they had so recently quit.

"Come on," he said. "Let's see what they have." He caught up her hand and began to pull her along.

At the top of a flight of steps above the marina she sat down abruptly like an animal on its haunches, resisting commands.

"You go on down. I'm tired. I'll watch from here."

"But what shall I reserve for us?"

"Whatever you like." She clasped her arms around her knees and prepared to wait. As Tony shrugged and took off down the stairs, it seemed to her that he was glad to get away. She rested her chin on her knees. To tell the truth—to approach telling the truth—she thought there was something in her that was glad to see him go. She breathed her own breaths, slowly. Probably it was laughable how weak her legs felt at this moment; probably some day she would remember this and laugh at herself.

An exceptionally pretty young woman in a heavy sweater, her golden hair blowing loose, was just starting up the stairs from the dock as Tony approached the bottom. Anne saw him stop to ask the girl something. She pointed and then said a few things, holding back her hair at her forehead. Tony said something else. She said something. They both laughed. A small motorboat was just put-putting in from the opening of the bay. Both Tony and the girl turned to look at it, and she pointed again, out toward the expansive lake. Her blowing hair was as fluid as if it were moving in water; it seemed to pick up all the light that was left in the day and send it out again shining and streaming into trees and water.

It was this sight, this image of extreme beauty, that came to Anne's mind when she found Tony's note the next morning, propped up in front of two of the oranges he had bought at the marina store the night before. He had taken the rest of the fruit with him, and the note said that she had been sleeping so soundly he hadn't had the heart to wake her, that he would be back before noon, and that he loved her and why didn't she take a walk? *Wish me luck,* he had written after his signature, and she stared at it and thought how he was the son of his father, the fishmonger.

She sat down on the edge of the bed and ate one of the oranges. From the window she could see a few boats on the lake, but of course it was impossible to tell who was in those boats. Then she got dressed. She changed her clothes twice before she finally went back to the sweater and jeans she had worn the night before. Her plain brown hair, too, was problematic. Up or down, it seemed to lack something.

"Pin it up so Daddy can take your picture," her mother had insisted only last week. "Get it up off your neck so we can see how much your bone structure is like Lucy's." And she had obliged. She had sat at the end of her mother's yellow and blue couch, turning her head this way and that at the directions of her father, the Judge, who was about to give his second daughter in marriage—his hands had been shaking slightly as he changed lenses—and when it was all over he had kissed her, first on the cheek and then on the nape of the neck. "There," her mother had said with a tone of finality. Celia and Caswell had come to stand arm and arm in the doorway. Even Lookout the dog had been watching. Of them all only she had been going away, again, this time across the country to Seattle; now she was on her way: here she was.

Tennessee was extremely far away. This country was huge. The lake they were on was very large, very high in the mountains. The hour, ten o'clock in the morning, was like no other ten o'clock she had ever known. She finished dressing, took some breakfast in the dining room, and then found a walking path by the lake. Who was there on earth who could tell her what to do now? From where she stood on the rocky ledge she could see across a curve of shore to one of the steaming thermal areas; it was just a taste of what was to come, she knew, deeper into the park.

The brilliance on the water was such that now and then one of the distant boats almost seemed dissolved by it. She squinted out over the surface until her eyes ached with the effort of wondering which of these bobbing, disappearing shapes contained Tony. A girl with long golden hair in a boat would probably be indistinguishable from sunlight, and from a boat it might or might not be possible to discern a figure on a high ledge, a person such as herself, standing straight, shielding her eyes. She stood straight and held inside a sickening dread. She stood so straight and so still that she thought it might be possible to die, right in that place, from the sheer desire not to have to move again. Then a thought came that for a moment gave her a thin, bitter, heady, defiant sense of invigoration. *If he's dumb enough to lose me, he's too stupid for me.* But this energy seemed false, artificial, a spur in the wrong direction for her; she stood straighter, even more still, shielding her eyes, aware that her stance was traditional, that of a woman waiting for a ship, but she bore it, she contained it, she endured what she imagined might even be shame, in order to explore the meaning of an ancient patience.

Instead, an extreme fatigue overcame her. Had she ever been this tired before? It seemed to take forever to make her way back to the hotel. Voices, languages, the universal sounds of children pressed around her in the lobby. She fainted down on the empty bed with the engulfing conviction that with this man, with this husband, she was coming upon happiness and pain such as she had never known before, such as she did not know she could endure. It was like falling in space, free-falling. A blackness took over.

"Are you all right?" Tony was asking.

"I've lost something," she said through her half-sleep.

"What do you mean?"

"What time is it?"

"Eleven, a little after."

"I thought I had lost more."

"Were you sleeping?"

"I don't know." He was sitting on the edge of the bed, and she could almost smell his energy. It was as if the air had become charged.

"My God, it's beautiful out there, Anne! I should have come back for you, but there I was, paying by the minute. But you could have slept in the boat. You'd have loved it."

"Were you alone?"

"Who would I be with?"

"Any fish?"

"No keepers. The little ones are too small, and the big ones you have to throw back for breeders. But I didn't mind. I really didn't mind. It was so incredibly beautiful."

His hand was absently lifting her hair from her forehead and smoothing it back; his words, though soothing, spoke of something that had happened only to him, that she could only imagine. She caught his warm hand in both of hers and brought it down where she could see it: long fingers, clipped nails, calluses, skin creases, new wedding ring. Simply to be touching him made her glad. She almost felt sheepish how glad she could be made how simply.

"You know, we've got to check out," he said. "Otherwise we'll have to pay for another day."

"We wouldn't want that, would we?" she said, still holding to his hand. She flattened her matching hand against his palm.

"Come on, rouse yourself. This afternoon we're supposed to be seeing the geysers, Old Faithful, all of that."

"The geysers? Old Faithful?" she repeated, her fingers now laced with his, holding tightly, playing, claiming.

He was laughing now. "What is on your mind, missus?"

She made her face wide-eyed, innocent. This game, she had not known she could play it; she had not known she would have to play it, this lighthearted game that was also a grave contest.

Suddenly she let go and began to sit up. "Yes, we have to pack. Instantly. The geysers must be seen. They must be seen to be believed."

Now he was the one to hold her. He was laughing and rocking her back and forth and saying over and over, in submission, "You and you and you."

But this person he was holding, what was being made of her? She felt an attenuation of her power, a stretching of herself over him, around him, around them both, a thinning of her former identity, and still this extreme fatigue. She could not shake it off, even while they rushed like the devil to get themselves packed and checked out. It was as if she had been drugged.

"Do you think there's something odd about the water here?" she asked Tony when they were in the car again.

"I think it's good. Why?"

"I just feel so dopey. I can't seem to wake up properly."

She looked at him, looking at her, and in his manner then, in his eyes, in the angles of his cheeks, in the questioning concern of his mouth there was a slight change; she felt it completely, something new from him dropping into her heart, a deeper note.

"I want you to be happy," he said. He reached out and touched her cheek.

She nodded, only knowing that she wanted to agree, to feel safer, to let down her struggle. He was driving in silence now. He didn't turn on the radio, or reach for his chewing gum, or begin to sing, as he often did, beating a rhythm on the steering wheel. She didn't open the black notebook to tally the last day, or spread out the maps, or rearrange anything in the car. They were both looking straight ahead as the road left the lake and wound through forest, higher and higher, until patches of snow appeared on the hillsides and then more snow and more snow. Anne opened her window to bring in more of the full, cold, percolating flavor of spring in the mountains. Twice they crossed the Continental Divide. Something new had sounded between them, which in the quiet they each might have been testing, testing. Every moment the topography changed. What was the exact moment, she asked herself, when they had become married? Had it been last November in the Madison streets, or in February in their first furtive rented bed, or in June in her parents' garden, or in St. Louis, or Kansas City, or Lincoln, or Ogallala, or last night, or an hour ago, or this instant, here, where the road was taking a downward turn and below appeared a steaming thermal valley, as strange as anything she had ever seen, a vision of a fuming earth, where they themselves, the new lovers, might make a difference, some little difference, or none at all.

"God, there it is," said Tony.

In their wooden room under the eaves in the old section of the inn, he sat down naked on a wooden chair and drew her to him. He held her by the hips as she stood in front of him, her hands resting lightly on his head, her eyes on the plumes and gushings of steam in the geyser basin beyond their window.

"Are you all right now?" he asked, his face persistently against her, nuzzling against a burgeoning heat, a swift, downward movement of her lifeblood, a fierce melting of her flesh. For an answer, she straddled him, and in the accelerating force of union she thought for an instant it might be possible to stay balanced together in a high awareness, securely possessed of exhilaration.

Downward they slid toward sleep, under sheets and blankets, the window open beside them, but what drifted in was not a mountain sweetness but an unsettling mixture of sulfurous vapors and sounds, human and inhuman. From a gathering of calls and shouts outside, a quickening of footsteps, a distant hissing, they knew they were missing the late afternoon display of Old Faithful.

"There she blows," murmured Tony unperturbably. "Too bad we're all cooped up here, isn't it?"

"Too bad, yes. We're lousy tourists." Her head was on his chest, one ear turned to his heart, the other catching the rush of outer life, and the dream she fell into was something like that: lovers in an enclosure, making connection but continually being threatened by a cacophony of public voices.

"Tell me a story," she said to him after dinner when they were following the boardwalk that threaded through the geyser basin. "Tell me something I don't know about you yet." With their next steps they entered an area of dense steam in which it would have been possible to disappear from one another in an instant. "This place is weird," she said as she caught hold of the back of his leather jacket.

"A story? All I've done is work, that's all there is to tell—school, my dad's market, college, now med school. It seems like all I know about is work."

"Then tell me a story about work." They were out of the steam now, but the dusk was so thick they could barely see down into the bubbling pools. "Let's sit on this bench. We can come back here tomorrow."

He sat bent with his elbows on his knees, his head hanging. "Have you ever cut up an animal?"

"A frog," she answered. "A rat. School things."

"I've cut up more than I've ever told anyone about. When I was in high school. I was working a lot for my dad, gutting pike and snapper and bass, filleting, chopping off heads, the works. We did a huge business. I got so good with the knife that he took me off sweeping and potato salad and the rest of it and just had me handling the shipments as they came in. Sometimes I even had to get up before school to go to work. There's a damn lot going on the customer never sees. Blood and guts."

He raked his fingers through his hair and looked up at her. "Then there came a day when I'd look at my mother and I wouldn't see a naked woman or anything like that, I'd see lungs and a heart and an intestinal tract and ovaries and a uterus. My father would bend over and I'd see kidneys and backbone and colon. It was like a new way of seeing, but I felt kind of nutty about it. I didn't know who to talk to. Some nights I couldn't sleep because I'd be thinking about my own body, what was going on, and what sleep was—could you see it if you looked—and what death was—could you make yourself die if you saw yourself dead. That sort of thing. I wanted to know what happens when the body goes from one state to another."

Suddenly he turned fully toward her, and she felt him draw his finger in a slitting motion quickly down the center of her throat and chest. "Like that," he said. "Quick as a whistle. First one condition and then another. Or else it's slow, like with my mother." He slumped back against the bench. "It was while she was dying—it was like sand going through an hourglass one grain at a time—that I started killing things. Hell, it was all like a dream, like a trance, and yet while I was doing it, it would be the sharpest, clearest thing that had ever happened to me. My uncle had a cabin outside of town in the moraines where I'd gone sometimes with the cousins, to ski and hunt and so on. I started going out at odd times, by myself. By this time my family was completely caught up in my mother's dying. It was what was happening to us, and there didn't seem to be much else that we talked about. My sister would sit with her boyfriend and my father in the front room, but I just got out; I couldn't take all that thickness. I thought they were missing something, but I didn't know what it was. I killed crows and squirrels and pheasants and took them apart organ by organ and bone by bone. I killed a yellow tomcat. I killed a female cat and found fetuses inside. I killed a raccoon. One day I killed a fox. I slit it open and took out all its parts and arranged them around the body in the snow, the way you take a machine apart, you know, so you won't lose anything important and you'll remember how to put everything back together again. I was working very slowly and methodically because I thought this might be the last animal for a while. Finally, I didn't know what to do with the hide. I knew it was worth something, but if I'd tried to sell it, then I would have lost part of my secret. So I put everything back inside the hide and wrapped it up and put it inside a hollow tree."

His hands as he spoke had dissected and arranged and wrapped and hid. Now he held them out in front of her. She took them both in her hands and began to stroke them.

"What did you find out, from all those animals?"

"I'm not sure. Here I am."

"And your mother died that year."

"Yes, the end of my senior year. April. But to me she had been asking for death, sort of calling it to her for way over a year. That's what I think. There was a failure somewhere. I don't understand it."

She rested her head on his shoulder. She had been so quiet that she felt like a container for his words.

"Don't you ever get like that," he said somewhat fiercely.

"Like what?"

"Like my mother. Don't you ever give up."

"That's not my idea. I didn't say yes so that I could end up saying no."

"I've got a long road," he said.

"We both do," she said, sitting up straight. Suddenly she felt irritated. The balance was off again. Something had to be done, or said, from her side. She poked him in the ribs. She got him in the place where he had been found to be most ticklish.

"Hey!" he said. "What are you doing?"

"Listen. Thanks for telling me that emotional story."

"What do you mean?"

"I mean that was a very, very emotional story."

"I just tried to tell it the way it happened."

"Thank you," she said. She leaned over and kissed him, provocatively, playfully.

"What are you doing!"

She kissed him again, surprised at herself, giddy. There was almost a danger, she thought, in kissing. It might look like a coming together, but it was really like taking life in your hands and trying to open it up, split it open, and then seeing how it might rearrange itself.

"What are you doing!" He laughed. He took her by the shoulders. "What are you thinking? When you get like this, I have no idea what you're thinking." He shook her shoulders.

She laughed outright, poised upon her own power, a dangerous moment. "Alive is the only way you'll ever get anything out of me," she taunted.

"That's awful! What a way to talk!" His hands dropped from her shoulders. "You make me feel like a monster."

As quickly as it had come, her bravado left her. She looked into his face and saw that what was asked of her was strength of a different kind. "I need to tell you something," she said. "You know the other morning, when you went fishing?"

"That was this morning," he corrected her.

"No, it couldn't have been."

"Yes, today is Thursday." He held up his hands and named the days since their wedding, six of them, and where they had stayed each night. "It's a good thing we have at least one historian in the family," he said, tapping his own chest.

"That's not fair," she said. "These days have been highly irregular."

"I'm sorry. Now tell me your story."

"Now I don't know if I can. You're such a bully—do you know that? Your tactics wear me out."

"My tactics? What tactics?"

"You're very competitive, you know."

"I have to be. I've had to be all my life. Just be glad I am."

She drew up her breath out of a well of patience she had not even known she had. Her body was trembling again. "This morning, then, when you went fishing . . ."

"And left you sleeping."

"And left me sleeping. I woke up and found you gone and do you know what I thought?" She searched his eyes. "I thought you had taken that blond girl out in the boat with you."

"What blond girl?"

"The one from the marina last night. The one you talked to on the steps. She was absolutely beautiful."

"Oh, that girl! There were some other pretty girls down there you didn't even see. At least six of them." He grinned at her and rested his arms on top of his head. "Luscious girls."

She got up from the bench and started walking away from him, back up the boardwalk, through steam and dusk, past bubblings and hissings, on heavy legs, her whole body gravid with fatigue and dismay. The softly lit inn ahead did not seem as if it could be her destination; a place like that belonged to people who knew how to talk and walk, who knew how to live and how to defend their lives. Out here was the place for her. She would wander until the earth swallowed her up.

"I want to ask you something," said Tony's voice, approaching from behind. "Have you ever had ideas like that before?"

"I don't think so."

He caught hold of her and stopped her. "I want you to take that idea out," he said. "It's trash. I want to put something else there instead." He kissed her. "Now listen. When I'm with you I feel I'm where I want to be, right at the center. I don't want to go anywhere else. I love you. No one was in that boat with me. That's not the way I want to behave."

She began to cry. "It's the way you tease me that I don't understand," she said. "And I'm so tired. I think I could die right here on the spot."

"No, you couldn't," he said sternly.

"I might. I just might."

"You tease me too."

"Not the way you tease me."

"I just don't take it the way you do. You know, maybe you think about yourself too much. Maybe you need more endurance."

"Tony!" She heard her voice wailing.

"I'm serious. Has anyone ever helped you to have endurance?"

"What are you talking about! I grew up, didn't I? I made it through four winters in Wisconsin. My father didn't think I'd last out the first one."

"That's what I'm talking about," said Tony. He started walking and drew her along with him.

"You men! I'll bet you've never had to wait for anyone in your life."

"I waited for you," he said, pulling her in close. "I think I must have been waiting a long, long time for you."

In the middle of that night she woke abruptly, as if by signal, but nothing untoward appeared to be happening, only the continuing and by now familiar strangeness of the sporadic geysers. She had to go to the bathroom, but for a few minutes she lay still, putting off the trek down the hallway. Tony was sleeping with the covers over his head, like a child. Finally, she made herself get up. She wrapped up in his robe, which she was finding she liked much better than the ruffled one her mother had given her, slid on her tennis shoes, took up the room key, and let herself out onto their balcony, two wooden stories up from the lobby, the whole interior illuminated to about half the brightness of the night before. Several clerks were talking softly at the desk below. The clock on the great stone chimney said half past three.

When she had come back from the water closet to the balcony area, she recognized in one of the armchairs a woman she had observed in the dining room the evening before, a woman of about forty with heavy long hair and remarkable eyes, large, brown, and urgent, and a set look to her mouth. In the dining room she had been sitting with a man and three half-grown children and another, younger woman, who had had a baby beside her in a high chair. The relationship between these people had not seemed clear. At this moment the woman was alone, wrapped in a plain white robe, her bare feet propped against one of the burled supports of the wooden railing. She was filing her nails.

She looked up as Anne crossed near her chair. "So. Another nonsleeper?" she asked.

"No, I've been sleeping," said Anne.

"Ah, very good. Sleep on, sleep on." The woman waved her nail file in the direction of the bank of rooms.

Anne hesitated.

"Well?" The woman waited, and Anne felt like a child who has been dismissed from a room but doesn't know how to make her exit. Then the woman's expression softened slightly, and her brown eyes looked even larger and seemed to float upon her face. "You should sleep when you have the chance. Don't think a thing about me."

Anne turned and walked in her loose tennis shoes to their room. She leaned against the inside of the door, trembling. Tony was burrowed into sleep, far away. She crossed the room and leaned into the open casement of the window. Alone, she leaned into the night. The steaming land was like a field after a battle, when the soldiers are gone and only smoke marks the place of ruination. But this was not ruination; this was just the earth, speaking from the inside out. Gradually her trembling diminished. This is where they found themselves; into this land, into this time they had appeared.

Mercy was what they needed, mercy and instruction. She said the words as she eased back into bed, into the shadow of her husband's body: have mercy on us, tell us. She drew herself in closer; she fused herself to his warmth. What, she wondered, was to be said through them, married together, that could not be said in any other way? Her question eased her mind, and for the rest of the night she slept more deeply than she had for weeks.

"Well, good-bye to fire and brimstone," said Tony the next day when they were leaving the geyser basin. Somewhat dutifully they had followed the geyser trail that morning in a hot sun. The sense of wonder, they discovered, was difficult to keep acute in the midst of so many plodding tourists.

"Next time we travel I want to camp out," said Anne. She was driving.

"You really do?"

"I do. I want to lie down on the ground, and I want to be further away from the main roads."

"I thought you liked to stay close to bathtubs."

"That's true. The water part we'd have to work out somehow."

"I bet there are hot pools in the back areas here where the rangers go and have a great old time soaking."

"Do you think so? Oh, I'd love to do that. We could pretend we were Indians in one of the sacred places."

"The magic wouldn't work for us, though," he said. "We don't know any of the ceremonies."

"Maybe an Indian ghost would come and teach us."

"He probably wouldn't come to me," said Tony. "He'd take one look at me and refuse to give up any of his secrets to a monster. But he'd tell them to you. He'd tell them to you, and you could whisper them to me."

"Why are you calling yourself a monster? Do you really feel bad now about those animals?"

"Yes and no. Hell, all boys go hunting, don't they? I was just a little bit more scientific about it."

"The Indians were hunters too," she reminded him.

"They walked on silent feet and said prayers," he said. "I know all about that; I used to try walking like an Indian." He walked his fingers silently across the car seat to her and rested his hand on her leg. "But the Indians ate everything they killed," he added.

"Maybe they didn't. Maybe some things were for their ceremonies."

"That's different. That's religion."

"Well, you had a reason," she said. "You were learning. Now you're going to have a chance to make use of it." It almost surprised her how much she was enjoying the feeling of his hand on her leg and the sound of their voices, blending. Today she felt rested; she felt good. "Thank you for telling me that story last night," she said.

"Your stomach wasn't turned?"

"I'm still here."

"I think I could say almost anything to you." His voice pleased and surprised her with its tone of feeling. He slid close to her and spoke into her ear. "I want you to promise to tell me everything this Indian says to you. I'm counting on you."

"What makes you think he'd tell me anything?" She was smiling because his breath, his kiss on her ear was so immediately pleasurable.

"You're a mother confessor."

She laughed. "Wise old Indians don't need mother confessors."

"You never know."

"They probably whisper everything into a hole in the ground or a rock."

He deposited an unintelligible, tickling sibilance into her ear. "There," he said. "Now you know everything about me."

She ducked her head, laughing. "I can't drive like this, it's too dangerous."

"Pull over up ahead. It's time for lunch anyway." He stretched his body taut and then relaxed into beating out a rhythm on the dashboard. He began to hum.

He was still humming and singing a few words as he swung the ice chest from the trunk and they carried it together under some pine trees and down a slope to a small river. The light fell on them, gently. It seemed so simple and innocent, what they were about to do, eat together in the sun, by rushing water, but at that moment the thought flashed through her that she might soon be deprived of him; it flashed through her with actual pain, a simulated catastrophe of the heart with actual power. Not yet, not yet, she was breathing to herself; not yet, we've only begun.

"What's that you're singing?" she made herself ask him.

He grinned and gave her the words clearly. "'Goin' on a picnic, gonna have some fun. I'll bring the wiener, you bring the bun.'"

She knocked the ice chest against his legs.

"It's a classic," he protested.

"Maybe you should teach me a few more classics."

"Any time, baby, any old time," he said with a mock smile that was both courtly and lewd.

"Do you know what I said to my father? I said, 'Daddy, he's a diamond in the rough.'"

"A very rough diamond in the rough, I guess," he said. "But

I'm here to strengthen your stock—you'll see."

As they spread out the food, she said, "What I'd like to know is what it's like to be you, really what it's like."

"Me?" he asked. He was building up a many-layered sandwich.

"Let me ask you something. Did you ever think of putting on that fox's skin?"

He stopped reaching and looked at her. His eyes were wide and dark, his hair tousled. Crouched there above the food he was within the present of human history. The cave was there in him, the mountain pass, the harsh desert, the lush green plain; he had walked the narrow streets of early cities, between the columns of temples, sandal-footed along Mediterranean shores. "I don't know whether I thought of it or not," he said. "It was awfully bloody."

"You could have put it on and pretended for a little while to be a fox," she said.

"It was pretty small. Foxes are smaller than you think."

"Maybe on your head and shoulders then?" She dropped onto all fours and crawled around the edge of the picnic blanket to him, nose first. "I'm a fox," she said. "Shoot me, shoot me."

He put his food down and caught her firmly under the arms, pulling her up and toward him with a strength in his shoulders that surprised her; she let herself be drawn forward.

"Right now what you're doing is teasing me," he said. "What are you getting at?"

She sat on his lap and looked at his face, inches away. "I don't want you to die. And I don't want to die yet."

"When did that all come up?"

"It's been here." She was so close she could see the faint yellow wheels around the darks of his eyes; she could see the shape of herself reflected.

"What makes you talk like this?"

It seemed that a space of stillness was surrounding them,

and then abruptly, as if a border had been crossed, she had it for an instant again, like a complete remembrance: that revelation of a pure and tranquil universe lit by love, brimming with love. Through her eyes his face shimmered as she said, "We have to stay alive. Do you see? We hardly know half of it yet."

At Mammoth Hot Springs late that afternoon the young clerk at the hotel desk assessed them before he answered Anne's question about whether there might be a hot pool—perhaps one off the usual tourist path?—where they might bathe.

"There is," he said finally. "If you're careful." He drew a few lines on their map of the park. The Gardiner River was the danger, he said. Twenty miles an hour at least it was going from the melt-off, and it was barely above freezing. "But if you're careful. . . ." He made a small cross with his pencil. The cold river was impossible, and they weren't allowed to disturb the hot one, but where the two rivers met, here, was a small waterfall just inside the cold current. Rocks had even been thrown in as a sort of protection, just space enough to sit. The rangers kept it under pretty close tabs, but it was all right to go in. "Just take it easy," he said. He handed them the map. "I go there every night when I get off work. It's heaven."

"I'm afraid my expectations are rather high," said Anne when she and Tony were in their room changing into their swimming suits.

"Let me do that," said Tony. He took the hairbrush from her and stood behind her in front of the mirror, brushing with long strokes. "You're looking beautiful," he said. He was lifting brushfuls of hair out into the air and letting them fall back. In the mirror her body in its close-fitting suit was superimposed upon his, two human shapes differing only slightly from each other, two parts, two pieces. She drew herself up tall under the pleasure of his attention. "Wear it loose," he said. "Just like this." He put down the brush and wrapped his arms around her, and she felt the length of him, all his hard and soft places, almost merging into her.

Regal was how she felt as they stretched their legs out along the path above the torrential Gardiner River: regal and long-limbed and easily upright in the warm dry air; firm on an earth that was itself by nature firm. They should become more and more like the earth, she thought as she led the way down the narrow path between sage and low-growing cedar and here and there a blooming prickly pear: firm and patient like the inherited earth.

"Oh, look," she said, stopping still. At their feet, just off the path, in a bed of yellow snapdragonlike flowers, was the small carcass of a fawn, partially picked over but also baked and dried by the sun. His body was rounded, his head tucked beneath his spindly front legs, the markings on his fur still recognizable.

"Spring didn't come fast enough," said Tony.

They stook still a minute longer, looking down, without words, but by then the sound of the waterfall was already drawing them forward, rushing them forward toward what they hadn't experienced, and by the time they had shed their sweat suits and climbed down the rocks to sit beneath the falls, Anne was firmly of a mind to consider water also as an element she wanted to claim as kin. It was glorious; it was heaven. Boiling River pounded down upon their heads from a height of about four feet, almost too hard, almost too hot to bear, but able to be borne in exchange for the exhilaration of being pounded and heated by innumerable moving particles of water. If they stayed crouched, they were totally within the heat; if they spread out their legs, the temperature instantly dropped to a cold carried down from the highest mountain peaks. A row of rocks protected them slightly from the icy main current of the Gardiner.

"God, this is something else," said Tony above the roar.

He closed his eyes and tipped back his head until he was completely soused.

After a few minutes Anne stood up, leaning her belly into the falls, so as to cool her shoulders and see how this water came about, for the small hot stream above with its fragile rock and many-colored algae did not seem strong enough to produce such a falls. Underground water, perhaps, had joined the current. From a distance away, they had seen nothing of the hot river. It was like a gift from the inside of the earth. They had followed a bare path. It was arid here, quite different from the other areas of the park they had seen. The hills were gray-green and purple. Swallows swooped across the water to holes in the opposite bank. She breathed in the fragrance of sage. All her senses felt opened, her limbs unwearied.

Settled down again beneath the falls, she did not move for a long time. She thought she was learning to breathe water, to become completely permeable, to turn herself into a liquid that at will could reappear as a woman. She would learn how to go underground, how to vaporize, how to freeze to absolute quiet, how to melt and sweep forward, how to hold to a placid blue. Water was wonderful, absolutely wonderful.

When she brought her head out from under the falls, Tony was sitting on one of the rocks at the edge of the current, balancing his body, holding his arm out into it.

"Be careful!" she cried. She inched forward and held on tightly to his near leg. To her eyes the earth reappeared from water: firm, commendable, commended to them. And then there was the sky: look at it, struck with late sun, filled with swallows, able to bear moisture, merging out there in space with who knew what else. They should become like air too, she thought: airy, expansive, bearing gifts.

"What are you trying to do?" she called to him.

He shouted something she couldn't hear.

She gripped both his legs as he made a bridge of himself from hot into cold, trusting her, and doused his upper body in the main stream. Through the water he looked pale, broken up by the movement over him, but after a moment he came up all in one piece, himself, streaming wet, whooping with joy.

In the swirling heat she held to him, and together they made a new pair in the new world, while all around them the general, age-old wedding was still going on, a limitless, continual, sun-warmed wedding of like to like, love into love, and how this was being accomplished and what was to issue from the heart of all this joining they were not yet to know.

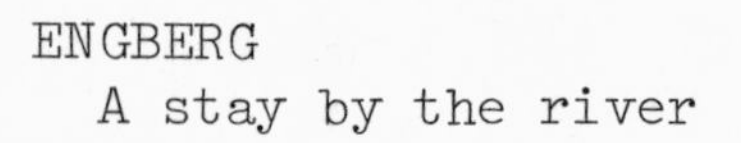